USA TODAY BESTSELLING AUTHOR

Dale Mayer

SIMON SAYS...
RUN

A KATE MORGAN NOVEL

SIMON SAYS... RUN (KATE MORGAN, BOOK 5)
Beverly Dale Mayer
Valley Publishing Ltd.

Copyright © 2022

All rights reserved. Except for use in any review, the reproduction or utilization of this work in whole or in part by any electronic, mechanical, or other means, now known or hereafter invented, including xerography, photocopying and recording, or in any information storage or retrieval system, is forbidden without the written permission of the publisher.

This is a work of fiction. Names, characters, places, brands, media, and incidents either are the product of the author's imagination or are used fictitiously. Any resemblance to actual events, locales, or persons, living or dead, is entirely coincidental.

ISBN-13: 978-1-773365-69-5
Print Edition

Books in This Series

The Kate Morgan Series

Simon Says… Hide, Book 1

Simon Says… Jump, Book 2

Simon Says… Ride, Book 3

Simon Says… Scream, Book 4

Simon Says… Run, Book 5

Simon Says… Walk, Book 6

About This Book

Introducing a new thriller series that keeps you guessing and on your toes through every twist and unexpected turn....

USA Today Best-Selling Author Dale Mayer does it again in this mind-blowing thriller series.

The unlikely team of Detective Kate Morgan and Simon St. Laurant, an unwilling psychic, marries all the unpredictable and passionate elements of Mayer's work that readers have come to love and crave.

Some cases are clear-cut and make sense, and then there's this one. Two women, avid joggers, out for a hard Stanley Park Fun Run. Both dead. Both at the same time. Both on the popular park trail. rail running up and down hills dodging rocks and trees is rough, sometimes deadly. But this killer has a unique method for taking out his victims—one that doesn't leave any forensic evidence. Detective Kate Morgan focuses on the victims, ... until two more are killed.

Awakening in the night with horrible nightmares, Simon St. Laurant curses his life and hates having ever traveled down this strange pathway, particularly when the visions come out of nowhere. This case, though, involves a much more personal element that terrifies him.

As Kate gets closer to finding out the truth, she finds herself following the path to becoming the next victim.

Sign up to be notified of all Dale's releases here!
https://geni.us/DaleNews

PROLOGUE

Saturday, One Week Later, Mid-September

KATE MORGAN WOKE up early in the morning, still at the penthouse apartment of Simon St. Laurant. She rolled over and tried to sneak out from the covers. Almost instantly an arm came around and pulled her back down.

"It's Saturday."

She froze. "It is?"

He nodded. "It is. You're off work."

"Jesus, I don't even know what day it is anymore."

"Well, if you would take some of the time off that you have coming and rest a little bit," he said, "I wouldn't have to worry about you quite so much."

"You worry too much," she replied instantly. The arm around her tightened, and she cuddled in closer. "In that case," she decided, yawning, "I'll just stay here a bit. Maybe we can have breakfast for a change."

"Normally, you're up and out of here before breakfast is even possible."

"And normally, you're up and out of here, buying and selling the world," she replied.

"Foreign markets and stock exchanges open up early," he explained.

"So, why the hell are you still here now?"

"It's Saturday. They can go screw themselves."

She laughed. Just then her phone rang.

He froze, tucked her up closer, and said, "Don't answer it."

She rolled over and looked at him. "You know I can't do that."

"I know." He sighed, then kissed her gently. "Go ahead, answer it then."

She reached over and grabbed her phone to see the Caller ID. "What's up, Rodney?"

"We got a new case," he said, his voice grim.

"Yeah, what kind of a case?"

"You mean, outside of dead bodies?"

"Bodies?"

"Yeah, two, on the Stanley Park jogging trails."

"Runners?"

"Yeah, both women, both late twenties."

"Shit. Shot or what?"

"No, we're not exactly sure what happened. But it sounds like something might have been sprayed in their faces. Gassed maybe, but Smidge'll have to tell us what it was," he noted. "Anyway, I got the first call. I'm here, and I'm tagging you."

"*Great*," she mumbled. "Simon just told me that I needed to take a few days off."

"And he's right. You do. But you didn't set that up."

"Nope, I'm coming," she replied. "You know me. Anytime somebody needs me—"

"More than that," he added, "I think this will definitely be your case. At the very least I want you on it with me." And, with that, he hung up.

She smiled at her phone. "You know what? I think that was actually a compliment."

"Remember that teamwork thing?"

"I'm working on it," she grumbled. "I'm working on it. Oh, and don't plan on jogging the Stanley Park trails today."

"Not planning on doing any jogging—especially now."

She smiled, got up, and said, "I don't even have time for a shower."

"Yes, you do," he argued. "Just make it fast."

She hesitated, then nodded. She was in and out in five minutes to find him with her clothes all laid out.

"And dirty clothes again." She swore softly.

"In this case it doesn't matter," he noted, "because we spent most of yesterday sitting around the house, doing nothing. So, you'll be good to go. These are the ones you came in the day before."

She looked at them in surprise. "Did you wash them?"

"Yeah, I did it last night."

"Shit, you're handy to have around."

She walked over to give him a quick kiss, but he snatched her up into a hug and kissed her thoroughly, then added, "And you remember that."

With that, she was gone.

CHAPTER 1

DETECTIVE KATE MORGAN slid under the yellow tape and headed down the slight slope to the running path. She glanced around, orienting herself. A lot of jogging trails were along the beach. Matter of fact, jogging trails wound around all over, not just up and down the beach, and she wasn't even exactly sure how far inland they went. A parking lot was off to the side, where four vehicles and numerous cop cars were currently parked. She glanced around but found no sign of Rodney.

As she headed in the direction where everybody was walking, she held up her badge twice, as people approached. They just nodded and let her go on through. She hadn't been on the job long enough to know too many of the running trails, but, when she considered the number of them in the area, she wondered whether they were even technically on Stanley Park land. She would have to pull up a map to figure that out.

She saw a group of first responders had convened up ahead and noted that the attack had occurred just close enough to the parking lot that anybody could have lain in wait. Nobody would even know whether the victims had gone for a run yet. She understood from the quick description she'd gotten from Rodney that two women were killed, which presented its own problem. How did you kill two, without alerting one of them that something was wrong?

Unless more than one killer was involved. Although it happened, multiple killers working together weren't the norm. And, if they were, they were usually couples. But then why would anybody attack two joggers? And two female joggers at that?

Kate shoved her hands in her pockets, frowning, as she contemplated the area. It was a warm sunny day, and there hadn't been any rain, so any tracks the killer and the victims left would be easy to find. Assuming, of course, that there were any and that they were distinguishable from all the others, since this place was a heavily used jogging path.

As she approached the crowd, Rodney separated himself and walked toward her.

He smiled. "You made good time."

She nodded. "Traffic was pretty light. I'm surprised we're so close to the parking lot."

"Yes, and that's just compounding things. There are no cameras, nothing along this area to give us any assistance."

"Of course not," she grumbled, "and the parking lot itself is off the main thoroughfare. So, even if cameras are on the main road, it would be hard to see anyone coming in or out of this corner."

"Yeah, we'd have to go back to that last main intersection," Rodney noted.

"We might have to. But, at the moment, we have absolutely no indication that this person even drove in. And how many stops are there along this path? Like half a dozen?"

"Three different parking spots have easy access to the path, but these jogging paths are like a spiderweb all around the area," he explained. "So really the killer could have come from any direction. It won't be clear and simple at all."

"Is it ever?"

He just laughed.

"So, what do we know about the victims?"

"Both easily identified, both carrying cell phones with those little attachments on the back for carrying cards. One had a credit card, and the other one had her ID."

"Students?"

"No, actually," he replied, "and that was my initial thought too, but they're locals. Both of them live on Pendrell Street by Stanley Park."

"Oh, nice area." She rolled it around in the back of her mind. "And makes sense, considering where they run."

"It does, and it's really been developed in the last ten or twenty years."

"Yeah, that's a joke," she said, turning to look around. "What square inch of Vancouver hasn't been developed? Property prices have gone so sky-high that anything even ten years old is worth dropping and putting up as something brand-new."

"No argument there," Rodney stated. "So, back to our victims. Both are married. Both have jobs, and apparently this happened just a couple of hours ago."

"Who found them?" she asked.

"A group of joggers. They meet every morning at six and come out this way."

"So, these women were out here before them?"

"Yes, although the bodies were still warm when they found them."

"How did they die?"

"Well, you can ask Dr. Smidge that question yourself."

She snorted. "Oh boy, he won't want to see me."

"Well, it's been a little bit of time since that last case

piled up on his desk."

She shook her head. "It won't matter." She sighed. "He'll still blame me for it somehow."

"Well, keep me out of the line of fire," Rodney suggested, with a laugh.

She shook her head, as she walked toward the crime scene. Smidge was there bent over examining something. But the medical staff had two gurneys at the ready, just waiting for the go-ahead to load up the victims and take them away. She had wanted to ask Smidge something, but, as he straightened up and turned around, he caught sight of her, and his glare was the first thing she saw. She raised both hands in mock surrender. "Hey, I didn't kill them."

"Well, you better find out who did," he barked. "Two at a time, really? Seriously, like I don't have enough work already? I've only just barely dug out of your last mess." With that, he shook his head and stormed back to his wagon, grumbling all the way.

She sighed and looked over at Rodney. "How come you got off so lightly?"

"Hey, I stay out of his line of sight," he admitted, with a grin.

"Well, at least he's still speaking to me."

"You're about the only one he talks to," Rodney noted. "You should remember that."

"Yeah, sure. I'll keep that in mind while he's barking at me all the time." Of course that didn't mean anything. She had to deal with him, and generally they ended up getting along. But he was hard at it and overworked, and that was nothing new. In a big city, like Vancouver, there was a steady stream of crime. It didn't ever seem to slow down, and the authorities had no short supply of murders—to the point of feeling as if putting two people in the same room would result in only one coming out.

She had learned a lot about humanity in her lifetime, beginning as a child—when her brother had gone missing, and nobody knew anything about it. Nothing they were willing to talk about at least. That's the part that really got to her.

She knew that people had to have known something, but nobody had ever spoken up. Whether it was out of fear of the person who committed the crime, reluctance to have the police looking into their own lives, or just because they didn't want to get involved—that inconvenience factor—she didn't know. It had been a hard-learned lesson. Now she just stayed on the side of cynical at all times. It made for less disappointment that way.

Dr. Smidge ordered the bodies to be collected; then he stepped over to Kate. "Hope you catch this guy."

"We will," she replied, a note of confidence in her voice.

He looked at her and rolled his eyes. "Preferably *before* he kills again."

She winced at that. "Depending on the motive, that could be a little tough. Do you have a cause of death?"

"At first glance it'll be strangulation," he stated, "but they were also sprayed in the face with something."

She nodded. "That's what I heard, and I did see something there at the neck. Plus, their faces looked very contorted."

"Well, that would go along with the strangulation," the coroner confirmed. "Something else I don't quite understand and will definitely have to take a better look at, but I don't think how we found them is how they were left."

"What do you mean?" she asked.

"The same ligature was wrapped around both necks."

"At the same time?"

He nodded. "As if they were both down on the ground and rolled over, kneeling or something," he suggested. "We found them side by side, but there was only one ligature mark on the front of one woman. And there's no mark around the back of her neck. So, both heads were together and yet slightly apart." Smidge demonstrated, cocking his head off to the side. "And just one rope wrapped around both necks."

"That sounds strange." Kate thought about it and asked, "It would take them longer to die, wouldn't it?"

"It's almost a garrote, so not necessarily," he countered. "It cut through the skin in places. I'll let you know more when I get through the autopsies."

She shoved her hands in her pockets again, as she watched the medical team load up the bodies. "Any idea what would have been sprayed in their faces?"

"From the look of it," Dr. Smidge replied, "I'd say it's probably bear spray, but again I'll have to test it."

"So, that would have immediately caused them to panic and to become disoriented. As they fought the burn, the rope was likely thrown around both of them. But it's not likely they were being cooperative," she commented, as she took in the scene. "They'll be freaking out, clawing at their eyes, definitely not standing still. It would be almost impossible to get a rope around both of their necks at the same time."

"There is bruising on one of the women," Smidge added.

"So, it's possible they were hit somehow and stunned, and then, after they were dead, they were separated?"

He nodded. "They were lying next to each other, and

the rope was off to the side."

"And it's an actual rope?"

"I said a rope, did I not?" he stated in a testy voice. "But I also said that it was more of a garrote as well."

"Whoa, whoa, hang on a minute. So, you're saying that he killed them and then came back with another weapon and killed them again?"

"I'm not sure," he admitted, "unless the rope has some wire through it."

She frowned. "I really want to see that rope."

"And you will, whenever forensics is done with it," he snapped.

She glared at him, and he glared right back. "Fine. ... Answers as soon as you can."

"Answers *when* I can," he corrected.

And probably more as a matter of form as anything, he generally didn't get along with very many people. The fact that he spoke to her at all, even in a testy voice, was a testament to the relationship she'd slowly been working on.

Yet he remained standing by her and the crime scene.

"I wonder if the rope didn't quite do the job or something," she muttered, her mind still caught on that one fact. "Particularly given the angles, with the two of them tied together."

"That's quite possible," the coroner agreed. "In which case it makes sense that the rope was left behind because it would have been deemed a failure."

"So instead he's taken the garrote with him," she theorized, "leaving us with next to nothing to work with."

"Not a whole lot anyway," he muttered, shaking his head. "Two at a time now. Jesus Christ, what next?"

"Don't even ask." She cringed. "You and I both know

that, when it comes to this crap, there's no end to what might come next."

"I know," he replied. "Time for me to find another job."

"That won't help," she argued. "Even if you did leave this career, these pictures won't leave your mind."

He stopped, looked at her, and asked, "Do they ever leave yours?"

She grimaced and shook her head. "No, they sure don't."

"Exactly, how can they?" he noted. "The best we can do is hope for a good night's sleep at some point before we die."

She burst out laughing. "You know that it'll probably be our very last sleep when it happens."

He grinned. "Very true. I think that's why they call it *going to sleep*. Forever."

"Well, that suits me, as long as it comes without dreams. Nightmares, I mean," she muttered. And, with that, they separated, the coroner heading toward the van. She walked over to where Rodney was talking to forensics.

He looked at her and asked, "Did you get anything from him?"

"A little bit." She quickly relayed the bits that Smidge had shared.

"So, maybe the rope itself didn't work on two at a time." Rodney frowned. "I'm wondering why he tried two at a time anyway, especially if they were both fighting it. And the bear spray would have had them struggling regardless."

"Yeah, that's for sure, particularly if he sprayed them right in the face, as he appears to have done. Smidge also noted some bruising on the temple of one of the victims, as if she may have taken a blow to the head."

"If you think about it, how do you bear spray two of

them at the same time and actually get a decent enough shot that it never incapacitates, yet completely disorients and blinds them? They never really get past that, when he's on them."

"Especially if he's there with a rope and a garrote maybe," she suggested.

"Rope *and* a garrote? Now that's something. And again, I think it goes back to the fact that he tried for two at a time. What was the purpose behind that?" Rodney asked, wondering out loud.

"Instinctively I want to say revenge," she replied, "but I don't know against who or why. It doesn't even mean it's against our victims, but he chose these two for some particular reason, and it could have just been opportunity."

"Which is always the worst," Rodney muttered.

"It never gives us anything better than that for understanding the whys. You die because you're in the wrong place at the wrong time." She shook her head. "That just sucks. There's never a good time or reason to die, I guess," she added. "But to think that just because you go for a morning jog, to be healthy and fit, this is what happens? That doesn't make a whole lot of sense either."

"But that's the thing, ... murder doesn't make any sense," Rodney declared. "Come on. Let's take a look around."

"I want to check out the layout from up on the hills around here," she stated, "just to see where this guy might have been."

"We have no idea on that yet," Rodney said. "He could have been another jogger too. Even jogging with them. No way to know."

"Well, we can case the area and can talk to other joggers

who are out here now, but the chances of finding anybody who was here around the same time is pretty slim at this point."

"Beyond slim," Rodney declared, "but not impossible."

And, with that, they headed out to speak to anybody on the trail. The police had cordoned off this trail's entrance and exit, and the two dead women hadn't been left right on the path. They'd been placed just off a bit, so anybody who saw that the police were here either had come in out of curiosity or were avoiding the entire mess, thinking that they'd find out what happened via the news later. Nothing would interrupt their jogging.

Kate had met people like that, those who wouldn't let anything mess up their plans, their day, or whatever it was they were doing; and, if anybody thought otherwise, they were wrong. She often wondered at the mind-set, but then she didn't give enough of a crap about anything but her job to actually follow through with that mind-set herself. Except for finding out who took her brother. She still refused to say *killed* because there was absolutely no proof that he was dead, and, until she found his body, no way she would accept that. Just no way.

Two hours later, Rodney had spoken to a few joggers, while Kate spent all that time walking around, checking for any evidence possibly related to this crime. She found three locations where somebody could sit and see the joggers coming from a good couple hundred yards away. She studied the distance, looking at how far she had to go to get back down on the path, and then called Rodney on her cell. He was down at the other side of the path.

"If you turn and look to the north, you can see me." Watching as he turned, she lifted a hand, and he acknowledged her presence. "I can see you, and I can see the joggers coming down the pathway," she noted, "so this is a possible scouting area."

"Anything out there?"

"Nothing at first glance," she stated. "I'll take a look, but I think we should probably send forensics up here to have a better look."

"Sure enough," he agreed. "They'll be a bit yet anyway."

"Has any civilian stopped you down there?"

"A couple people asked what happened, you know, and was it accidental—which, really? You'd think that wouldn't need to be asked," he said. "I told them not to run alone, how they should always run in pairs, but even that sounds pretty stupid, considering two women died here together."

"No, I hear you," she concurred. "Did you find anything down there?"

"No, not yet. I'll keep walking farther up though, so, if you don't hear from me for a bit, that's why."

"Good enough," she replied. "You're a big guy, so chances are that you're safe."

And, with a laugh, she waved at him again and got a thumbs-up in return. It wasn't anything to laugh about, but making jokes and finding something lighter to think about made the job easier to cope with. She knew the public probably wouldn't appreciate it if they overheard them, but everybody had to find a way to deal with the stress of these cases. And for her and for many of the police, it was good-natured teasing and laughter.

She studied the area around her again. Just enough potential was here that she wanted to find a way to keep track of anybody who came here. But that was almost impossible, short of setting up cameras, and then what? Would this guy ever use the same spot again? Was this a one-off? Did he have an affair with one of the women and not care about collateral damage and so he took them both out? There was just not enough information to have the slightest idea what was going on here. She sent Rodney a quick text message, asking if the families had been notified.

No, not yet. We can go do that now, if you're ready.

She looked around at the final spot that she'd chosen as the best—or at least most likely—location and sent back a text. **Sure, let's get that done. We need info and fast, before panic sets in.**

Unless there's a long history of murders on this jogging trail, I doubt anybody will panic.

Shaking her head, she wrote back. **The jogging nuts might, when they realize two were killed at one time though. When they find out the buddy system they've been using to feel safe all this time isn't enough, that's when they'll panic.**

Rodney replied right away. **Right, so information first. In order to get that, let's get to the families.**

Kate met him at the parking lot and asked, "Do you want to take one family, and I'll take the other?"

He nodded. "Sure, looks like they both just live a few blocks away from each other." Rodney checked his watch. "Chances are people could be at work."

Kate nodded. "I'm running the one woman, the blonde. Oh, wow, she's recently divorced and has a DUI charge," she noted, sounding surprised.

"What?" He turned toward Kate, staring at her, with a confused expression on his face. "What's so odd about that?"

"Nothing," she said, "but so often we run these reports, and nothing pops at all."

He smiled. "Well, in my experience, a recent divorce can

cause all kinds of shit."

"Isn't that the truth," she muttered. "I'll take that one, I guess."

"Are you expecting anybody to be there?" he asked.

"No, I'm really not," she replied, "but I'll give it a try. Let me go get the lay of the land, then I'll contact the parents."

"Good enough. I'll take the other one."

"Do we know anything about her?" she asked him, as she walked over to her car.

"Nope, not a whole lot. I have an address though, so I'll go see what I can find out."

They both drove to the same area. As they got out, he pointed to both townhomes and noted, "They're neighbors, so chances are good they could be long-term friends with similar fitness goals, and it is nice and convenient to have a running buddy nearby."

"Yeah, it also gives us good potential to find people who might know their patterns. I mean, if they've been here for very long," she suggested, "then the neighbors will probably all know that they run together, and we can find out whether they were friends before or something."

He nodded. "Who knows? We don't want to assume too much. We might get surprised."

As he walked up to the front of one house, she headed over to the door of her victim's as well. She wasn't expecting anybody to be here, so when an older woman answered the door, Kate was surprised. "Hi. Is this Jenna Barney's home?"

"Yes, of course this is the Barney residence," replied the woman, who Kate thought might be her mother. The woman looked at her, then frowned and asked, "You're with the police?"

"Yes, I am." Kate held up her badge.

"What's the matter?" asked the woman, puzzled, then she panicked. "Oh my God, is it about Jenna?"

"May I come in?"

The woman looked at her, wordless, and stepped back so Kate could enter. "Please don't tell me that it's Jenna." Tears had already formed in the corners of her eyes as she waited, hoping not to hear the bad news she already knew was coming.

"Are you her mother?" Kate asked. When the woman slowly nodded, Kate continued. "I'm very sorry." She held up her phone, showing a photo of the face of the dead woman. "Is this Jenna?"

"Yes," she cried out, tears pouring down her cheeks. "She's dead, isn't she?" she asked, staring at the picture.

"Yes," Kate whispered quietly. "I'm so sorry for your loss."

She shook her head. "No words can ever make this right." She looked over at Kate, squaring her shoulders a bit. "Please tell me that you've picked him up already."

"Picked who up?"

"Her ex-husband," the woman said, frowning. "You know he did this."

"Why do you say that?" Kate asked.

"They fought terribly. He swore he'd kill her before he'd let her have the house and everything else." She waved a hand around the home. "You can see that Jenna is—was— still in it."

"And you're living here with her?"

At that, the old woman gasped. "Oh my God. Yes. Yes, I have been living here. Am I in danger?"

"And is that because you don't have another place to live

or because you wanted to be here with Jenna?"

"She actually asked me to move in with her. She said she didn't want to be living alone."

"And what was the ex-husband's problem?"

"He's an awful man, and I know that she was really worried about him. He was very abusive, very aggressive, and she was scared of him."

"Did she have reason to be? Was there a history of abuse?"

"Oh, yes, absolutely," she declared.

"Did Jenna go to the police or tell anybody?"

"No," she replied, "it wasn't good for her business."

"What was her business?" Kate asked, looking confused.

"She was in real estate."

At that, Kate just stared.

"That's what I said to her too. Big deal if you're in real estate. It's not as if you're a celebrity, protecting your reputation. Wife beaters come from all walks of life."

With her notebook in hand, Kate wrote down the name of the ex-husband and asked, "Do you know where Barry is living these days?"

Jenna's mother shook her head. "I just know that it's an apartment somewhere. I don't know that I ever heard her say where. But he was not very happy about downsizing, while she stayed in this house."

"Has the divorce been finalized?"

"No. Well …" Then she stopped and shook her head. "I actually can't confirm that. She did meet with the lawyer yesterday, and I'm not at all sure what the latest is."

"Okay, good enough. Do you happen to know the name of her attorney?"

The woman looked at her, and her bottom lip trembled.

"No," she whispered. "Why is it I don't know these things?"

Kate reached out a hand to the obviously distraught woman. "I'm sorry. It's not as any of us are ever prepared for this conversation."

She looked at her and blinked. "No, you're right. It's not like we say, 'Hey, honey, before you go for a run this morning, do you want to tell me who your lawyer is in case you get murdered by your ex-husband'?" Such bitterness and raw grief filled her voice.

Kate added, "Maybe you'd better sit down. Is there anybody you can call to be with you?"

She sagged onto a kitchen chair and shook her head. "She's my only daughter. My son lives on the other side of the country."

"Did Jenna have any children?"

"No, she always really wanted children, but Barry didn't."

"And what about your husband?"

She waved her hand. "He's been gone a long time now. It's one of the reasons why I was quite happy to move here with Jenna," she shared. "There's just the two of us. I knew that she would find another partner soon enough, and I'd be in the way again, but—you know, for the moment," she whispered, "I was just going to enjoy it. And hopefully, before too long, it wouldn't be an issue."

Her odd wording caught Kate's attention. "What do you mean by that?"

The woman looked up and gave her a half smile. "I have stage four breast cancer," she shared. "We've been trying to decide about going through more treatments, though they can really do nothing more but delay the inevitable a bit."

Kate took a moment as she absorbed the news she'd

sensed was coming. "I'm so very sorry this is all happening to you."

"You never think that the end of your life will come like this, and I was prepared to do what I could to squeeze every day I could out of this life, but now? I'm just thinking, 'Please, let this be over, and then I can at least go join my daughter.'"

The shock was taking a toll, and she looked unsteady. "Are you sure there's nobody I can call to come be with you right now? Or I can get social services to come in."

"No, please, that's the last thing I want," she said. "I'll just go upstairs and lie down and think about what I'm supposed to do now." She looked over at Kate. "How long before I can have my daughter's body?"

She hesitated and then spoke. "I'm sorry, but because of the circumstances of her death—"

"Not for a while then. I suppose that means there will be an autopsy."

"Exactly. I'm sorry. ... Do you happen to know Robin?"

"Oh, yeah, that's her friend. She lives almost next door. They went running together every morning." She stopped, turning to face Kate. "Wait. I just realized that I didn't even ask how Jenna died. What did he do to her? How did he kill her?"

"First off, we don't know for sure that it was Barry," she reminded her. "We'll need to do a full investigation before we can determine that."

The woman just waved it away impatiently. "How did she die? Where did he take her?"

"They were running," Kate explained. "Jenna and Robin, I mean. They were found together, just off a nearby jogging path. Both dead."

The woman stared at her in shock and then slowly sagged back down onto the chair. "Both dead? What? Both my Jenna and Robin are dead?"

Kate nodded slowly. "Yes, while I understand that you feel sure it was the ex-husband, would he have had any cause to kill Jenna's friend?"

"No, no. My God, they have two little children." She stared blindly out the window, her hand over her mouth. "Oh, my goodness, Agnew will be just devastated."

"Agnew?"

"Robin's husband." She pointed out the window. "A vehicle is over there at their place now."

"Yes, that's my partner. He's another detective in my department."

"You've told Agnew as well?"

"Yes, ma'am, that's why my partner is over there."

Looking pale and distraught, she asked, "Why would he kill both of them?"

"That's what we must determine, and, of course, the autopsy is a part of that investigation," she noted. "We need to get every bit of information we can to make sure we know exactly what's been going on here and why this happened."

"What could possibly be going on?" she asked. "Why would he kill two?"

"And that's one of the many questions we have to get answered," she explained. "Are you sure you'll be okay here alone? Maybe I could go get a neighbor for you?"

"No, no, I'll be fine," she said. "You go figure this out. I need to bury my daughter, before my time comes."

And such a note of pain filled her voice that Kate didn't really know what to say. Death notifications were always the worst part of the job, and it was better if one didn't get too heavily involved. But, at the same time, what do you do when you have a situation like with this poor woman, all alone now with nobody to help her? "Look. People can help, if you do need something."

"No," the mother repeated, with yet another wave of her hand. "It's fine."

Another thought occurred to Kate. "Maybe Agnew would like your help with the children?"

The woman seemed concerned, considered it.

"But look after yourself first." With that, Kate took her leave. She stepped out onto the front steps, then realized she was leaving empty handed. At the door, she looked back and asked, "Do you know whether your daughter had an address book, a laptop, or anything like that?"

"A laptop, yes, of course," she replied. "She kept all her business there. Do you need it?"

"Yes, ma'am," Kate said immediately, "I do. One thing we'll need to figure out is who else might have known that they went jogging in the morning, for example."

"I have no idea," she stated, "but we all knew. They've been doing it for years. They laughed about it. They used to do some racing for fun, as they were very competitive, but there was never any animosity between them."

"Was it always just the two of them?"

She frowned, then looked at Kate. "You know what? I don't think so. It seems like another woman went with them as well. But something happened to that, yet I can't remember just what." Her face lit up. "She had twins. That's what happened. I forgot for a moment."

"Good for her," Kate said. "Hard to get back to the same running schedule after that."

She nodded. "Let me go get the laptop for you."

"Oh, and if she has a cell phone."

The mother stopped. "She would have had that with her."

"Right," Kate noted. "I'm sure we have it then."

Relief passed over the mother's face. "That's good. I know it shouldn't matter, but somehow it does. She was so connected to that phone that I think I'd actually like to bury it with her." And then she turned and dashed off to get the laptop.

"Bury the woman with her phone," Kate whispered to herself. "That's a new one." Did people love their technology so much now that they would want to be buried with it? Personally she'd just like to be cremated and her ashes taken out to the woods and thrown back whence she came. But she knew burial rituals were important to a lot of people; they'd just never been important to her.

SIMON ST. LAURANT opened his eyes and stared around his bedroom. It was early Saturday morning, Kate had left on a case hours ago, but his heart raced, as if under attack. He had an instinctive need to jump up and to race away. But this was definitely his bedroom, and nothing was wrong here. He slowly sat up, his body wanting to run and run and run. He shook off the sensation and hopped out of bed. Then slowly, almost as if in slow motion to combat the panic in his brain—still telling him to run—he headed to the bathroom. It was barely light outside. He wasn't sure what was going on, but it felt like the residue of some sensation.

Some *psychic* sensation.

Shaking his head, he washed his hands and crawled back into bed again. As soon as he closed his eyes, it was like he was racing down a path, his feet pounding on the dirt beneath him. But he was laughing, and there was something light about the movements. And he realized that it wasn't him; it was somebody else. When he heard the laughter, he realized it wasn't his laughter either. A woman's.

He turned to look and saw another person, a woman running just behind him, not close enough to actually see as he would like though. The air was fresh and bright, and joy filled his heart. He smiled because, for the first time ever, it seemed that this psychic experience was about something great. Most of the time his visions involved connecting with pain and torture.

He just enjoyed the sensation of a wild run like this, controlled and yet almost at full speed. This person was a runner, somebody who jogged every morning, but right now this was a sprint for a finish line. Some conversation was going on between the two runners, but this woman he was connected to laughed as she ran.

She ran faster and faster, and it was such a weird sensation being in a female body, as he felt her breasts bounce with every step. Thankfully she wasn't massive, as, for the first time in his life, he experienced the discomfort of that on a run. She wore a sports bra, and he felt the band around his chest. A part of him wondered at such a thing, even as the rest of his mind was fully encapsulated in this vision. The vision itself was an anomaly because he was awake and yet not awake.

He was not asleep, and yet his subconscious was taking over, but his eyes were open. Plus, he knew that he was in his bedroom, but he felt this run, this absolute flat-out joy of being healthy and fit and out running on a pathway in nature. And obviously there was such a sense of camaraderie with whoever she was with that just added to the fun.

He didn't know how many people were in this group. The path wasn't very wide at this spot, although it widened up ahead, and, almost as soon as they got there, the other person raced past. She wore blue jogging pants that looked more like leggings, made of that fancy special tech material to whisk away water, to keep you warm, and to keep the sweat from cooling you down. That woman wore a sports bra too, and that's about all he saw, as the woman raced past, her long blond ponytail bouncing behind her. She was also fit, laughing and having fun as well.

The person Simon was connecting with swore and picked up the pace, running faster and faster, until the two were neck and neck. She was so focused on the path that she wasn't looking at her friend. She caught glimpses of a long ponytail but that was it. And she kept going faster and faster, as the path widened ever-so-slightly up ahead yet again.

Then *bam.* He jerked back several steps, shocked, his head screaming at him, as something came out of nowhere and slammed into his head. Almost as if he'd run flat into a tree branch. He was on the ground, and then there was just pain—something cold, wet, and then burning hot in his face. He started to scream, as he rubbed his face, trying to get rid of the hot stinging pain on his skin and in his eyes.

He got up and stumbled into the bathroom and poured cold water all over his face, but it didn't help. He stared into the mirror, but that didn't help either. All he saw were trees all around him. He stared down at his hands, but they were elegant, with long fingernails, not his short, thick muscled hands.

He was still caught in the same damn vision.

Yet, as he looked in the mirror, he didn't see the victim.

All he saw were the trees and the bushes and the pathway. Slowly he made his way back to his bed, trying to figure out what the hell was going on, when a rope came around his neck and his partner, friend, or whoever it was slammed up against him. She seemed to be unconscious, while he was awake. He couldn't think at all because he was choking, his hands at his throat, the rope cutting his fingers as he fought it. Consciousness came and went, and then he felt something even worse. Something metallic, something thin and cutting, and then he knew no more.

He laid back down on the bed for a long moment, his breathing erratic, as he tried to go over the events in his mind. As soon as he thought he had a handle on it, he called Kate. When she didn't answer, he groaned, then waited to leave a message. "I need you to call me back," he demanded, his voice harsh.

And she didn't, at least not right away, but, about an hour later, she called him, her voice distracted. "What's up?"

"You have a runner who died."

He heard the gasp in her voice, as she whispered, "What do you know about that?"

"I just saw her death," he stated, his tone harsh. "She was so happy, so full of life, and so fun. She was out running, racing with her friend. And then something came out of the blue and dropped them both. Then something burned their faces, and a rope choked off their throats. And yet there was a bit of consciousness, in and out, before something cut her throat. And I don't know beyond that."

"Yeah," she said, her tone grim, sad. "That pretty well sums it up. So, through all of that, I don't suppose you saw who did it, right?" she asked in a wry tone.

"I couldn't see anything after that stuff was thrown in

her face," he stated. "Isn't this a little overkill?"

"Any kill is overkill in my opinion," she snapped. "In this case, we're trying to figure out why. It was both of them, you know?"

"Both of them?"

"Yes, the one running with her also died."

"Interesting," he murmured. "I did sense that they were together, but I don't know anything beyond that."

"They were both killed at the same time," she added, "at least as far as we can tell, with what we have so far. What we don't know is why and how somebody was able to handle the two of them."

"Well, the blow to the head would have done it right off the bat," he noted. "My head is still killing me."

"Sorry," she replied gently. "You need to find a way to shut this off."

"Shut it off?" He huffed. "Great idea. That would be awesome, but something that isn't likely to happen."

"Well, it could happen," she said. "Couldn't it?"

"Maybe," he whispered, "but it isn't happening right now. Whoever this is, he took away something very precious."

She was silent for a moment. "No connection to the other one?"

"No, I don't even know which one I'm connecting to, just someone full of life. Yes, I remember. The other one, the blonde, wore a blue tracksuit and a matching sports bra," he said, "but, when I say *tracksuit*, it's not like the old kind with the stripes down the outer side of the pants. These were like tight leggings."

"Yes," she agreed. "That special running gear they're wearing these days. These two women ran together for years."

"And that was obvious," he confirmed. "A lot of joy filled their voices, and I felt so much joy in this woman's heart as she ran."

"Well, I'm glad the last hour before her death was good," she noted, "because that death really didn't give them a chance to defend themselves."

"No," he agreed, "not at all. This person didn't come to hurt. He came to kill."

"And still, the question is why? Did she have any thoughts, anything you could recognize?"

"No," he replied. "That's the biggest problem with all this. There are never any answers. It's just more of the same bullshit. I can see—and, in this case, even feel—it happening, but I can't stop it. I can't do a thing about it."

"In this case," she added, "you're also behind."

"What do you mean?"

"It's over. It happened several hours ago."

He stopped. "Really?"

"Yes."

"We had a bottle of wine last night. Usually it takes more than that to delay a vision."

"Maybe the vision didn't come through at first try, or maybe it came through, but you couldn't remember it until later."

"No idea," he admitted. "Can't say I appreciate the thought that it waited for me to sober up."

"No, and yet maybe that delay has to do with the fact that the vision was important."

"Maybe, but then why? What about it is so important?" he asked bitterly. "Seems like none of this is important, now that it's already too late."

"I hear you," she said calmly. "That doesn't change any-thing though."

"And again, that's my point. Nothing ever changes. It's always the same old, same old. People get hurt. People die. I can't do anything about it."

"You've done lots in the past," she reminded him, with what seemed like forced cheerfulness. "So let's not go down that pathway. If you come up with anything helpful, just let me know."

"Wait. Do you know who they are?"

"Yes, Jenna is the blonde divorcee. You connected to her best friend, Robin. She was a mother of two, and they both lived in the same townhome complex on Pendrell Street by Second Beach. They've been running together for years. Apparently all the neighbors knew it."

"So, a lot of people could have known about their jog-ging schedule."

"Yes, they were also found on a pathway, a common running path, which is quite hilly. So a lot of vantage places exist, where somebody could have stopped and waited for them."

"But he would have had to know exactly when they were there," he argued.

"I'm not sure that would have been a difficult thing. These two women went before work every day and some-times ran twice a day on weekends. So, anybody who's out in the jogging community would have known. Or anybody who's looking for a victim and chose that area would see them on a regular basis."

He nodded. "Well, let's hope you find the killer fast."

"Any reason not to?" she asked, curious.

He frowned.

"Just wondering," she said, "considering that we have two of them here, if you had anything helpful."

"They were blindsided," he noted. "At no point in time did I get any sense of recognition from either of them. Whatever happened was very fast, and they weren't at all prepared for it. They weren't expecting it and didn't have time to do much more than try to fight. And honestly that didn't last very long either."

"No, so the surprise attack was well-thought-out, and, although the killer may have had some issues actually handling the killing," she murmured, "in the end, it didn't take very long at all."

"What do you mean by that?"

"As far as we can tell, he used a rope to strangle them jointly but couldn't really do a decent job with the two of them together, since they were tied up with the same rope around their necks. He then used a garrote and sliced into their necks."

"Definitely overkill."

"I think he wanted to be thorough," she noted thoughtfully. "Make sure they were really dead."

"Well, that's thorough all right, but there has to be more to it than that."

"I'm on it. You just need to rest and to let this one go."

"Yeah, like I'll let *that* go," he noted, his tone bitter.

"If not, then lean into it," she suggested, "and come up with something useful." And, with that, she hung up.

He stared down at the phone. "Like I can just do that either," he snapped. No point in getting angry at her though. He was angry at himself for his inability to do just what she mentioned. Wouldn't it be nice to think that he could just turn around and decide to become a "gifted" person, who could get into the head of a killer, instead of being an unwilling eyewitness to their victims' deaths for a change?

It seemed like he only ever connected with the victims. He knew in the back of his mind that probably something was there for him to work with, but the fact remained that a small part of him still saw himself as a victim too and was determined to never be one again.

Whether that was why he connected with other victims, he didn't know, or maybe it was because of that determination that Simon was reaching out to help other victims. Again they probably needed a shrink to handle this, but any shrink who knew what Simon was doing and going through would have a whole lot to say, and none of it would be what Simon nor the shrink really needed or wanted to hear. Simon wouldn't let himself be medicated either, and too much of the medical and mental health community was all about drugging you up and drugging you down, until you didn't know if you were coming or going. Not Simon's style at all.

His world had to function somehow, and it wouldn't function if he were on drugs. No way could he be making the decisions he needed to make on a day-to-day basis if he were under any chemical influence. Plus, the damn drugs were scary as shit. If you got off them cold turkey, it led to more depression and suicides—the *very* drugs given to depressed people who were suicidal. Simon shook his head at the insanity of it all. More patients needed to realize this before swallowing just anything a doctor gave them.

Besides, giving up control was something Simon was never very good at. As a matter of fact, it was something that he would never allow to happen, no matter who the hell told him differently.

CHAPTER 2

AS SOON AS Kate got back to the office, she brought up a map of the jogging area. These were readily available; apparently it was all part of some popular runner's circuit. So much of the park itself was developed, but the larger portion was still wild and full of walking and jogging trails.

What she needed to do was connect with the husband of the other victim—Agnew, per Jenna's mom—and see whether the two women had a regular running route that they could count on, one that changed on a regular basis, or one that they chose randomly as they ran. If it changed, that was a different story. If it was the same, day in and day out, all Kate needed to do was find somebody who frequented that area, since other runners would have seen the two women on a regular basis.

Also, Kate needed to follow up with Agnew about that third party to the wives' runs and confirm what had happened there.

Of course, even a permanent running schedule over the years didn't mean somebody who knew them had killed them. Somebody could have followed them or was on the running path too. There could be any number of options. As Kate sat down, studying the pathway, she looked over at Rodney. "I want to walk the running path."

"You mean, you want to *run* the running path?"

"Actually that's not a bad idea either. I wouldn't mind seeing what time frame we're talking about."

He looked over at her. "What good would that do?"

She shrugged. "I don't know, but I need to go for a run either way, and I want to check it out, and that sounds like the best idea yet."

He shrugged. "You go for it. I hate running."

"Maybe so, but you still do it."

"Yep, I do it to keep fit, but it's not something I'd choose to do for fun."

She laughed. "Well, that's exactly what our victims did," she noted, "so I want to take a look at it."

He smiled, then nodded. "Have at it."

She took that to mean she was going alone. Well, that was fine with her. "I think I'll head over there now." She looked at her watch. "The day is almost over anyway."

He frowned. "You'll go for a run now? It's really hot out there."

"It might be hot, but it's also a good way to see the area."

He shrugged. "As I said before, go for it."

She smiled and stood. "See you tomorrow then."

She headed outside and then home, where she quickly changed into her running gear, then walked back out to her car. Once outside, she drove to the location that she was interested in and parked in the lot closest to the crime scene. If nothing else, it would give her ground zero. With that in mind, she left her car behind and set off down the trail to where the bodies had been found and, from that point forward, picked up her pace and started to run.

She wasn't even sure where she was running or why, but she did want to check out these endless loops with multiple entrance and exit points. So possibly any number of places could be all along here, where this guy watched the joggers. As she passed each ingress/egress, she checked the areas. She noted people walking their dogs and people running; this area was busy.

That really struck her. It was busy even now. People were all over these trails, coming and going throughout the day, and, although it was hot, it wasn't deadly hot. Vancouver didn't get crazy hot like in some places. It certainly did get hot enough though that you'd leave your jogging for later. "That or early in the morning," she murmured.

She kept on going, her lungs expanding, her body stretching, her muscles pulsing with joy, as that lovely energy flowed through her. The first couple miles were spent getting used to the different terrains. She didn't run much on uneven ground, like this was. Yet the change-up was good and made her muscles work a little harder. She came to a rise, where she pulled off the path and took a look around.

As much as she didn't want to stop running, she needed to check out how far she'd come, where she was, and if it made one damn bit of difference. From where she stopped, she noted other vantage points. And this one actually looked down on where the bodies had been found. It was a distance away, but, even as she watched, she saw a couple people in the distance heading toward the area where the bodies had been. All crime scene remnants had been removed at this point in time, even the police tape, so nothing was left to hint something had happened.

She was pretty sure the rumor mill was working overtime, and it would probably hit the news tonight, something she always tried to avoid watching, if she could. It never ceased to amaze her how they could get information on something like this, when supposedly there was a ban on all information on active cases. If the police wanted to release an official statement, that was a whole different story, and that came from the actual PR section of the department.

If left to Kate, she would have told them all to fuck off and to leave her alone. But that would never go down properly in terms of publicity. And it was all about good PR and keeping a good impression of the department fresh in everybody's mind. Didn't matter whether it was all bullshit or not.

Pausing to survey the area and checking her time to see how long it had been and how far she'd gone, she picked up the pace and ran again. She passed several people—some pushing strollers while talking with friends; others jogging alone, talking on Bluetooth as they went down the path; still others listening to something on earbuds. Some men, some women, some groups, some singles. Mostly pairs. She thought about that as she ran.

Why had the killer attempted to take out two at once? No, not attempted, he'd succeeded. But why had he chosen two? One would have been a better bet. Unless he was after the one and realized that the two could never be separated. Still, it was hard to see how someone could conclude that this would be the best place to take them out. Two was taking more of a chance, more likely to be seen, harder to control. Double the trouble literally, so why two?

That question was a constant thought that sat at the back of her mind. Until Kate found an answer for it, she knew it would bug her. She found it hard to believe it was just a casual choice because, if that were the case, this crime hadn't been well thought out at all. Nobody would choose to take out two victims with twice the trouble and twice the headache, not if there was any way for it to be easier. Serial killers were just as lazy as everybody else.

Not that this guy was a serial killer by any means. Even having that thought go through her mind made her cringe. She'd been on too many cases lately that were bad news all the way. She didn't want another ugly case right now. What about a nice run-of-the-mill homicide or a simple escalated-argument shooting? But, no, this one had all the earmarks of something much deadlier.

In the back of her mind, she couldn't let go of the thought that this could be a random stranger-killing. And, if that were the case, they couldn't assume this guy was done. The minute that thought crossed her mind, she winced again because who the hell even knew if this was his first killing? Maybe he'd done this before. They hadn't even considered that; at least she hadn't.

She shook her head because she knew better. Assholes were just out there who seemed to prey on the weak.

At least the women didn't appear to have been raped, although Kate would have to leave that determination for the medical examiner. Only then would they have clarity on that and many other issues. But, at this point, it didn't seem like sexual assault was part of the motive. So why these two women?

Were they specifically targeted, or was it just a matter of opportunity? Were these women just unlucky random victims, who came by at the wrong time, unwittingly becoming the successful applicants to whatever trial or test the killer was running? The very idea sounded gross when Kate thought about it that way, and she didn't mean any disrespect.

But the way serial killers talked about their victims, it's

not as if they were mentally well either. They disassociated from their victims in order to not have to deal with the reality of it all. In some cases they were psychopaths and sociopaths and really didn't give a shit to begin with.

She scrubbed her face, feeling a sweat coming on. She wasn't exactly sure where the hell that came from, except that she was on uneven terrain, and she'd pushed herself harder and faster. As the fatigue creeped up through her, she slowed down, not happy with her own performance on the trail.

As she walked, she found another vantage point that looked out over the water, with hills up and around, that could look down on this trail as well. She disappeared into the grass and deeper into the bushes, and she had excellent viewpoints of several pathways. What were the chances that the women had felt like they'd been followed or watched at some point in time? Maybe this guy had stalked them earlier or watched them from a distance long enough to learn their habits and actually knew where they would be, choosing them specifically. Or, this killing could be a one-off whim.

Of course that brought Jenna's ex-husband to mind, as they tended to make great suspects anyway. It wasn't necessarily the truth though, and she couldn't focus solely on that and forget about everything else. Once again, they needed data, and what she'd really like were the autopsy reports. But that would take a couple days yet.

Frustrating, but true. She didn't dare push Smidge into doing it earlier. Not only did she know perfectly well that other cases mattered just as much as hers but anything that pushed her rocky association with the coroner into the drink would make it even worse on everybody.

So far, she was keeping up and cultivating some sort of a

relationship with Smidge, and that was working out well. As long as she didn't push it and go too far into the deep end, they would keep working on their interactions. She wasn't the best at relationships in general and was definitely not the best at communication.

She would bet that Simon considered her the shittiest of all on that topic, but that wasn't fair because he'd never actually told her that. She just assumed he felt that way. Seemed like she was always on a case, always busy, never having time to really settle down into their relationship. She felt that he wanted more, but she was too afraid to ask—in case the answer was something she didn't want to hear.

She didn't want to do anything that would rock the boat, so what she did was nothing. She was fine with this situation as it was, but she wasn't so sure he was. Again, if she didn't ask, she wouldn't find out the truth and wouldn't have to fix anything.

Swearing at herself, she picked up the pace and headed down the pathway again. By the time she'd gone five miles, she felt it. Five miles on a flat stretch, five miles on a treadmill, five miles in the gym was nothing, but five miles out on the trail? What a difference. She felt her lungs burning, as she finally made her way back around to where she had parked her vehicle. She walked the last couple hundred yards to the parking lot. People were coming and going in a steady stream.

One guy was off to the side, stretching, so she walked over and asked him, "Is it always as busy as this here?"

He nodded. "Yeah, it's popular this time of day," he noted. "Saturday mornings are bad too."

"Got it," she replied.

He looked at her, frowned. "I've never seen you here

before."

She smiled. "My first time. I'm just checking out some places to run."

"Well, if you can handle this," he stated, "you can pretty well handle any of the paths in Vancouver."

"Good to know," she said.

"Although," he added, "I don't know how safe it is."

She looked at him inquiringly.

He raised his eyebrows. "Two women were murdered here this morning."

She winced. "I know. I'm actually a cop."

His eyes lit up. "Seriously?"

She nodded. "Most people don't react like that. Why the interest?"

He laughed. "I don't know. I always think what people do is fascinating."

She frowned. "It's not always a terribly fascinating job though," she stated dismissively.

"I don't know. It depends what department you're in."

She didn't answer and just waved. "Thanks for the info. Maybe I'll try it again on a Sunday."

He replied, "Well, Sunday is actually a busy day too. I mentioned Saturday, but really it's the weekends, you know? It's nice. It's outside, and it's challenging but not superhard. You'll get a pretty wide range of people here, everything from those out for a stroll with their babies or walking their dogs to serious marathon-running athletes out here."

"And that's the joy of Vancouver too." She laughed. "It's all here, all available, and everybody is happy to mingle."

He nodded. "If they stay out of my way, I'm happy," he said. "I get pissed off when they fill the whole pathway, going four across, and some places it narrows down to two across. It just takes a little bit of respect to make people happy at a place like this," he explained, "but, when you get assholes out here, who step in your way or slow down your pace, it gets to be a problem."

Curious, she asked, "Any confrontations out here?"

"It happens."

"What? Like road rage on a running path?"

"Sometimes," he replied, "but I don't know that *confrontation* in the word I would use. You know when you're running in the zone, and you think that the place is yours? So, when somebody steps in your way because they're not being terribly thoughtful about what's around them or about why people are here, it can be irritating. It's pretty much just like any place else really."

"So true," she muttered.

She headed back to her car and leaned against the door as she drank some water, thinking about his words. That scenario was possible too. Maybe the two women had pissed somebody off on the pathway. Maybe that's why the path had been chosen. It still seemed like an odd place because it was too busy, too exposed, too likely that somebody would see the dead bodies. But then again, maybe that's what the killer wanted. Maybe he wanted them found fairly quickly.

In that case, why? A lot of runners came to this park, and you could guarantee that the bodies would be found right away here. So why would somebody want them found quickly? Why now versus later? She thought about it, but no answer came to mind. Unless this person wanted something—or could avoid something—by having the dead women found earlier. And again that didn't make any sense.

Frustrated and tired, but with her muscles humming, she climbed into her car and headed home. It might have been a shitty day for some people, but she felt good after that workout.

Once home, she crashed for the night.

Sunday Morning

THE NEXT MORNING Simon woke up, missing Kate. Even though it was Sunday, he went about his normal daily business routine—except the markets were closed. He couldn't help himself, and, at the end of the day, he waited outside her station. He hadn't told her that he was here, and he wasn't planning on it. He was hoping to catch her when she came out. He didn't know whether she'd driven to work or not, since they hadn't spent last night together. That was something else that was starting to piss him off, but he didn't dare say anything. He didn't dare push any harder. He wanted her to want to be with him as much as he wanted her by his side.

She wasn't to that point yet. She'd come a long way, but she wasn't ready. He didn't know how much of it was his supposed *gift*. She didn't like his psychic gift, and, so far, it had been somewhat helpful with her cases, yet not helpful enough. As she had told him before, what he shares with her is not the stuff that she could put before a judge and jury. So, to date, he would say she found his psychic gift was probably 50/50.

He often had nightmares and dreams, caught whiffs of bits and pieces, but they were in the distance, as if a curtain obscured them. He liked it that way because he could turn his back and carry on. But this last vision wasn't that way. This last time he was actually *in* the victim, like a possession or whatever, as she'd been plowed to the ground and strangled. He had experienced her horrible death. That was *so* not what he wanted.

He could still feel his heart pounding, the adrenaline pumping through his body, as she raced down the trail, filled with the sheer joy of what she was doing, the exhilaration of feeling her muscles burn, as she pounded and stretched them further and further to the max with her efforts. And then the complete shock as something came out of nowhere and slammed her to the ground. He sat here—outside, on a street bench, in the heat of the summer afternoon—almost shivering. He huddled over his coffee, wondering if this sense of foreboding would ever go away.

There also hadn't been any numbers connected with this latest vision, as seemed to be prevalent with his previous sightings, at least he didn't think so. He didn't know if numbers were even part of this case.

As he waited, studying the traffic that came and went around him, he kept a close eye on the front of the station. It's also possible she'd go out the back, in which case he was completely screwed, or rather had just wasted his time. But anytime something like this happened, it wasn't necessarily a waste of time, but maybe he needed it anyway as a break. Maybe he needed a few moments of resting time, either before he headed off to another job in order to keep himself busy, or went home alone. When a woman called out to him, he looked up, startled to see Kate standing across the street, glaring at him.

"Off to a great start," he muttered to himself, as she walked over to the corner, waiting for the traffic light to change, and crossed. When she reached his side, she sighed. "You know that you could tell me that you're here."

"I know," he said, "but I like sitting here."

"That's creepy," she announced.

He snorted. "Given what I do, and what you do, you find *this* to be creepy?"

She stared at him. "Why are you here?"

"I wondered if there was any news," he replied quietly.

Immediately her shoulders sagged, and she plunked herself down beside him. "Not enough. And I'm not done for the day." He looked at her in surprise, and she shrugged. "I'll go see the husband of the other victim. He's at work. Apparently he went to work even though his wife just died."

"Sometimes people need work to bury themselves in," he suggested, thinking of himself. "It helps to turn the focus away from something you can't change."

"And a lot of people just like to grieve too," she reminded him, "because they are so shocked and so horrified by what's happened that they can't even begin to function."

"And sometimes people go into auto-pilot mode," he argued, defending this nameless guy. "And they just go on in a robotic way because that's what they can do. You can't take that away from him, if it happens to be his coping mechanism."

"If it's his coping mechanism, then fine," she replied in exasperation. "I'm not judging him."

"Yes, you are," Simon snapped.

She glared at him. "Is that what this bench-sitting is for you, a coping mechanism?"

He shrugged. "Probably. I don't know why the hell else I'd be here when you're cranky."

"You didn't know I was cranky before you got here."

"You're pretty much always cranky," he snapped back. She stared at him, and he saw the hurt and realized how quickly they'd slid into a destructive pathway. He reached over and gripped her fingers gently. "I'm sorry."

"No," she admitted, "you're probably right. That's exactly why I don't get along very well with a lot of people."

"You get along fine with people, when you want to," he reminded her. "It's just that, a lot of the time, you don't seem to care."

Her lips twitched. "Not with the work I do. I want people to give me the answers, and too often they're just sitting there, being stubbornly silent about it. Or they're lying or cheating."

"Sure, but they're also trying to outwit the cops, so they don't spend the rest of their life in jail."

She shrugged. "I'll get to the truth anyway. Wouldn't it be easier to just give it up right away?"

At that, he stared at her in shock and started to laugh. "Do you really think it'd be easy if they thought that way?"

She frowned. "Why are you laughing at me?"

"I have this image in my head of your expectation that criminals should see you coming and say, 'Oh, here she comes,' then lie down and hold out their hands and say, 'Take me away, Officer.'"

Her lips twitched in spite of herself. "Okay, so it sounds pretty stupid when you say it that way."

"Besides, you wouldn't have a job then. If there wasn't a need for somebody to sort out the puzzles, there wouldn't be any need for people like you. You could just have officers walk over and pick up all the criminals who are standing there, with their wrists out, saying, 'I'm guilty.'"

She groaned, slumped into the bench seat, and stated, "Okay, so it's a stupid idea."

"No, not stupid at all. I mean, if we live in Heaven, we might as well dream what we want," he added. "I personally would like to have no crime, but, if you want the criminals to just walk over and say they are guilty and roll over, that's a different story. Maybe that's something we could stop, before it got to that point."

"Fine," she moaned. "And obviously we're not in that world."

"Nope. … Last I checked, it was still full of assholes."

She smiled. "I agree. So where are you going from here?"

"Well, I was hoping to spend some time with you, but apparently you're not off work yet."

"I'm not," she confirmed, "although the visit with the husband probably won't take all that long."

"Well, in that case, let me come along," he said, yet a part of him hated that he even had to ask, but that's just the relationship they had. She was busy, and he was busy, but her busyness seemed to take priority over his, or maybe he was letting it. He didn't know. But the truth was, he could also do an awful lot of his stuff on the go. As long as he had a laptop, it didn't really matter.

But her work was very different, and it required going out, meeting people, checking up on their stories, and doing all kinds of related stuff. He'd never really been exposed to her side of the police before. It was fascinating work that she did—time-consuming, demanding, both emotionally and physically exhausting—but watching her mind work was truly a wonder.

He wasn't sure that she even understood just how analytical she could be or how well she could fit herself into the mind of a killer. She did it with such ease that he thought it was something she didn't even see as unique, which was also an interesting aspect.

He wondered if God, in His wondrous form, actually

considered the fact that, for every criminal out there, He needed to provide somebody like Kate to handle them. Was that part of what this good-and-bad balance was all about? Simon wouldn't doubt it, but, at the same time, it seemed like a foolish process, when God could have just wiped out the criminals in the first place.

But it all came back to that whole free-will thing, as far as he was concerned. People made choices, and those choices sometimes got them in trouble. This shouldn't have happened, and terrible crimes like murder should never be, but people were people. That was one of his favorite sayings.

"I guess you could come along," she relented. "Too bad you're not in your running gear. We could go for a run."

"We can go home and get my gear," he offered. "I only need a couple minutes to get changed."

She frowned.

He added, "A run down there would be great. Maybe I could give you a different insight into the layout of the run."

"I ran it late yesterday afternoon and again this morning," she stated thoughtfully. "I was thinking of just doing a walk, not another run, tonight."

"Well, a walk would be good," he agreed. "Come on. Let's go." He hopped up, and she looked at him with a frown. He shrugged. "Hey, the only way I get to spend time with you is while you're on the job," he explained, "so don't hold it against me that I'm trying. I'll take whatever time I can get."

"It's not exactly quality time," she noted slowly.

"But it's time," he declared, "so I'll take it."

She smiled. "Is it that bad?"

"It can be," he murmured. "You're always busy."

"No," she began, "it's just that some cases ..."

"What is it about this one?"

"It just seems so random. No suspects for one of the women potentially, and the favorite that everybody likes to consider for the other is an ex-husband and an ugly divorce."

"Yep, that's often a good suspect, isn't it?" he agreed, with a smile. "But you're right, it's also very cliché. It doesn't mean that he had to kill the second woman though."

"Unless they were inseparable, and that's what people keep saying," she related, "but I'm not buying it."

He looked at her in surprise.

She continued. "Killing one is pretty intense. To take out both of them with no real reason for the second one doesn't make sense to me."

"That's because you don't yet understand his motivation. What if the ex blamed her girlfriend for the breakup of their marriage? What if the relationship with the girlfriend was stronger than what he thought the relationship with him was? What if she had sided with her friend and had helped her make the choice to leave him, or things like that. In his mind, she could be equally responsible for the breakup."

She muttered, "Oh, now that's an interesting point." She hopped up and said, "Come on. Let's go."

"And where are we going?"

"First to talk to the husband, and second something else instead of a jog because I'm not sure I'm up for it," she shared. "I was thinking about suggesting a walk down at the beach tomorrow."

"I'm always up for a walk on the beach." He chuckled. "But why wait?"

She smiled. "You are way too amiable. You know that, right?"

"Oh, don't say that," he replied in horror. "I don't know

too many people who would take that comment as a compliment."

"Come on. You're easy to get along with, probably way too easy. It's seems to me you never really argue about anything."

"Well, I do actually. I just realized that some of the stuff that you do matters a great deal to you, whereas my work is more easily juggled around to different time frames, or I can shift to a different type of work."

"But you shouldn't have to," she replied, as they crossed the street back over to the station side.

"It doesn't matter whether I have to or not," he countered. "If I choose to, no force is involved." She frowned, and he held up a hand. "Don't even start."

"What do you mean?" she asked.

"You're looking for a reason for me not to do what I do."

"I'm not looking for a reason. I'm just considering whether you need to be saved from yourself."

He snorted at that. "Don't even start, and, by the way, you don't get the right to psychoanalyze me either."

She shrugged. "I didn't think that's what I was doing."

"Well, maybe you should take another look," he stated quietly. "Just because I'm shifting things around so I can spend time with you, when I know that you can't do it yourself, does not make me weak, abused, or somebody who needs saving." She shot him a sideways glance, and he shook his head. "I know you. Even if you didn't put words to it, I felt the meaning."

"I don't want you to have any less of a relationship than one that's all in," she stated.

"I'll tell you what relationship I want, if and when I decide to change it," he replied shortly. "Don't start telling me what I need." And, with that, he fell silent, but inside he was furious.

Finally, after a few moments, she said, "I'm sorry. I didn't mean to upset you."

He shrugged. "You never mean to."

"And see? That is just what I mean." He turned and glared at her. She raised both hands in surrender. "Fine, I just won't say anything more."

"Perfect. Now, let's get in the car and drive."

He sat in the passenger side of her vehicle, and she got into the driver's seat. She turned to look at him and murmured, "Simon, I really am sorry."

"Don't say another word," he bit off, as he turned and buckled in. "Come on. Let's go take care of business."

CHAPTER 3

KATE DROVE STEADILY to the running path parking lot. She didn't know what possessed her to have him do a reality check on their relationship, since it was potential suicide on her part and not at all what she wanted, no matter what he was thinking. But then again, if it wasn't what she wanted, why did she keep doing this? Because what the hell? A breakup was not what she was looking for and would be devastating.

But, by the same token, she just felt he could do so much better with somebody who could be there in the time frame he needed them, instead of somebody on the run all hours of the day and night like she was. There was no peace with her job, no calm evenings in. Oh, sure, there were a few of them, but, at any minute, she'd get a call and be off and running.

Yet it was the work she wanted to do, and she wasn't willing to change it.

She certainly wasn't asking him to make any changes, but she also knew that he wasn't getting a fair shake in this relationship. It wasn't even that he was giving more than she was, and that alone bothered her. Normally it didn't. Normally there was nothing to even be discussed, but, for some reason, she wasn't terribly impressed with the imbalance in their relationship. She just didn't know how to shift it or how long it could last if she didn't. Surely it wasn't fair to have something so unbalanced go long-term.

As she kept driving, he finally spoke up. "You don't know what you're talking about, so stop."

Surprised, she looked over at him. "What?"

"*You*," he said, "just stop thinking about it."

"Thinking about what?" she asked, cautiously looking at him, while trying to hide the horror in her gaze. "Please don't tell me that you can read my mind now. I don't know if I could take it."

"I don't have to be a mind reader to read your mind," he declared in disgust. "You're trying to figure out how to save me from myself."

And since his response was just close enough to the truth, she flushed.

"See? No mind-reading involved. You're sitting there, muttering about what a bad deal this is for me."

"Well, it is," she cried out.

"Don't go there," he snapped.

Staying quiet, she headed for her destination, her mind buzzing about what he said. And with what they weren't saying.

Finally she gave up delving into their relationship, pulled into the parking lot, then looked over at him and said, "I just want to take another look around at the crime scene, before I talk to the husband."

He nodded. "That makes some sense to me. I'd like to see the scene of the crime for myself anyway."

"You do have a morbid curiosity, don't you?"

"No," he replied, "but I do get an intimate look from you, and it helps to put pictures and places together." Especially in his head.

"You also seem to understand the criminal mind," she noted, tossing him a look.

He smiled but didn't say anything. She frowned, but he shrugged. "Hey, we've all done things in our past, whether we acknowledge them or not," he shared, "and anybody with a childhood as rough as mine certainly had occasions when it was best if the police didn't take a closer look."

She opened her mouth and then thought better of it.

He nodded. "Good choice," he muttered, when she didn't ask. She just glared at him. "Come on." He walked over, hooking his arm through hers. "Let's go take a look at your crime scene."

"I actually wanted to take a look at the light at this hour," she noted.

"But the women were killed early in the morning, weren't they?"

"Yes, and I guess what I want to know is why."

But it became readily apparent as they headed out.

"A lot of people are here," he murmured quietly. "It's really popular, isn't it?"

She frowned at that. "I guess the early morning timing does make more sense. I thought it would be busy this time of day, but I didn't think it would be this busy."

"Yet you were here yesterday evening or at least late afternoon, weren't you?"

"Yes, but you know how news gets out, and, instead of staying away, a lot of people come. So I was trying to figure out if that's what I saw yesterday toward the evening."

"Looks like it's just a popular place, and maybe it's too bad we didn't bring our running gear after all," he added. "We could have gone for a nice run."

"Maybe tomorrow," she replied, looking over at him.

He nodded. "I think that would be a great idea."

"I don't think we've ever done a run together, have we?" she asked thoughtfully, as she studied the area around her.

"Nope, not that I remember," he replied. "We haven't done any martial arts training or physical exercise together at all."

"Well, except for the one," she stated, with a smirk.

His lips twitched. "Except for the one. And, since we're so well matched there, I can't imagine that we would have a problem anywhere else."

"Interesting thought," she noted. "We might be physically well-matched, but that doesn't mean that mentally or emotionally we are."

"I think we're better matched than you think." And he reached down for her hand.

She slipped hers into his, as they walked down the pathway. She pointed out where the bodies were found and noted that already a million footsteps had covered the area.

"It's sad to think of the passage of time already," he said. "So many people have run right over the same place, where somebody suffered so greatly."

"And yet it was over quickly," she murmured.

"It was. That was the thing that really got me. It came out of nowhere. She had no expectation, no understanding even. At the time, it took her a while to even grasp what was happening. By then, it was way too late."

"Yes," she murmured, "that's the effect of a surprise attack, isn't it? Catching them while they're unaware, knocking them to the ground, long before they have a chance to even fight back, effectively taking them out before they really get any defenses up—not to mention the bear spray to take out their sense of sight. Both women were incredibly fit, but I have yet to find out if they had any self-defense training. Not that it's necessarily a game-changer, with a surprise attack like this, but you'd think, if they had some, they might have recovered enough to kick his ass."

"Was the ground scuffed up?"

"I took photos of it," she noted, "and so did forensics, but, with no fresh rain and the effects of a million people running over it day in and day out, it was really hard to tell. We didn't see any tracks going sideways or anything that looked kicked up, like from a fight. But you know it's so pounded down here from all the traffic, that's probably not surprising."

"Sad that it's to be expected," he stated, "but obviously this guy took his time, figured out the perfect timing for when to hit them, and got it just right."

"That brings up another question," she added. "If it was *just right*, how many times did he have to practice and get it wrong first?"

He looked at her in surprise. "Are you thinking he has done this before?"

She frowned. "No, not necessarily, I mean …" Then she stopped. "I don't have any reason to think either way, but it does bother me to consider that, right out of the gate, with no warning, this guy kills two people."

"Yet we don't know it was without warning, do we?" he asked. Although his vision said it was. Still he'd been wrong before.

"No, we don't," she agreed, "but I didn't find any similar cases in recent years." She turned, looked around again. "Now I want to go talk to the husband."

He nodded, and, as they got back into the car, she saw still more vehicles pulling up, more joggers getting out, some in groups, some singles, but most had somebody with them.

"I wonder what the stats are about joggers these days," Kate mentioned out loud, "like whether they run in packs, in pairs, or alone."

"I think you'll probably find more are alone than you'd expect because it's hard to find running buddies who can consistently function at the same time frame that you do."

She nodded. "That's why these two women ran together all the time because they both wanted to run in the same time frame, and it worked for them. Plus, they liked trail running, not like jogging on a flat rubber track. They also were good friends and were well matched to do the same level of trail running. Like some people enjoy running on the sand, but, for me, it's not my favorite."

"Why not?" he asked.

"Because I never did enough to build up those calf muscles. Running on the sand exhausts me," she admitted. "I've been working on it, but I'm not getting very far."

"Just the fact that you're working on it says a lot about you," he stated. "You don't like to see something defeat you."

"No, I don't." Then, with a laugh, she added, "I'm the same at work."

He nodded. "And that's also why you're good at what you do. Once you get your nose into something, you don't let up."

"Should I?" she asked curiously.

"No. Why would you? There's just so much shit in the world around you, and everybody else needs somebody like you to keep the system functioning."

"Sometimes I wonder," she muttered. And, with that, knowing that he was studying her in bafflement, she changed the subject. "Let's go." And they walked back to the car. As soon as she got to the vehicle, she turned it toward the address on Pendrell Street, just a block back from the beach.

As they got out, he looked at the area and smiled. "A really nice development is here."

"Sure, it's the rage now," she stated.

"Yes, but you can see houses have been dropped and rebuilt, as new money moved in."

"It takes new money to do it," she noted. "That activity isn't cheap."

"No, it's not," he murmured.

"So why do you do it?" she asked.

"Because money isn't the be all and end all. You have to understand the motivation behind why you're doing something and what it'll cost you—whether time or money."

"Everything has a cost," she agreed. "We just don't always take account of what way we have to pay."

He smiled. "And again we have such different views but still end up at the same place."

She frowned at that but didn't say anything. She walked up to the front door.

He looked at her and asked, "Are you okay if I come with you on this interview?"

She nodded. "It's probably not kosher but whatever." She waited, and, when the door opened, a tall thin man answered her knock. He looked like he'd been weeping. She smiled, gently introduced herself. "I just have a few questions for you."

He looked hastily behind him into the house and asked, "Do we really have to do this now?"

"No," she replied, "of course not. But the sooner we're able to get answers for our questions, the faster we can get to the bottom of this investigation."

"I thought it was the ex-husband," he replied in surprise, staring at her, with a weird blinking stare.

She frowned. "Now who would say that?"

He pointed across the road. "She did."

"Well, Jenna's mother might have made that assumption," Kate noted, "but we don't have any proof of that at this point."

Agnew frowned. "If he hasn't been picked up, you should be doing it right away. I mean, he killed two women. Isn't that enough for you?"

"We don't know for sure it was him," she repeated. "May I ask why you're so happy to pin it on him?"

"The guy is an asshole," he replied, some of his spirit returning and his body straightening up in outrage. "He always hated my wife."

"Why is that?"

"Because Jenna and Robin were such good friends, Barry blamed Robin for his divorce." He shrugged. "And honestly I'm not sure he was wrong in that regard because my wife did think Jenna should leave him. He was abusive. He was an asshole. He was emotionally corrupt. Just no reason for Jenna to stay with him. Threats were hurled from one side to the other. When they did finally split up, I know he blamed my wife. I would think you'd want to pick him up and throw him in jail."

"We still must have evidence first," she added tartly. "And I guess that, from your perspective, you may believe who did it," she stated with emphasis, "but we, as cops, don't know that yet and need to prove it."

He asked, "How can you possibly prove something like that? Motive is everything, and, in this case, this guy has got all kinds of it."

"Maybe so," she admitted, studying him. "I would like to ask you a couple questions about their running pattern. For example, did they always go to the same place? Did they choose different trails? Did they always go at the same time of day? Did they go every day? Were they always running together?"

"Every day, same trail, all the time. Robin used to laugh that she could remember each and every branch and knew how to duck and when to jump. She told me that half the fun was anticipating what was coming, so she could actually guess the best lift, when she went over roots on the pathway."

"They never got bored of it?"

"No, they used to sprint and run and dash around, and basically it was an excuse to go have fun," he muttered, and she heard an almost disgruntled tone in his voice.

"You don't run?"

"No, I've got bum ankles."

"And how long had these two been running together?"

"Years," he stated flatly. "Several years. Probably at least five, if not longer. We moved here about seven or eight years ago now, and the two of them hooked up right away, as best friends. I have never seen anything like it," he shared, shaking his head. "I have to admit, at the time, I felt a little bit odd, maybe even jealous because they became so close so quickly. But it seemed foolish, as we were happy and had our kids here, and she was such a great mom," he explained warmly, with a catch in his voice. "They'll be so devastated growing up with this." His voice thickened, as he added, "No children should wake up without their parents."

"I know. I absolutely agree, and I'm so sorry for your

loss."

He sniffled and nodded.

"Did they see each other outside of running?"

He nodded. "They often went shopping together. They attended seminars on health nutrition stuff," he replied. "They were both real health nuts."

"Interesting," she noted.

"Not particularly, they were just that kind of people. That is what they did. They loved it and really adored the fact that they could share their interests with each other," he added.

"I understand a third woman used to run with them as well. Why is she not still running with Jenna and Robin?"

Agnew frowned, then murmured, "Right. I forget her name at the moment. That was years ago. Maybe five or so years by now. I believe she started a family, so running took a backseat."

She made a note of that in her notepad, then hesitated. "I know you'll find this offensive, and I apologize, but I do need to ask. Was there anything more there than friendship with Jenna and Robin?"

He looked at her in shock and then shook his head. "Good God, no. They were just, you know, like two peas in a pod. They could have been twin sisters. In fact, that's what I imagined being a twin was like," he replied. "And I can't begin to think about what life will be like without her, without them." Agnew paused. "They were both over for coffee and whatnot at the other's house all the time."

Kate saw the tears starting to creep into his eyes, as he swiped at his face.

He reached into his pocket, pulled out a business card. "Look. I'll give you my card, and, if you have any other questions, maybe you could just call or text me. I really am trying to keep all this away from the kids."

She nodded, accepted his card, and gave him one of hers in response. "Did Robin ever have anybody threatening her? Or following her? Anybody who liked her too much, or didn't like her at all?"

He shook his head. "No, no, no. She was very well loved."

"I know that Jenna was in real estate. What did your wife do?"

"She worked in a dental office," he murmured. "She was working part-time now because of the kids and planned to go back to full-time when our youngest started school in September, but she was having a rough adjustment. So Robin wanted to wait until after the holidays this year," he told her. "In the meantime, she was doing what she could to balance family and work and running."

It's what he didn't say that Kate found interesting. "And please, just a couple other questions, and I'll go. What was your marriage like?"

He stared down at her. "Oh, don't you even go down that path right now." The anger built in his tone. "We loved each other. We had a great marriage. Whoever this killer is— and I swear to God it was Jenna's ex—whoever killed my wife should rot in hell for it. We had wonderful years together, and a beautiful future all mapped out, and that was stolen from me," he snapped. "She was so young. She had so many years ahead of her, and now she's gone."

"I get it, but obviously we have to ask as we investigate. Where did Robin work exactly?" He gave her the name of the dental office; she nodded and thanked him. Turning, she noted Simon stood at the bottom of the porch steps, quietly listening. She nodded again to the husband. "If you think of anything else, just call me, please."

He nodded but didn't go back in right away.

As she got into the car, Agnew remained on the front porch, staring at her.

Simon saw it too. "It's always nice to end on that note, isn't it?"

"Hardly, but, if I do it any sooner into the interview, I won't get the other information I need. He's just making sure that we actually leave, and, honestly, being pissed at me is probably a welcome distraction from everything else he's dealing with."

As she pulled onto the road, he asked, "Where to?"

"I want to go to past the dental office where Robin worked. It's Sunday and they aren't open, but I want to just take a quick look. You can sit in the car."

He snorted. "No way. This is too much fun. I want to come with you."

"What did you think of Agnew?"

"I think some of his comments were telling. Like the fact that Robin was balancing her running, her job, and her kids. But there was no comment about family, as in him. My impression is that he felt disassociated from her life. Maybe because of her other strong interests, or maybe they were just starting to drift apart."

"I had the same idea," she confirmed. "It's fascinating when you talk to people, isn't it?"

"Yeah, it is," Simon agreed. "It's amazing what you can figure out in a conversation. I'm just not usually talking to people about criminal activity."

"What are you looking for?"

"Whether they're trustworthy, whether they're lying,

whether they're likely to actually do what they say they can do. Plus whether they can do it in the time frame they agreed to, whether they cheated the last person they worked with, and mostly whether they're working for me or against me," he ended, with a half laugh.

"Still, it's very similar, isn't it? You're looking for signs of deception underneath it all."

"Exactly," he agreed, "which is why I find this so fascinating. People will be people, and, no matter what you're dealing with, you'll get some who are good and some who are not so good."

"Yet instant judgment is something we try hard not to do," she noted, with a yawn. She shook her head. "Jesus, I need more sleep."

"You can't keep burning the candle on both ends without consequences," he said. "That tends to backfire eventually."

She smiled. "I know, and I keep trying to get more sleep but—" She shrugged.

"How are the nightmares these days?" he asked.

"Mine are fine. How are yours?"

He laughed at that. "Another topic we better avoid for now."

"Sounds good to me." She pointed up ahead. "That's the dental office where she worked. I'll just run in for a few minutes."

"Well, I'll run in with you," he repeated. And, true to form, he stuck by her, as they walked inside. The building was open as it was a mixed use building, but the dental center itself was closed. She wasn't sure whether it was curiosity, as he had pointed out, or if it was something more, but she did find it interesting to have him here. He also had good insights, and she realized that she respected his opinion. He was good at reading people and circumstances in so many ways and had a very different viewpoint on life than her own. Mostly because of his own background, she assumed, but it was fascinating to talk to him. There was a little coffee shop on the main floor. She asked the woman who made them two cups to go, about Robin.

"I don't know her," she replied as she handed the cups over. "I can say that everyone I've served here has been great. No issues at all."

She asked a few more questions but there wasn't anything to find, apparently.

"Was that helpful?" he asked curiously, once they were back in her vehicle.

"No, not really. All she said is everyone here has been great but didn't know Robin personally."

"What is it that you're looking for?"

"I want to get some insight into how Robin's marriage was," she murmured, and she looked over at him. "The husband can say all he wants, but a close friend or coworker would have given me something more truthful. And, since Robin's best friend died with her, I'd love to talk to the one coworker who Robin was close to but the office isn't open so I'll just call her at home instead. I figured maybe we could go down to the beach, and I'd call her from the parking lot." And that's what they did.

When she finally connected with Robin's coworker on her cell, the woman broke into tears. "I've taken a few days off work because I'm so upset," she shared. "I didn't think I could be there and stay calm and professional around the patients, you know?"

"Sure, I understand. I'm so sorry for your loss. Were the

two of you close?" Kate asked, as she paced along the beach.

"Yes," she replied, "we were very close. I don't want to say best friends because I know Jenna was her best friend and neighbor, and they spent a lot of time together. Yet I was her best friend in a work sense. We did everything together. It'll be so damn lonely without her."

"I'm so sorry," Kate murmured, trying to ease the other woman's pain. "Can you tell me anything about her life? We're still figuring out who did this to her."

"I hope you catch the bastard, castrate him, and throw him away," she snapped. "How could anybody do that to her?"

"I'm not sure what you might have heard in the news," Kate began, "but, at the moment, we're still looking at any and all aspects of this case."

"Of course," she replied. "What do you want to know?"

"First off, did anybody bother her or follow her that Robin was scared about? Was she worried about going out alone at night or anything like that?"

"God no." The woman laughed. "The opposite, in fact—Robin was fearless. It would never occur to her that anything like an attack would even happen, so she never considered herself a sitting duck. She had no idea that something like this was going on."

"What do you mean by *something like this going on?*"

"That somebody could lie in wait for her like that."

"We don't know for sure that somebody *did* lie in wait," she corrected.

"Oh, I thought that's what they mentioned on the news?"

"No, only that she was killed on the running path."

"*Huh,* I'll have to—no, never mind. I won't," She had

immediately interrupted her own train of thought. "I would say, *I should listen to the news again*, but I don't want to know the details."

"None of the confirmed details will be released by the authorities for a long time," Kate explained, "because it does impact our investigation."

"Of course it does. I understand. Anyway, Robin wasn't the person to be afraid to go out in the dark. She ran early in the morning because that's when her friend could run, and the two of them absolutely loved it. She really looked forward to it and would go to bed early, so she could get up the next morning and run better and faster and farther. She was very fit, and her body was a machine," Robin's friend commented. "That's another reason I'm so surprised somebody could overpower her."

"Did she do martial arts or anything like that?"

"No, but, man, she could run. I mean, she could sprint like crazy. Probably faster than a cheetah. She often wanted to get tested to check her speed because she was so darn fast. And she just kept getting faster and faster. I know it was something she took a lot of pride in, and it breaks my heart to think of all the time and effort she put into it, only to be dead at such a young age."

"So, nobody bothered her, like following her? She didn't get strange phone calls? Nothing like that you are aware of?"

"No, not at all," she said, bewildered. "Do you really not know who it was?"

"No, I really don't," Kate confirmed. "Do you?"

"No, I guess I just always assume that, on things like this, you detectives would probably already have a good idea."

"Well, we certainly have some persons of interest, suspects if you will," she explained, "but, as you know, in our world, you're innocent until proven guilty."

"Of course, of course," she rushed to say.

"Did Robin have problems with anybody at work?"

"No, not that I know of." She sighed. "She was well loved at work. Everybody was kind and generous to her. I know that she was really feeling sad over her friend, who was going through a divorce."

"And yet she approved of her friend going forward with the divorce, did she not?"

"Yeah, she used to tell me that the guy was an absolute asshole and that her friend Jenna needed to get away from him. But just because you need to get away doesn't mean you actually, you know, can get *away*, away."

"No, that's quite true," Kate stated. "And did Robin tell you anything about her own marriage relationship? Was she happily married? Did she ever talk about her husband at all?"

"Not about him so much, but she always talked about her kids. She was a really great mom," she stated. "She absolutely adored her children. She never really spoke about her husband much—*hmm*—but I know they were happy. I find that most mothers don't talk about their husbands anyway. They talk about their kids," she added, with a smile in her voice.

"Isn't that the truth." Kate nodded. "And was there anybody at work who had a problem with her?"

"Nope, she worked part-time and planned to come back to do more hours come the new year, and she was looking forward to that. She was the type of person who always needed to be busy, always needed to be on the go with something to do," she told Kate. "Which was great for us because, anytime there was any overload of work, she was right there to step up and to take it. Now, of course, it'll be a whole different story."

"I'm sorry," Kate added. "Hopefully we can get to the bottom of this quickly."

"I hope so too," she agreed. "The longer it goes on, the more unnerving it is."

"Do you ever run along that same path?"

"God no," she quipped. "You couldn't get me in a pair of sneakers. Not to mention the fact that I can barely bend down and touch my toes," she added, with a jovial laugh.

"Well, if you think of anything else that might be helpful, then please give me a shout." Kate gave her a telephone number to the department.

"Will do. I sure hope you get this guy fast. He shouldn't be allowed to continue living after what he did to her."

"You mean, killing her?"

"Yes." Then she stopped and whispered, "She was raped, wasn't she?"

"No, as far as we know, she wasn't sexually assaulted. Where did you get that from?"

"I don't know," she said, "but you know how rumors are."

"We don't have anything back from the coroner yet, confirming any such thing. Besides, there were two of them, and I'm not sure he would have raped both."

"No, that's true," she answered thoughtfully. "I just assumed, in a case like that, he would have just knocked one of them out."

"I don't think it's that simple," Kate noted, "but, if you think of anything else, let me know, please."

After getting off the phone, she turned and looked at Simon. "Do people just assume details in cases like this or just make shit up?"

"I think their imaginations go wild, and misinformation runs rampant," he replied. "Nobody really wants to get the right information. They just want to get details they can pass on to others."

"It's a sad world."

"We've already been over that a couple times," he noted, a laugh in his voice, "because, indeed, it is. At the same time, it's fairly common that they only hear little bits and pieces, and they add to it until they get a whole story. If you guys haven't released any details about sexual assault, then it'll just be whatever assumption people can make because the victims were females. It's almost automatic to think that the women were knocked out in order to become sexual assault victims."

"Interesting world," Kate murmured, "because—of course, in this case—there wouldn't have been time. And I don't think that was his interest anyway."

"No, I don't think so either," Simon agreed. "This was too deliberate. I just don't know if it was deliberate to take out two, deliberate to take out those two specifically, or just deliberate to try out a methodology."

"None of which makes me feel any better at all," Kate noted.

"Nope, I'm sure it doesn't." He chuckled. "Now, can we finally go enjoy a stroll along the beach?"

She nodded, reached out her hand, and together the two of them walked the beach. She looked at the sand, smiled. "I feel like walking barefoot." And that's what she did. Socks and shoes off, she headed to the water's edge, only to find Simon beside her, with his pant legs rolled up.

She laughed. "You know, when you get to this point in time, a barefoot walk on the beach can sure make a shitty day end up better."

"That it does," he replied. "That it does."

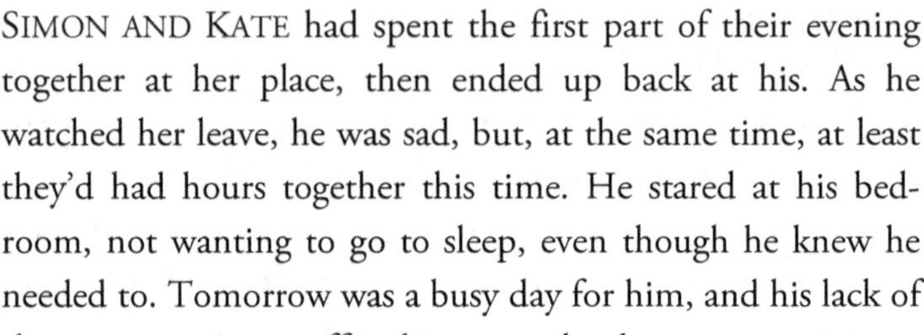

SIMON AND KATE had spent the first part of their evening together at her place, then ended up back at his. As he watched her leave, he was sad, but, at the same time, at least they'd had hours together this time. He stared at his bedroom, not wanting to go to sleep, even though he knew he needed to. Tomorrow was a busy day for him, and his lack of sleep was starting to affect his energy level.

At some point in time, he would have to beat this dragon called nightmares. But it all seemed to be connected to the visions, so he wasn't sure how to make that happen. He could dull his sleep with some drinks, and he did want a whiskey before bed, but that wasn't enough to knock back all the visions as they came through. As he had learned recently, the booze just delayed the visions.

He showered, stripped his bed, and made it back up with fresh bedding, then curled up and crashed almost immediately. When he woke a little later, he found himself wandering around in the dark. He stopped and stared, wondering what the hell was going on. He walked himself back to the bed, got back in, and sat here for a long moment, a little more unnerved than he'd thought. "Since when is sleepwalking part of my world?" And did it mean more visions? Less? Or foreshadowing of something else?

And that brought up an element that he really didn't like. Determined to not let it happen again, he did drift off to sleep, but, when he woke up the next time, he was getting out of bed.

"Oh no, hell no," he said out loud. "If this is a vision, it needs to stop. I'm not walking around my place in the nude in the dark without any idea why. So, whatever the hell this is, knock it the hell off."

And then realized it wasn't his bedroom he saw.

He frowned. "Whoa, whoa." The walls were blue, the curtains closed. There was a great big bed and a fluffy duvet. He stared down at his body and saw long legs. A female's body, just the lower part. Immediately the thought kicked into his head that they were legs built for running.

The woman quickly dressed, while he tried to disassociate from the vision. Yet it was happening so fast that he didn't understand. She got into running shoes at the doorway. When a man called out from the bed, she hesitated, and he whispered, "Please."

She sank back down onto the bed beside the man and kissed him on the forehead. That immediately snapped Simon back into his own vision. "Good Lord," he moaned, "like I need see that."

But, at the same time, he had to wonder. She was about to head out on a run and stopped. Somehow that seemed important. He just didn't know what it meant and what the importance of that stopping meant too. Was she meant to be a victim and then didn't become one because she changed her mind? And, if that were the case, why the hell was Simon even connecting with her?

Dissatisfied with it all, and unnerved by the change in the vision, he tried once again to go to sleep. This time he zoned out, until bright light streamed through his bedroom window. He woke up with a start and realized he was late. He swore, got dressed, and raced out of the penthouse. This had to stop. If he could just gain some control over his visions, his daytime would be a hell of a lot more manageable because he would get some sleep at night.

Something he rather desperately needed at this point in time was some way to make that all happen. He really needed to take control of that area of his life—before something else went crazy and things really went wrong. Something he didn't need in the least.

CHAPTER 4

Monday Morning

KATE WOKE UP late and with a sudden start. She instinctively reached for her phone, her heart slamming against her chest. Without even giving herself a chance to question why, she called Simon. When he answered, his words calm and measured, she immediately relaxed. "Jesus, I just woke up and immediately thought of you."

"Well, that would be a good thing," he replied, amusement in his voice, "except I don't think you were thinking the right things."

"Honest to God, it felt like something was wrong," she blurted out. "Please tell me everything is okay."

"Everything is okay," he repeated instantly.

She took a long slow deep breath and let it out noisily. "Thank God for that," she murmured. She reached up to rub her face. "I'm not even sure how the hell I slept in, but it is definitely later than I would like it to be."

"You've been running yourself down," he noted, "and I'm sure your dreams are not exactly peaceful."

"No, that's not the word I would use for them," she stated. "And it's kind of pissing me off because there's so much to get done right now."

"You're only one person," he reminded her.

"I know."

She got up and yawned. "Well, as long as you're okay … Man, I don't know what the hell that was, but I just woke up, and my immediate thought was that something was wrong with you."

"Well, something was wrong a little while ago," he admitted. "Maybe you're getting a delayed reaction."

"What?" she snapped. "Are you serious? What's the matter? Are you okay?"

"I'm fine," he said gently. "And I'm really glad to hear you care."

"Of course I care," she snapped, then groaned. "Please tell me what's going on."

"Just something weird happened," he began, "but it's really not a problem, and we don't have to talk about it now."

"I think we do," she argued. "If it had anything to do with that feeling waking me up, we definitely do."

"Well, that would mean," he suggested, "that you are getting psychic vibes all on your own."

Such a note of laughter filled his voice that she glared at her phone. "That's not funny."

He chuckled out loud at that. "Maybe not, but I do know that you guys swear by your instincts."

"And gut feelings," she added.

"Absolutely. In this case, it's all good. I just had some weird things happen overnight."

"Like what?"

There was silence for a moment. "It seemed like I was sleepwalking."

"Sleepwalking?" she asked in confusion, "You?"

"Well, that's what I thought the first time, only to realize that it really wasn't me. It was somebody else. I was just caught inside their vision."

Then he quietly explained, as she stared at her phone in shock. "Why would you connect with this person who got back into bed and kissed her partner?"

"Do I sound like I have any answers?" he asked in that flat note of finality.

"Look. I'm sorry. It just threw me. I was expecting all kinds of horrible things, and that's not horrible at all."

"No," he replied slowly, "until you consider that maybe she was heading out running and may have been another victim, except that she changed her mind."

At that, she stopped in midair, one pant leg on, one pant leg off, and sat down hard on her bed. "Jesus," Kate said, "you mean you're connecting with somebody else before they die?"

"I often do. Remember Robin, most recently."

"No, I know, and I guess the kids. They weren't dead yet, but neither were they well."

"Some were, not all of them."

"Jesus," she repeated. "I really don't want to think that this is somebody else who'll die. Did you see their faces?"

"No such luck. First the room was dark. Second, I saw only her legs. Third I didn't want to see the kiss and the rest. Besides, she kissed his forehead, and I saw above that."

"Too bad. As much as I keep telling people we can't assume it's the husband, I really don't want it to be another serial-killing scenario."

"Well, what you want isn't necessarily what you'll get," he stated, "and I certainly can't say this latest vision was related to your current murders. All I'm saying is that, this woman got up and then went back to the bed with her partner."

"Well, good for her," Kate said. "Let's hope it means nothing. Look. I have to go. I'm really late for work."

"Bye then," he immediately replied, then hung up.

She stared down at the phone *again* because she's the one who had called him. It's not as if he had been interrupting her. She immediately sent him a text. **Sorry. I just realized how late it is.**

And it was late. It was damn late, and she would get shit for it. Then she stopped and shook her head. Of course she wouldn't get shit for it. This is the job. Some days she could make it at a certain time; some days she couldn't. She did her best to always make it there consistently, but it's not like she hadn't been working around the clock on this case, starting this past weekend.

When she did finally get to the office, she grabbed a coffee before heading to her desk. She looked around to see who else on her team was here, frowning at Andy's empty desk. *Right, he took off this week. Lucky guy.* She sat down with a heavy *thud* that resounded around the room.

"Wow," Owen said from behind her, "you okay?"

"Fine." She yawned. "I need to catch some sleep though."

"Yeah, that gets to be a never-ending problem for us," he noted, with a knowing glance.

"We do the best we can"—she yawned again—"and sometimes, when you think that you're all good and that sleep should be right there, it's just not, and that's damn irritating."

"Yeah? Wait until you have kids," Owen added.

Sergeant Colby entered the bullpen and added, "If you're having trouble sleeping, you can always make an appointment with the department's shrink."

She looked up at him, shook her head. "It'll be one hell of a long time before I ever do that willingly. You know that, right?"

He glared at her. "They're not all the same."

"Maybe not," she agreed, "but just the thought of that one we had previously, talking to her pedophile brothers, while talking to us, is enough to make my insides creep out completely."

He nodded. "I have to admit that I've had a similar thought or two. Try taking a sleeping pill then."

"Nope, not going to," she stated. "I can't stand what drugs do to me."

"You're just being stubborn," Owen remarked, with a chuckle.

She shrugged. "Whatever. I'll deal with my sleep problems in my own way."

"As long as it doesn't affect your job," the sergeant noted.

"It hasn't yet." She glared at Colby, as if challenging him to argue with her. But, of course, she also knew he wouldn't. She had done a huge amount of quality work for the department, and their case closing rate had skyrocketed since she had arrived. She knew he was pleased with her and with the team. And if she had trouble sleeping? Well, she'd deal with it in her own time, in her own way, like everybody else.

"We got two other cases that came in overnight—unrelated," the sergeant relayed.

"I want to keep working on the runner case," she stated instantly.

He looked over at her. "Is it complex?"

"I hope not."

"Hope not? I thought we were looking at the ex-husband

being the guilty party in this one," Owen said.

"You may. I'm not," Kate stated.

"And why is that?" Owen asked.

"It's too cliché," she replied. "He makes an easy scapegoat, and I haven't even talked to him yet. So, until I can lock down any evidence that says that he's the killer, I'm not going there."

"But it looks like he's good for it?" the sergeant asked her.

"In a way, sure," she admitted quietly, "in that he is somebody who would know both women's habits and schedules, had a grievance against his ex-wife, and had threatened her in the past."

"Yet you don't like him for it, why again?" Colby repeated.

"Well, like I mentioned, I haven't talked to him. We don't know whether or not he has an alibi for that time. We don't know that he doesn't have a completely different story about the marriage and the divorce than everybody we've talked to—who has been on the wife's side, by the way. And the killer took out not just the ex-wife but her best friend."

"But," Rodney reminded her, "they were best friends, so the ex-husband could potentially have a grudge against her as well."

"And that's true. He may have," she agreed. "I spoke with Agnew, the other victim's husband yesterday, after Rodney had done the initial interview." She looked over at Rodney. "Agnew did confirm the theory that the two women were best friends and that Robin had been cheering on our other victim, Jenna, to leave her husband."

"So that would give motivation for killing both of them," the sergeant noted.

She nodded. "Yes."

"But?"

She shrugged. "Methodology. I mean, why go to such an elaborate method, not to mention one with such a high chance of being seen? Seems like there's a million other things he could have done. I don't know, but," she added, "it just, it feels wrong."

Colby frowned, as he studied her.

She shrugged. "I know. I know. We don't have much time. We need to close it as fast as possible. I'm doing my best. I just have to make sure I'm comfortable with everything, and, right now, let's not forget we don't have anything other than motive. And that means I need to find out where he was and if we can put him anywhere near the place of the murders. We can't just assume it's him. We have to prove it."

"Well, get after it then," the sergeant ordered in a sharp voice.

"I will. I will." She raised both hands. "Lots of people are here. Assign the other murderers to somebody else."

"I'm happy to take something different," Owen offered. "Running exhausts me, and that's just thinking about it."

The laughter dissolved any tension in the room, and the discussion quickly moved away from Kate. She was grateful and suspected Owen had done it intentionally and for that purpose. *Maybe he uses that trick in his marriage and with his kiddos too, which maybe made his familial unit such the touted success—most unusual in their line of work.* She gave him a slight tilt of her head in recognition. Maybe this team thing wasn't so bad.

Sighing, she returned to her murder cases. She couldn't explain why, but she was still so puzzled and upset about this one.

Although the ex-husband looked good for it, that didn't actually make him good for it. And, of course, nobody here was trying to railroad anybody, but, when you had something so clear-cut—or what looked to be so clear-cut—she always got suspicious. How hard would it be to make it look like the ex-husband did it, so somebody else got the heat of killing Jenna? Kate also didn't know if that woman was even the target of the two. It could have been Robin, the other one.

Maybe someone at the dental office hated her. Maybe a patient held a grudge against her, or someone in the office and made her the target. Or maybe Robin had an argument with a teacher at one of her kids' schools. Kate didn't know until she managed to get to the end of her questions, and she still wouldn't know for sure, even after all that. The trouble was, the department always had more cases than they had time and effort to deal with. By the time the next murder arrived on their doorstep, they were deemed through with the previous murder investigation. She shook her head.

She did her best though, and, as long as she got another day's grace, or two or three if she were lucky, she could focus just on this one case. And she realized it looked like she would be given that leeway today.

As she got up, the sergeant called her into his office. She walked over and stood in his doorway.

He looked up at her. "Any reason for the misgivings?"

"Not yet." Then she hesitated. "Well, maybe."

He looked at her, crossed his arms, and frowned. "Speak up."

"You won't like it."

He groaned. "Simon again?"

She replied, "Not in total, but one vision he had was about another runner."

"*Another* runner?"

She nodded grimly.

"You're not talking about a serial killer or some copycat killer who's waiting to strike again, right?" he asked in a sharp tone.

"Well, I hope not," she stated, "but you know as well as I do that only time will tell."

"No, no, no. I don't want any more of these cases."

"I wish," she whispered. "I really do, but there's no way to know yet."

"Then get to the bottom of it, fast. The last thing we need is another killer running around, picking off people at will."

"Got it." She hurried back to her desk. There she called Jenna's ex-husband again, and surprisingly she got him this time and identified herself. "I need to speak with you."

"Fine," he snapped into the phone. "I didn't kill her. I'm not all that upset that she's dead, but I didn't kill her."

"Then you won't have trouble telling me that to my face, right?"

"Of course not."

"Good. Then come on down to the station, and we'll talk here." And, with that, she gave him a time and added, "Don't be late."

When she hung up, Rodney looked over at her. "Was that the ex?"

She nodded. "Yeah, I figured it might put him off balance a little bit if we met with him in this setting."

"Let's hope it doesn't put him on edge so much that he shows up with a lawyer, and then we don't get jack."

"He might," she agreed. "That also says something about him, if he does."

"Only that he's more aware of the law than a lot of people. And it doesn't take much to think that somebody so soon after a bad divorce is a potential murder suspect," Rodney added.

She looked over at him. "How are your cases going?"

"Still just waiting on the tox screen for the one, but I'll help Lilliana on hers," he told her. "But, any time you're ready for a hand, let me know."

"I will," she said. "So far, this is just a case of running around and crossing *T*s and dotting *I*s, until something doesn't add up."

"So far?"

"Yeah, so far." She gave him a grim smile. "Let's hope I get something sooner rather than later." She got up and headed over to the coffee room, where she poured herself another cup. She stood here, staring out at the city from the window. And then she got another phone call. She looked down at her phone and noted it was the ex-husband.

"I came in early," he stated briskly. "I'm at the station."

"Good, I'll meet you up front."

As she headed down, she called out to Rodney, "The ex-husband just showed up."

"Came in early, huh? That's a good sign," Rodney noted.

"Depends on whether he's trying to confess or not," she quipped, tossing him a smile.

"Not likely. He's just trying to be cooperative."

She nodded and soon approached the man. His name was Barry Little, but nothing was little about him. He was tall, six-two, with broad shoulders and a clean-shaven face.

He looked like a salesman but could also have easily been a lawyer or some other professional. He definitely had a businessman look to him.

She held out her hand and introduced herself. "Thank you for coming down."

"It's always the husband—or ex-husband—who gets looked at first," he stated bitterly, "even if we didn't do anything."

"Which is why, the sooner we can count you out," she noted, "the better. Then we can focus on finding the real killer."

He studied her in surprise. "Well, that's a refreshing attitude."

She shrugged. "Listen. I'm not here looking to nail you, unless you did it. What I want is the killer. If that's not you, then the sooner we get there, the better," she explained. "Follow me, and we'll head into an interview room."

Once there, she sat down, started the recorder, identified the both of them, and then began. "Okay, so can you give me your whereabouts during the time frame in question?" She went on to specifically describe the time span she was interested in.

He nodded. "At home, sleeping."

"Anybody else with you?"

He shook his head. "As you are undoubtedly aware, I'm an ex right now," he said, "and I haven't hooked up with anybody new."

"Do you have anybody in your life right now?"

He shook his head. "No, I don't."

She nodded. "So, you don't have an alibi."

"No, I don't. But the thing is, most people are at home still sleeping at that hour," he declared. "Honestly, it was one of the problems in our marriage."

She looked at him in surprise. "What do you mean?"

"The running," he stated. "I get that it's healthy and keeps you fit and all that good stuff. But she was fanatical about it, and it wasn't just a morning jog for her. She was competitive and absolutely wouldn't miss a morning run."

"Some people are fitness crazy," she murmured.

"Yeah, that was her all right. *Fitness crazy* is a good phrase for it."

"And I take it you were not?"

"God no," he said, "absolutely not. She wanted me to be, but I'm of a much more moderate nature."

"Yet I understand you were quite abusive," she stated.

He flushed angrily. "No, I wasn't. She put that into the divorce papers, and her friends went to bat against me," he replied. "I never hurt her. We had plenty of yelling matches, but she always yelled back just as much."

She frowned at that. "So, you never hit her, and are you saying that you never abused her?"

"God no. That was her and her bloody BFF," he snapped. "The two of them were against me from the beginning."

"The beginning of what?"

"Since she started the divorce. I tried hard to fight against it. I wanted to go for marriage counseling. I signed up. She didn't show. I tried to coax her to go see somebody on her own, but she wouldn't do that either. Everything I tried to do in order to save the marriage she avoided, saying it wasn't worth saving."

"And yet in her paperwork filing, she actually lists abuse."

"I know. I think it's almost become a standard cry sometimes," he suggested. "It doesn't matter if there actually is any abuse, but they twist it all around to make it sound like you are this horrible person and how they never did anything wrong."

"Did she do something wrong?"

He stopped, looked at Kate for a long moment, and sighed. "You probably won't believe this, but Jenna was the abuser. It's not something I'm proud of and sure as hell not something I wanted to make public, but it won't matter if I've got a murder charge on my neck. You got to understand. She's the one who hit me. And it was more than once."

CHAPTER 5

KATE SAT DOWN at the beach, a cup of coffee in her hand. She was an oddity here in more ways than one, with the beach still full of sunbathers. The smell of suntan lotion and fries permeated the air for some reason. The fries really spoke to her. She lifted her nose and noted a couple food trailers off to the side. She was tempted to take a look, but fries were hardly a meal, and she wasn't sure what her plans were at this point. She was still processing the information she had just picked up from the ex-husband. It didn't really surprise her to hear Barry claim that Jenna was the abuser.

It was something that she had heard several times before. Everybody automatically wanted to think that the man always beat the woman, and 95 percent of the time it was true. Yet there was that other five percent, and, if Barry's words were true—something Kate would have to confirm— she wasn't sure how that actually helped him. Didn't it potentially make him even *more* of a suspect? Yet, if that were the case, why would he have said something? He had clearly had a very hard time telling Kate about the abuse, and the shame was heavy in his voice. He had left soon afterward.

But she was more bothered by the fact that this didn't seem to help anything. So, was it a red herring to throw her off the track or to garner sympathy, so she would have a harder time looking at him as the killer? She wasn't even sure how all this fit together.

Just wanting to have a time-out from all of it, she was out here among the sunbathers, in her jeans and shirt, with a jacket covering her holster.

As she sat in the blazing sun, drinking a cup of hot coffee, she shook her head. On display all around her were beach bodies, many of which were barely covered. People were in the water. People were on the sand. People were all around her, most of them ignoring her because they were intent on enjoying their own experience. And who could blame them? It was a gorgeous day—and hot—but the sun was finally beginning to ease up, reducing that intense heat, as it started to cool down for the evening. Still not cool enough yet for her.

Plenty for her to do yet today, although she could call it quits and start again tomorrow. It's just that every day that went by was another day without anything happening. Therefore, in no time at all, she would run out of days. On every case, the first forty-eight hours were incredibly important, and she had already exceeded that in this joggers' case by almost twelve hours, counting from the approximate time of the murders early on Saturday morning. It didn't stop her from wanting to sit here and to pull on all these threads she had. Yet, if she didn't get any answers, she really had no place to carry on with her investigation.

As she sat here, her phone rang. She looked at it and saw Dr. Smidge's phone number and sighed with relief. "There you are," she greeted him. "I've been dying for answers."

"I got to it as soon as I could," he declared in his customary testy voice. "At least you haven't brought me any new ones."

"No. ... However, I'm not sure there won't be more."

"Why do you say that?" he asked curiously.

"I don't know. Just something very odd about this case."

"Hell yeah, there is, but I wasn't expecting you to say that without any information."

"I have to say that," she stated, "because none of this makes any sense at all, unless it's a personal thing."

"What's wrong with it being personal? Isn't that why most of these things happen?"

"Yes and no." Then she told him what the ex-husband had told her.

"Oh, now that's a twist, isn't it? But is it a twist we believe?"

"That's where the trouble comes in."

"Well, it just makes him look like he's a bigger suspect, I would say."

"I know, and that's the problem. Why tell me, if that's the case?"

"Because he's thinking emotionally, not rationally. He's finally able to tell somebody and hopefully got them to believe it."

"Do you believe it?" she asked.

"I don't know. That's your job."

"I'm working on it, but I have to confirm it somehow, and that'll be difficult," she began. "He never went to the hospital, never got photographed, and never contacted the cops."

"No, that would be embarrassing as hell."

"And yet it shouldn't be," she cried out. "Abuse is abuse, no matter who's dishing it out."

"Yes, but so much of the male psyche is tied up in being the strong male and not being a victim," he reminded her.

"And certainly not at the hands of a woman. So, in this case, I can see why he wouldn't have told anybody."

"Yeah, and that doesn't help me confirm it now."

"Did you ask him if he told anybody?"

"No, and I need to." She looked down at her phone, making a mental note. "Maybe he told his parents or a buddy at work or something."

"I doubt it because that would make it even more embarrassing."

"So, chances are, he *didn't* tell anybody, and that won't help."

"But that doesn't mean other people didn't know," Smidge suggested, "especially the other girlfriend."

"And, therefore, the other girlfriend's husband," she muttered, with a nod.

"That's quite possible, isn't it?"

"I would think so."

"Hell, who knows? Maybe he had nothing to do with it."

"Maybe not," Kate agreed. "Did you find anything forensically?"

"Well, we've got the rope—your general average yellow poly, which is probably why they had trouble getting it tight enough."

"*They?*" Kate repeated.

"I don't have proof of two killers," Smidge quickly added, "but these were two very healthy, very fit females."

"Yes, but they were also blindsided," she noted, "as in running full-out, until they came headfirst against something."

"Yes, and that does line up with the facts, with the injuries," he said. "Did you happen to find a tree branch?"

"You're thinking a tree branch?"

"I'm thinking that maybe it was suspended, like pulled back, then came out of nowhere and hit them together. The second woman may well have been hit again separately, in order to knock her down. Because, if one was ever-so-slightly ahead of the other, the blow would have impacted the first one much harder."

"Right," she agreed. "Any proof of that theory?"

"There's definitely branch and bark particles in one, Jenna, so she was hit by a tree branch. The other one, Robin, was the same, but to a lesser extent. Then an additional minor blow just to knock her out maybe or to finish the job," Smidge suggested. "Honestly, they both died from the garrote, but, at that point in time, I suspect they may have been unconscious already. So, it was literally just to finish them off. It's actually very hard to strangle a person with your hands and especially with two people tied together with a nylon rope like that. He might have panicked and realized it was taking too long."

"Right, so I wonder, how he didn't think about that, yet how did he just happen to have a garrote on him too?"

"Well, the thing is, anything can be used, like if he had used wire or something to help hold back the tree branch."

"But that would more than likely be the rope."

"Hey, I'm just telling you what was used to kill them," he retorted. "It's up to you to find it."

"Got it. So any fingerprints, DNA, or anything like that?"

"No."

"Were they sexually assaulted?"

"No, although the one, Robin, did have semen, probably from a sexual encounter with her partner that morning."

"And not the other one?"

"No."

"Good enough," she said, "I'll have to check with forensics and see if they've come up with anything."

"I'm sure there'll be a little bit of blood splattered all around. There'll be footprints, but that doesn't mean it will be anything other than your garden-variety runner."

"Wow, you're being really positive, aren't you?"

"Just being realistic," he said.

"Right." She sighed. "In that case I'll head back up there and take a look and see if I can find the branch."

"I would like to head up there myself actually," he shared, "because, until I know for sure, I won't be satisfied."

"I'll meet you there in ten," she said, jumping to her feet.

"That'll be about right," he murmured. "I'm already in the car."

"Good, I'm not far away. I'm just down on the beach."

"You're at the beach?" he asked in surprise.

"Yeah, I just came from talking with the ex-husband, and I needed five minutes to digest this information on the abuse."

"Just park it," he advised. "Take it under consideration with the rest of the information you gather, but don't let it be more than it is."

"I won't," she agreed, "but it's troubling because abusive wives are always hidden. We never really think about it, even though we know it happens. I can't remember any case I've personally dealt with where an abused husband was a factor."

"No, and chances are you won't. In order for that to happen, you'd actually have to find out about it first, and the male victims are especially silent on these things. It's slowly becoming recognized as something that happens, but we're a long way from the male victims routinely coming forward."

"I know," she added quietly, "that abuse is never acceptable, no matter who it happens to, but there is such a component of shame associated with it—even more so with the men."

"I hear you there. I'll see you in about five minutes." And, with that, he hung up on her.

She stared down at her phone. "Goodbye to you too." She headed to her car, while chugging down the rest of her coffee, then dropped the cup in the closest trash can. Interesting that Smidge wanted to return to the crime scene. But then that was Smidge. He wanted to have a damn good idea of what was going on here, before he signed off on his reports. And, if anybody had missed something or hadn't thought something important enough to worry about, he wouldn't be a happy camper.

Back at the crime scene, she parked in the nearest parking lot and walked down the pathway to where the two bodies had been found. She studied the area once again, now with the information in mind that Smidge had given her. Looking at the site, she didn't think it was likely to have been a stray branch that had hit them, but the theory that one was pulled back and secured was worth exploring. She studied the nearby tree and found one that had potential.

Walking closer, she looked carefully and saw where the surface of one of the branches was stripped clear around, and it looked like it had been pulled back by a rope or something. As she followed the branch farther back, she realized that it pulled back easily enough and would send quite a whip flying into somebody's face, if that were the plan. As she studied it, moving it back and forth, Dr. Smidge arrived.

He looked at it, nodded. "That's exactly what I was coming to check."

"You're thinking he pulled this back." She demonstrated. "It looks like the only place would be to try and secure it right here."

He nodded. "Yes, so now look where the other end of the rope was tied and related footprints—but carefully though."

Cautiously the two of them moved around to the most likely spot.

"It's also possible," she suggested, "that he just stood right here, holding the rope himself."

Smidge immediately grabbed her arm and pointed at the nearby ground. "You see where the heels were dug in over there? Either he strained to pull it back to tie it off or stood here, holding it back himself."

She frowned. "The only way you could do that is if you knew they were coming." But, as she understood by now, that wasn't difficult information to come by. She turned and looked up the hill. "Look over there. See those tracks sliding down the hill?"

He nodded, and, slowly walking on either side of the footsteps, they headed up to where more tracks revealed where the killer had stopped and watched and waited. They both crouched to get a better look at the ground.

"So, chances are," Kate suggested, "that he had the rope tied to the branch with the rope hanging where he could get to it. Then, as soon as he knew that they were coming, he slid down here, grabbed the rope, and pulled it back. When they came around that corner, he let it fly right in their faces."

"So Jenna must have been slightly in the lead at that

time and took it right across the bridge of her nose," Smidge noted, "which is why the damage was here." He pointed across the brow area on his face. "It's actually cracked. She would have gone right down, probably without a fight. The other one, Robin, would have been stunned, and he must have come with a stick and hit her over the head. There's no evidence she got a shot of bear spray off."

"And then what? He grabbed the rope off the branch, tied it around their necks, and tried to strangle them with it?" Kate asked the coroner.

"Unconscious bodies are not cooperative at all," Smidge declared. "It would have been quite hard to get their heads into a position where he could have choked the life out of both of them simultaneously. And who knows? He might have heard somebody coming and pulled the bodies off into the shrubbery here. That could have been a change in his plan, causing him to panic a bit."

"But he must have had the garrote with him."

Dr. Smidge nodded. "I suspect he did. You know, a contingency plan perhaps."

She winced at that. "And it could have been any wire?"

"Yes, and garrotes are not hard to make. They just need some handle on either end. They're damn impossible to get away from, and it would have taken just a matter of minutes to kill both women. Particularly since both were most likely unconscious by then."

"No defensive wounds then?"

He looked at her and shook his head sadly. "Not a one. They were out cold, but apparently he didn't want to leave them to be found alive."

She murmured, "He wanted to be positive they were dead."

"Yes," he confirmed. "We'll need to bring forensics back to take a look at these areas."

"Okay." She nodded. "Though I'm not seeing much. No cigarette butts, no trash, nothing's here." She tracked around the area. "And I know that I saw forensics over there, when they worked the scene, but I don't think anybody was thinking of a branch that came out of nowhere."

Smidge snorted. "If you look at the extended crime scene, very little is here." Finally he stood, brushed his hands to clean them off. "Well, I'm good. I can go home and smile now."

"Good for you," she said, "your job is done."

He laughed out loud, perhaps the first real genuine laughter she'd heard from him. "Mine is, now the baton passes to you."

"Wait, what about tests?"

"Not back yet, but I'm not expecting much, and nothing was found in the first round. Both were incredibly healthy, strong individuals," he repeated. "Now it's up to you to fill in the blanks."

⚬⚬⚬

WHEN HIS PHONE rang at home, Simon was surprised to see the front desk of his apartment building calling. "Hello, Harry. What can I do for you?"

"The detective is here."

"By all means, send her up," he replied in surprise.

"I already did," Harry replied, but he hesitated.

"What's up?"

"She, … uh, she doesn't look all that great," he stated in a rush.

"Ah, okay, good enough. Thanks for the heads-up."

And, with that, he hung up the phone and walked over to the elevator.

When it opened, she stepped out, stared at Simon, and asked, "Harry let you know I was here?"

"Yep, he did." Simon smiled. "It's his job, you know."

She nodded. "And he better do it because we don't want you ever blindsided. If you ever get a new doorman, and then somebody comes, saying it's me, but it's not me—"

"Well, generally speaking, I don't have anybody coming up here trying to take me out," he noted, with a smirk.

"No, but you did have a lot of girlfriends coming up, using all kinds of different tricks to get into your bed," she argued, waggling her eyebrows.

"Well, you, my dear, are welcome in my bed anytime."

She snorted at that. "If only it were that simple." She gave him half a smile.

"You don't think it is?"

"Nope, I sure don't," she murmured. "An awful lot is going on these days."

"You want to talk about it?"

She shook her head. "You know I don't really, but I probably need to."

"Oh, that's interesting. What's going on?"

"I just wanted a male take on this."

He stopped and stared at her, his head tilting to the side. "So, it's very gender specific."

"Yes." She glanced at the beer in his hand and smiled. "Have you got another one of those?"

"I do. Are you driving?"

"I don't know," she admitted. "Am I getting an invitation to stay?"

He stopped, looked at her, and frowned. "You know

there is always a standing invitation for you."

She smiled. "I do know that. Either way, I'd still like a beer."

"Good enough. And is that suntan lotion I smell on you?"

She shuddered and then laughed. "If you do, it's by osmosis or something. I was down at the beach to clear my head, and far more people were down there than I expected."

"Well, on a beautiful summer day, late in the afternoon? It's a perfect time for a swim and for people just getting off work. It's a great way to spend the evening."

"You're right," she agreed, rolling her head. "Clearly I haven't done enough of that stress relief."

"No, you're too busy putting away all these killers."

"I wish to God they would stop with the killing," she muttered.

"Don't we all," he agreed. "Now what's going on?"

She frowned and hesitated.

He handed her the cold beer and pointed. "Come on. Let's go sit and enjoy the view."

"Outside maybe?" she asked, sounding hopeful.

He looked at her in surprise and replied, "Absolutely."

He opened the patio doors, and they stepped out onto his huge balcony.

She sighed. "I don't spend enough time here," she noted, walking over to the edge.

"You do know that you're welcome to move in, don't you?"

"Not happening," she stated instantly. "I just meant that, when I'm here, I don't spend enough time enjoying this." She waved her arm around the wide-open space and the view completely open before them. She tilted her face up to the sun. "It's so gorgeous."

"It is." He reached out, gently placed an arm on her shoulders and coaxed her over to one of the huge long couches he had set up outside. "Let's just sit and relax."

She nodded and collapsed onto the nearest couch. She laid back, her eyes closed, the sun on her face, and didn't say a word.

He waited, not wanting to push. Obviously something was going on, but he had no idea what, and the reality was that she'd tell him when she was ready and not a moment before.

Finally she opened her eyes. "Outside of the awful child abuse that happened in your world," she began, waving a hand as if to move quickly past it, "were you ever abused in an adult relationship?"

He stared at her in surprise, not even sure where to start with that one. "Are you asking about something specific?"

"Yes." She nodded. "I guess it's something that I don't really understand, even though I come from an abusive history myself."

"But not sexual abuse," he confirmed, "right?"

"No." She shook her head. "Not really. ... I mean, like you, I was a victim way back then, but in a different way. And no, I was never raped, although a lot of people would say tough relationships spawn their own sense of emotional and mental abuse."

"They absolutely do," he agreed. "So why don't you tell me what this is about?"

"I spoke to the ex-husband today, Barry Little." Then she slowly went on to explain about his claim that the victim, Jenna, had been the one to beat him up.

"It happens," Simon stated, staring out at the city. "I

think it happens more than we'd like to think. Guys are conditioned to not hit women. You'll get the abusers for sure," he noted, "but any decent guy has learned somewhere along the way, and many from a young age, that we're not allowed to hit women. They're smaller, frailer, and they can get damaged a lot more than we think from the blow of our fist, simply because we're so much stronger. So, to think that some female would actually hit me would be difficult, but, yeah, I'd probably take it without telling anyone," he answered, with a nod, "at least until it became something that was obviously a bad scenario for me."

"What do you mean, a bad scenario?" she asked. "When does something like that become too much?"

"It should never happen in the first place, but just because somebody loses their temper and reaches out and smacks me across the face, I can't say that I would sit there and cry foul. I mean, it's not right maybe, but it's still not something I would do."

"And if it were ongoing?"

"That's a different story," he declared. "If ongoing, I would break off the relationship."

"But what if you really cared?"

"This really bothers you, doesn't it?"

She shrugged. "I guess I need to understand it, and I don't know if it even changes anything."

"In a lot of ways," Simon noted, "it makes it worse for Barry, doesn't it?"

She nodded. "That's what I was thinking, and I was just discussing that with the coroner. Because it does add another element, making it not so much about revenge but about stopping the abuse."

"Exactly," he agreed, "but this was a well-thought-out

murder, wasn't it?"

She nodded.

"So, we're talking premeditation, so first-degree murder in this case, and the question is, if it was this guy trying to kill his ex-wife, he might have been happy to take out the running partner and best friend as well because she may have had elements of the same bitchiness," he suggested quietly. "You may want to check with the other husband on that."

"I was thinking about that," she said. "What are the chances that the two women were also that much alike at home in the family relationships?"

"It's definitely something to check up on," Simon noted. "Yet you can be certain that Agnew will be ashamed of it too, and he won't want anybody to know. And so, if it was him doing the killing, he'll be incredibly cautious about anybody finding out. Motive can be everything, and he won't want anybody to understand that he had one."

"So, if he killed them, he'll be even harder to prosecute," she stated, with a nod.

"Obviously you'll have to do everything you can to track it down because he knows that, if he does get caught, his motive will come out, and that will be a double whammy. So, for Agnew, it may not even be as much about the guilt over killing her but more about the shame of being an abused husband." After a moment of silence, Simon added, "And to answer your question, no, I've never been in an abusive relationship with a girlfriend. But have I ever been hit by a woman? Yes, but never twice."

She nodded. "That's what I expected. It just brings up a whole new perspective."

"I get it," Simon agreed. "The question is whether there'll be another murder as well."

She looked at him, startled.

He shrugged. "Remember that woman in my last vision?"

"Yeah, I remember." She winced. "I was just hoping that there hadn't been any further connection."

"Well, there isn't, and yet there is," he added. "I feel her again, like she's right here, breathing, always beside me, always just connected."

"You can't tell her to take up tennis instead of running?"

He burst out laughing. "No, and she's a runner, but she's not as hardcore as these other two women were."

"And yet she was ready to get up at some godforsaken dark hour and go out onto the paths."

"You know you would do it too, don't you?"

CHAPTER 6

"I'M CONSIDERING GOING running tomorrow morning." Kate glanced at Simon.

"Do you think he'd kill again that fast?"

"I don't know," she admitted. "If I could install some cameras up and down the pathway, that would make me happy."

"Can you get a surveillance team to do that or something?"

"There's a million reasons why we can't," she replied.

"And that just makes it that much more awkward. Even with cause and effect."

"Public security, privacy rights, *blah, blah, blah*," she complained, with a shrug. "We're going through the street cameras around the area, but it's such a heavy traffic spot that it will be difficult to pinpoint anybody. And the same vehicles come and go on a regular basis. The IT department's got a long list—and we've got Reese and her two assistants helping them as much as they can—but, short of something to narrow it down, nothing is happening. The rope that was used was cheap and could have been bought in any hardware store," she added. "They were killed by a garrote, probably handmade, according to the coroner, or at least it wasn't an easily identifiable piece of wire, just plain old wire. And they were knocked out by a branch first." She explained the setup to Simon.

"Wow." He relaxed a little farther back, bringing his knee up to rest his beer bottle on. "When you think about it that way, it actually takes quite a bit of planning."

"And the mode of killing wasn't random. Whether it was random that he chose them as his victims, it wasn't random once he decided on them."

He frowned at her.

She shrugged. "Think about it. He's up on the top of a nearby hill, and he's looking for his victim. Is he looking for *that* particular victim?"

"Maybe. Is he looking for those two victims?"

"Maybe," she murmured. "So, it might have been that they weren't random in the sense that he chose them because he saw them coming. But it's still possible that they were random in the sense that anybody could have been coming along and would have been good enough to have done the job on them."

"Right, and those random killers are much harder to catch."

"They're damn hard to catch," she murmured. "Stranger killings are always bad. In this case, if it happens again, then you know there'll be a massive outcry from the public—and with good reason. This is a popular running trail, and, all of a sudden, it's been tainted by killers."

"Not to mention the ongoing danger of the killers," he noted, with a sidelong look at her.

She nodded. "It's a PR nightmare, and the department would obviously do our best to try and solve it quickly. Stranger abductions generally take longer because we can't solve them until we get more victims and find a pattern or connection."

"Ouch," he murmured.

"Exactly," she said. "You know I've done everything I can so far, and it's only a matter of time before I get pulled off the case."

He nodded. "Anything else you can do?"

"I'll do it tonight. … Or maybe I can just call." She frowned. "I really want to talk to that other husband, Agnew, and ask if he was in the same boat."

"But you won't know that over the phone."

"No," she replied quietly. "He might be capable of hiding it over the phone. I need to see his face." She checked her watch. "I think I'll run up there right now." She hopped to her feet. She tossed back the rest of her beer, handed the empty bottle back to him, and said, "Maybe I'll go for a run afterward."

"Or go tomorrow morning, like you said earlier," he suggested.

She frowned, then shrugged. "Or how about I do both?"

"You need the exercise?"

She nodded. "Honestly? Yes. This tension is coiling up inside me."

"Then we'll both go," he stated. "Let me get changed real quick, and we'll go talk to Agnew now. Then you can run the pathway and wear off some of that energy at the same time."

She thought about it for a moment, then nodded. "Good idea. Let's do that."

It was a good thirty-five, almost forty minutes later, when they pulled up in front of Agnew's townhome. Kate studied the area, shaking her head. "It's so beautiful here. You can smell the salt water. You can hear the waves and the birds even. … The beach is literally one block from here, yet they obviously preferred the park trail," she noted quietly.

"Given the subject matter tonight, I'll stay here," Simon offered, leaning against the car.

She nodded, then walked up the front steps and knocked.

The door opened almost immediately, and Agnew stepped outside, closing it behind them, glaring at her. "Detective, I thought I'd made it clear I'm shielding my children from all of the investigation. That's why I'd asked that you call instead."

"I'm sorry, and I understand why you feel that way," she replied, "but, until this is settled, I may have to come back and forth a few more times."

He groaned. "Do you have any idea how painful this is?"

"I do, and I understand your frustration, but I'm presuming that you also want us to find out who killed your wife."

That stopped him.

She nodded. "In that case, we need you to answer some questions."

"Isn't there any forensic evidence you can use?" he replied fretfully. "Like something that, you—that you don't have to involve me in?"

"No, there isn't."

He sighed. "So, what is it then?"

"I have what I guess is a bit of a delicate question about your wife."

He nodded and asked, "What?"

"How was your relationship?"

"I've already told you that our relationship was great," he cried out. "Why are you asking me these questions?"

She stopped, hesitated, and then asked, "Did she ever hit

you?"

He stared at her, but she watched his eye dart to the left, and his jaw firmed up ever-so-slightly.

"She did, didn't she?"

"I don't understand why you're asking me that," he said, his tone turning stiff. "Why would you defile the memory of my wife by bringing up things like this?"

"I'm not defiling anything," she corrected. "I'll get to the truth, and right now it's looking a little sticky."

"Sticky?"

She didn't clarify. "Back to the question. Your wife, did she abuse you?"

He stared at her in shock. But it was manufactured, and she could tell almost immediately from the look on his face that he was figuring out how to act and what to say.

"So, let me change the question. Are you aware that your neighbor, the other victim in this case, was abusing her husband?"

He stared at her in surprise. Surprised that Kate knew.

She nodded. "At least that's according to him."

Immediately Agnew's face turned scornful. "And you believe that liar?"

"Any reason I shouldn't?" she asked quietly. "And obviously we're checking out his story. He said that she used to hit him on a regular basis. But she's the one that wanted the divorce, not him."

He shook his head. "I don't know the truth about that. I don't know anything about it at all."

"Are you sure about that?" She paused. "Are you sure that your wife didn't also abuse you?"

He shook his head. "You don't know what you're talking about."

But she watched as his hand gently rubbed his ribs. "So, maybe I should get a subpoena and photograph the damage to your body," she suggested.

He stared at her, his gaze hardening up.

She nodded. "Obviously you don't want anybody to know. If that is the case, I get it. Nobody wants something that you consider an embarrassment to be known publicly, particularly now that the women are both gone. I can see that, from your perspective, it won't help anything."

"Of course not," he spat. "It's despicable to just ruin their memories."

"That's not what I'm doing. That's just a statement of fact."

"So, what difference would it make?" he asked. "Why would I even want to talk to you about something like that?"

"Because, if we don't get a clear picture, we don't know exactly what's really going on, and currently everybody is pinning the blame on the ex-husband."

"Well, if he was being abused, wouldn't that give him more motivation?"

"If it had been an abused-woman-turned-killer, yes, at least potentially," she stated. "With men who are abused, there are additional issues, I believe. I'm sure the shrinks would have a heyday with this one as it is, though they would anyway because this guy killed two women. However, there's also another part of the story. If Barry were the killer, and he is prosecuted, then his whole motivation in all this would be made public knowledge. The whole sordid story would come out, and everybody would know that he was an abused husband."

She caught just the barest wince cross Agnew's face. She nodded. "Just like you felt just now. Obviously you don't want anybody to know, and it would be something that we would try very hard to keep under wraps," she noted. "Your self-esteem is very important, as is the children's memory of their mother. But hiding that abuse will never be a good thing in the end."

"Sure, it is," Agnew argued. "So what if she did hit me every once in a while? She used to lose her temper on a regular basis." Kate just continued to stare at him, and finally he flushed. "It wasn't very often. It wasn't that bad."

"How bad does it have to be?" she asked. "I'm struggling with that whole concept. When is something like that enough to raise an alarm?" she asked. "It always seems to be a 'bad enough' issue. It wasn't bad enough?"

He shrugged. "You're making too much out of it."

"No, I'm not. Yet I understand that you don't want it to be made public."

He stiffened and glared at her.

"So can you please help me—and you too—and confirm whether or not you heard that the same thing was a problem in the marriage of the other couple?"

He nodded slowly. "Robin did mention it every once in a while."

"In what context?"

"That Jenna should have beaten up Barry more often. Tuned him up, made him more amiable. And that it was sad that it had come to this."

"So Robin advocated for the abuse?"

Agnew didn't say anything.

Kate nodded. "Of course she would because she was abusing you." Kate sighed heavily. "You know that there are professionals you can talk to if you need help, right?"

He just curled his lip, as if that were the worst thing that she could have suggested.

"Did Robin think that you needed a tune up, when she realized that the other couple was getting a divorce?"

"I think she finally realized that the divorce was a good thing," Agnew shared quietly. "I gathered the ex-husband was getting more and more difficult to control, and this was deemed a better option."

"Interesting, and so you never ever went against Robin, did you?"

He stared at her for a long moment, before responding. "What difference does it make now?"

"Because I need to know who these two women were, whether they were abusive to anybody else, and whether anybody else had a motive for killing them."

"Well, you know the ex-husband, Barry, he was in that situation, and it was ugly," Agnew noted. "I admit I saw it every once in a while. However, I also knew how my wife felt about it, so I just stayed out of it. No good could come from criticizing her best friend."

"And did you and Barry ever talk about it?"

"No. We never discussed it. Barry never mentioned anything about it, but she could be quite ..." Agnew hesitated and then added, "Jenna was a shrew."

"So, she would humiliate him publicly as well, so most of his friends probably thought he needed to get the hell out of there too, correct?"

He shrugged. "I didn't meet any of his friends, so I don't know."

She nodded. "Well, thank you for confirming his story on that."

"God, I don't even know why he told you. It just makes him look even guiltier."

"Unless he is innocent and didn't think it through in terms of the additional motive. Yet I find that, typically, honest men don't have anything to hide, and they put it all out there for us to draw our own conclusions." And, with that, she thanked him, then turned and headed down toward the car, where Simon still leaned against the vehicle.

He looked at her and asked, "Ready for a run?"

"Oh yeah," she replied. "I really need a good run tonight."

After the first mile, she realized just how much. She ran hard and fast, but he kept up the whole way. At times he pulled ahead; other times she did, laughing, joking, and screaming with joy. She ran her body to a fitness level she hadn't been able to achieve lately. By the time they both came to a stop back at the parking lot, she was exhausted, exhilarated, and wired high with energy. She turned, looked at him, and grinned. "Now that was a lot of fun."

He nodded, gasping for breath. "It really was. I forgot how competitive you are."

She looked at him in surprise. "Am I?"

He just gave her a droll look.

She shrugged. "Maybe, but I don't think it's bad. Is it?"

"I didn't say that," he replied, "but, as soon as I would gain on you, you'd be right there in front of me."

She chuckled. "I was just putting you to the test."

"*Uh-huh*, sure you were," he teased, with a grand smile.

"Besides," she added, "you did really well."

"Oh, thank you," he replied, rolling his eyes. He stopped and started to stretch out his legs and his shoulders.

She immediately followed suit. "I can see what a joy this place would have been for the two women. A place like this, so close to home, and a best friend to run with? I totally get it."

Simon nodded, his arms stretching high above his head.

She nodded in return. "It could become something you look forward to each day, almost like a drug even, and then you start craving it."

"Particularly if you're a runner at heart," he stated. "A lot of runners are out there, but this trail requires a definite type of runner."

"Yes," she murmured, as she looked around at the spot. "So does that mean our killer was a runner too? I would think so," she answered her own question. "Not only a runner but somebody who loved the sport as well."

"Or *did*," he reminded her. "It could very well have nothing to do with these particular women, but him finding anger in the fact that he can no longer run like he used to."

"That's possible. Jealousy and rage are a powerful combination." She frowned, rolling the idea around in her head. "But that still doesn't help us find the killer."

Simon replied, "Unless you have a group of people who had accidents here or maybe some confrontations. Or maybe who just always used to run here."

"Yeah, but it's not as if we have to sign in to run here," she noted. "These are free open areas, and part of the joy of them is the fact that you get to come and go as you want."

"Oh, I get it," he said. "Believe me. I do. I'm just wondering if there is any way to know whether or not anybody around here had some sort of an accident or a hardship. I'm thinking of a scenario where they would have come to this place with the intent to stop others from having what they could no longer have."

"Aren't motives great?" she stated, turning to look at him.

"Yeah, it's like any excuse will do to take a life and to make you feel better because you can't do something anymore," he stated, with a chuckle.

"You know what? People are really simple. It's usually about greed, selfishness, power, or sex," she pointed out. "It's often about sex."

"Which is all about power," he added, with a nod of his head.

She frowned at that.

"You really should talk to the staff shrink about this case," he suggested. "It could go in all different ways."

"*Nah*, it's a single case," she argued. "I can't be bothered."

"Or you just don't want anything to do with her."

"You know how creepy it is to think that her predecessor is up on charges on all these other pedophile cases?"

"I know," he declared. "Believe me. It's something that I've woken up to in the middle of the night myself, wondering where her head was that she would actually continue to feed her brothers' fantasies in order to keep herself in the loop."

"And yet she's denying all knowledge of it."

"What about the murdering pedophile suspect himself?"

"Oh, he's singing his tunes just fine, pulling his sister into it all."

"Of course, because misery loves company. Once again back to that criminal mind thinking that, *If I can't have a good life, you're not getting one either.*"

"Is that what this is about, you think?" she asked, turning to look around at the jogging trail. "*I can't run anymore, so you can't either?*"

"Well, it's thin," Simon admitted, "but it's certainly a

motive."

"It is," she murmured. She shook her head. "Now I need a shower and food."

"Definitely food," he murmured. "And, if we had brought our swimming stuff, we could have gone for a swim."

She frowned, looked at him, and considered that. "We're already soaking wet with sweat—at least I am. I don't care about getting wet. It's just shorts and a T-shirt anyway. It'll dry fast." As a matter of fact, all she had on was a sports bra, a loose tank over that and her running shorts. She asked, "You want to hit the beach?"

He nodded and grinned. "Yep, even if I lose these clothes to the salt, it'll still be worth it to round out this day."

She laughed at that. "I didn't think to bring towels, even just for after a sweaty run," she noted. She dug around in her trunk and pulled out two plastic bags, which she draped over the car seats. "This will have to do to help keep the sweat smell out of my car." They got into the vehicle, drove down to the beach, and, as they parked, she pointed. "And look. It's almost empty."

"Well, the sun is going down, and it's been an absolutely gorgeous day."

"We hit the running trail just right, didn't we?"

"Just right," he confirmed, with a nod. "Just enough light to see and not enough light to be hindered by it."

"That's how the killer hit it in the morning too. He has to know that trail," she stated, shaking her head. "He had to know the trail, had to know the victims, and had to know that they would be the only ones there."

"Only if he'd seen them on a regular basis."

"Which also means he's scouting, either for them specifically or for somebody who would be there at that hour."

"So then the victims fit the time slot because the hour is what he focused on."

"Well, it makes sense," she stated. "It's still damn thin. A stretch, really. I'd like a lot hardier, heavier motive than that."

"Yeah, your prosecutor won't think much of it."

"Nope, he won't think anything of it at all because he'll be locked on Barry, the ex-husband."

"And you seem to have knocked him off the suspect list?"

"No," she replied, studying Simon. "I definitely haven't knocked him off, but I have knocked him down on the list."

"Why?"

"Because I don't think he wants anybody to know what happened to him."

"So, saving face is a bigger thing than stopping the abuse?"

"Absolutely. Everybody would have preferred to just completely ignore it. And then the fact that he was getting divorced means that the abuse was coming to an end – but according to what he'd said earlier, she was the one who wanted the divorce, so maybe he didn't want to get out of it."

SIMON WATCHED AS Kate kicked off her shoes and socks and raced into the water, her tank top flowing behind her as she ran. When the water was midthigh, she dove into the water. He wasn't far behind, but watching her brought such joy to his heart that he couldn't tear his gaze away. She was so calm, so confident, so natural—and, in this moment—so full of joy. He knew that the reality of this case, the other cases to come, and the ones that still weighed on her from the past would always be there, but she was doing so well in handling them.

He admired her and didn't think he could do the same work, not without being pulled down to levels he didn't want to even begin to go. And, of course, some of it was more interesting because it did bring up these other issues, like the men being abused by the women.

He knew it was a sensitive topic. He had heard rumblings about such things, but nobody he knew personally had ever been abused to that extent—that he knew of. Yes, he'd been hit, but, as he told Kate, it wasn't something that had continued, and he would never allow that. Either the relationship itself needed to be terminated or something different had to happen.

But he couldn't imagine a case where he would kill somebody in order to get out of that situation. It would bring up all the cops and all the questions, and he could imagine how any man would immediately not want anything to do with that because it would then become public, and keeping this private was the whole goal.

Simon sighed and dove in beside her, and, when he popped up, she was there, laughing at him, splashing him in the face. He grinned, caught her in his arms, then pulled her up tight and kissed her, the heat flashing between them, even though they were in the icy cold water.

She wrapped her legs around his hips, climbed up higher, then leaned down and kissed him tenderly. "This was a wonderful idea," she murmured.

"Definitely," he agreed, holding her close.

They turned to see the sun starting to set.

She cried out in joy. "Look at that," she whispered. "Is there any prettier place in the world?"

"I'm sure lots of people around the world think the same thing," he noted, with a chuckle.

"Maybe," she said, "but they'd be wrong because we are right."

He burst out laughing at that, and she just grinned down at him.

"We're blessed," he added, with a smile. "That's for sure."

She nodded. "What a stupendous evening."

He smiled, held her close, and whispered, "I'm so glad you came by."

"Me too," she whispered back. "I didn't even have a real reason to."

"Do you need a reason?" he asked, tilting his head back to look up at her.

She smiled, gently pulling his wet hair off his face. "Sometimes I feel like I do."

"We'll have to work on that," he noted.

"Maybe," she replied, "but not tonight."

They stayed in the water, just floating, talking, holding hands, enjoying the company and the downtime. Then finally, she started to shiver.

He looked her over. "Your lips are turning blue."

She shrugged. "The cold has been a problem for a while," she admitted. "I just didn't want to move."

"I get it. Come on though. It's time to go home."

"We didn't bring towels," she noted, with a shrug.

"Nope, we didn't. So fast trip home, hot showers, then we'll sit outside and have dinner."

"Yeah, is there any dinner at your place?"

At least she hadn't made any comment about *not* going to his place. So he smiled and said, "I can have it delivered by the time we get there."

"Oh, now that's a good idea," she noted. "Chinese."

"Seriously, Chinese again?"

"Yeah," she repeated, "Chinese."

"Fine."

As they grabbed up their shoes and socks, he made the phone call and placed the order.

At the car again, she quickly brushed off her feet. "Wet shoes and socks, not a cool idea."

"It won't be for long," he added, "so you can live with it."

"Not a problem." She drove them home. And, true enough, dinner was waiting for them. As they got up to the penthouse, she raced to the shower, calling back, "Last one there'll get the cold water."

He roared, jumped into action, and got in there, just as she did. They jostled for room to get inside the shower, and finally he just picked her up, stepped in with her, turned on the jets, and they made hot ferocious love under the cascade of water. When she collapsed, exhausted, against the wall, he smiled, then leaned over to give her a tender kiss. "I've been wanting to do that since we were in the ocean."

"You and me both," she murmured, looping her arms around his neck. "And I'd go for round two, except I know food's out there."

"Oh, look at that," he said, with mock humor. "I've been forsaken for food."

"Well, we could always come back later," she replied, waggling her eyebrows.

"Deal," he said instantly. The speed of his response made her burst out laughing. He grinned as he found some clean clothes. "And what about your clothes?" he asked.

She groaned. "Damn it."

"I told you to just bring a couple outfits here."

"Didn't I leave some clothes last time?" she asked, rooting around in his closet.

"I think you did actually." He went over to the dresser, where he had cleared out the top two drawers, and pulled out a pair of leggings and a T-shirt and held them up.

"There's no bra," she noted, "but I'll be good to go without one anyway."

She quickly dressed, and they headed out of the bedroom. Moments later, with the Chinese food served, they were sitting outside, enjoying the meal, the perfect end to an absolutely glorious evening. She gave a happy sigh, as she put down her empty plate. "Now, with a perfect night's sleep, I would be completely restored and could begin to rebuild my faith in humanity once again."

"Any reason not to get a good night's sleep?"

"I hope not. I sure need it."

CHAPTER 7

Tuesday Morning

KATE MIGHT HAVE needed a good night's sleep, but she sure didn't get it. Not even at Simon's penthouse. When the phone rang, she dragged herself out of her sleep and groaned as she saw her phone. "Morgan," she answered.

"This is Dispatch. You have a new potential homicide at the running path where your previous two DBs were. You've been tagged on this case specifically."

She slowly sat up. "Do we know anything about it?"

"No, only that it was reported as two bodies."

"Shit." She muttered to herself as she disconnected, throwing back the covers, and standing up, looking for the clothes she'd had on. Not that they were appropriate for the job she was about to do, but she had no time to go home and get changed. She hung up and called Rodney.

"Hey," he said in a sleep-induced tone.

"Two more bodies on the running path," she noted briefly.

It took him a moment. "Shit, seriously?"

"Yeah, I'm just getting dressed and heading there now."

"I'll meet you there," Rodney replied.

She hung up, looked in Simon's closet, and found a sweatshirt to borrow, then stepped into the living room. Shoving her phone into her purse, she took a last look around and stepped out onto the balcony. It was a gorgeous morning, and the cool air was just enough to wake her up. She'd have to pick up coffee on the way. As she stepped back inside, Simon—completely nude—stood in front of the coffeemaker, getting her travel mug ready to go.

She looked at him and smiled. "Thank you."

He leaned over, kissed her gently, and said, "Stay safe."

With that, she bolted out the door and headed to the jogging paths near Stanley Park. She got there before Rodney. As she walked the trail, she caught sight of the cordoned-off area. She frowned because, at the moment, it looked like it was exactly the same location as the first two murders, and that would be as suspicious as hell. She walked down the pathway to see the cops and the bodies. She frowned because this changed everything. Not only was it two more bodies but this time it was a male and a female.

She walked over to the nearest cop. "Do we have IDs?"

"I haven't looked yet," he replied. "I'm just securing the scene and keeping the traffic back."

"Any weapons? Anybody disturb anything?" she asked, looking around at the ground.

"No, we're just getting enough daylight in here to see now," he noted. "We've set up some lights but—"

"Who called it in?"

He pointed to the side, where a woman stood, shaking.

Kate walked over to her immediately. "Hi, I'm Detective Kate Morgan."

"Oh my God," the woman blurted out, staring at her. "I came for a run."

"I'm sorry you found them," Kate said. "That had to be a shock."

"It was terrible. I don't ever want to see something like

that again," she cried out. "I don't get it. What happened? Why? This was such a great area to run in."

"And it probably still is. We just have a problem with this killer right now," Kate explained.

"Was that supposed to be funny?" the woman asked, staring at her in outrage.

"No, it's not funny at all," she noted. "I actually ran here myself last night."

The woman seemed to relax a little at that. "I've been running here for years," she shared.

On a hunch, Kate pulled out the photos of the other two women and asked, "Do you know these two women?"

"Sure, they run here all the time."

Kate nodded. "Right, well they were murdered three days ago."

"Murdered?" the eyewitness asked, and she stared at Kate in shock.

"Yes, here on the pathway."

She looked around. "But why has nobody said any-thing?"

"We always recommend a buddy system, and, of course, we had no idea that there would be a second crime."

"Not to mention," the woman added, relaxing ever-so-slightly, "how do you even stop something like this? So many of us have been running here forever. If I even saw the yellow police tape, I wouldn't have thought anything of it. I would have just gone under and come from the other side. And then I tend to go back down and loop around and then walk the last half home."

"How long have you been doing it this way?"

"Years," she replied, "literally, years."

"Did you know these two women, outside of running

here?"

"Not really. I mean, we were friendly because we saw each other on the trail all the time, but we didn't really know each other."

"How did they seem?"

"Competitive, all the time." She shook her head. "I'd never run with them. They were always talking about who won that day, who was better, who was faster, who was stronger. It seemed like their relationship was more than running."

"Well, they were best friends," Kate noted. "They lived only a couple townhomes apart, so their families shared a large part of their free time as well."

The woman nodded. "That makes sense, though I wouldn't have guessed either one of them was married. There was just something about them."

"Like what? Did you think they were together, like in a serious relationship?"

She looked up at her and frowned. "I don't know. I wouldn't want to say for sure on that."

"Fine, did you run here Saturday morning?"

"I did," she confirmed. And then she stopped and put a hand to her mouth. "And that's when they were killed?"

She nodded. "Did you see anything on that day? Anything unusual? Anyone acting odd, suspicious?"

She shook her head. "I don't think so." She considered Kate's question, a frown line forming on her forehead.

"And when you say you don't think so, what does that mean?"

"Well, I mean, a guy was here, and he had a rope, but I didn't think anything of it. I just waved at him. He laughed and told me to have a good run."

"A rope, *huh*? Was he just standing here, looking like he would climb a tree or what? Why would he have a rope?"

"I don't know. I mean, you get runners out here." Then she stopped. "I don't know why he was here with a rope. I didn't even think. It never occurred to me that anything could be wrong. I've been here for years, and there's never been a problem. Obviously I didn't think that there was a problem this time either though." The woman started getting more and more agitated.

Kate eased back on the questioning. "Here's my card. We'll have to get a statement from you. One of these officers will come over and take it, and, if you come up with anything later that you might have seen that was unusual or suspicious, please let me know."

She nodded slowly.

"Oh, by the way," Kate asked, as she turned to look back at the present crime scene, "did you know this couple found today?"

"Not really," she said. "I've seen them here before, but not anywhere near as often as I'd seen the other two women."

"So, you've seen this couple around, just not as often."

"Yes," she agreed.

"You know," Kate suggested, "it might be better, from now on, if you took another route to run."

The woman looked at her in horror. "No, you don't understand. This is my route. This is what I do."

"You can't change it?"

"No, no," she declared in outrage. "He needs to change who he kills, but he's not taking my pathway," she stated loudly, with so much indignation that several of the cops turned and looked at her. She immediately flushed. "Oh

God, I'm sorry. That's obviously not the right thing to say. But it's how I feel."

"What? That this guy is ruining the run for you?"

"Yes," she agreed. "He's ruining it for everybody."

"Have you seen the guy with the rope before?"

She stopped, frowned. "Well, *probably*. I mean, I've seen so many people here. He didn't strike me as somebody I'd *never* seen. He wasn't giving off any creepy stranger vibes or anything like that."

"Can you describe him?"

"Sure. Tall, slim, and fit," she noted, "just like the rest of us. Now, I mean, if he was like, you know, 275 pounds, obviously overweight, and didn't fit in with the runners who often run here," she noted, "then he would have stood out more. But because he was exactly what I do expect to see here—particularly at that hour of the morning, it's usually the hardcore runners," she explained, "he didn't stand out at all."

"And that's very important too," Kate murmured. "But you can't identify him any more than that?"

"He had black tech leggings, runners, and a tank of some kind," she said. "He was fit, and I didn't notice any jewelry."

"Any tats, hair?"

"Brown," she replied instantly. "But it was just a fleeting glance. I saw the rope mostly."

"What color was it?"

She looked at her and grimaced. "It was yellow. I think that's why I recognized it. It's that nasty stuff. It's got like a coating on it. It's cheap. I told my husband not to buy that rope anymore because it always comes undone."

"Interesting," Kate noted. "Well, the next time you see him, I suggest you run in the opposite direction—and fast."

The woman stopped and stared. "Do you think it was him?" she asked in a hushed whisper.

"I think there's a very good chance that you're lucky your timing was off today."

"And it was off," she confirmed. "I'm actually ten minutes late." She stared down the pathway, and her face paled. "Oh my God, … that could have been me."

"But you saw him earlier today too, right?"

"Yes," she stated, "he was here. I headed down and swung around and came back, as I usually do. Only, as I was coming back up this way to head off in that corner—see? It's an intersection here. Runners can come down. They can come up, and they can cross over," she said, explaining some of the routes. "And it's only as I crossed over that I saw the bodies."

"But you didn't see him then?"

"No, no sign of him. But then he could be still running the trail," she suggested, "as if he had nothing to do with this. He could still be up there running now. Hell, there'll be any number of people coming through here, probably dozens of them over the next hour."

"Well, today," Kate noted, "and for a while, they'll be disappointed because this is now out of bounds."

"Too bad you didn't make that clear before today," she stated, with a note of bitterness.

Kate turned to face her and asked, "You said you came down to this trail from the other side. Would you have followed all of the various intersecting trails normally anyway?"

"No," she replied. "I often come in off the side. I don't drive here. I just walk over, so then I pick and choose wherever I want to start."

"So how would you have known if we had to close this off?"

She stared at her, and her bottom lip trembled. "Fine. I get what you're saying. You couldn't have blocked off the trail entirely. But please, dear God, get the message out now." And, with that, she sat back down again and curled up, with a blanket around her shoulders.

Kate turned to see a man rushing toward her. When the woman looked over, she bolted to her feet and threw herself into his arms. Oddly enough, he fit the description that she'd given Kate of the man with the rope. This guy was tall and slim, wearing black running pants and a muscle shirt, and he had brown hair. Kate eyed him carefully, as he walked over, with his arm around the crying woman.

"This is my wife," he said. "I understand that she found two bodies."

"Yes," Kate confirmed. "And there's a good chance that she may have seen the killer."

He looked at her in shock.

Kate asked, "When did you get here?"

He frowned and looked at her. "Well, we just live over there." He pointed to the apartment buildings. "She called me, and I came running. I was in the shower. I would go for a run myself, but she starts work earlier than I do."

"So, you don't run together?"

"No," the woman replied, her bottom lip trembling. "He doesn't like running with people."

"Well, that's not true," he corrected her.

"Sure, it is," she wailed. "And now it's even more important, which means I'll not run because I don't have anybody to run with."

He held her close and said, "Look. If we've got a problem, and it's dangerous, obviously we'll run together."

She relaxed ever-so-slightly.

Kate looked at her and asked, "Have you always run alone?"

"Mostly," she replied. "I was jealous of those two women because they were obviously best friends and had something special like that." She shook her head. "I think most of us would like to have somebody to share our passion with, and, when it doesn't work out, it becomes a problem." She slid a sideways glance at her husband.

Kate was interested in him too. "And you run later. Why?"

"I told you," he stated. "My wife starts work earlier than I do. No need for me to get up at that hour and run. I'm more of a night owl, and she's more of an early riser."

Kate nodded. "Well, take care of her now because we don't know if this guy saw her or not. And we don't want to have her out alone on the off chance that he did."

"Do you think he'll come after me?" she asked Kate.

Kate looked at her and frowned. "We don't have any reason to think that, but anybody who thinks that they might have been seen should do whatever they can to protect themselves. Just find another running path for a while and don't run alone."

At that, the woman turned to her husband and said, "Both people were killed. I saw both of them."

And there was such shock and horror in her voice, he immediately gathered her up in his arms. "Somebody killed two people?"

Kate nodded. "Yes, a man and a woman today. Plus two women on Saturday morning," she murmured. "So, when I say, *Find another route, and don't run alone*, I really mean it.

Do *both*. Don't run alone *and* do find another route."

And, with that, she turned and walked back down to the crime scene.

<hr>

SIMON DIDN'T KNOW what it would take to get control of or to block these visions, but, in random spare moments, he found himself searching the internet, looking for anybody who might have similar skills. Of course several came up, mostly under the sponsored ads. He looked at the heavily painted faces under colorful turbans and shook his head. "Where the hell are the real people caught up in this nightmare?" he murmured to himself.

Putting away his phone, he tossed his bagel wrapping in his empty coffee cup, then got up and headed toward his next rehab building. He currently had seven projects going. That was about two more than he was comfortable with, and he was still trying to buy one more. He shook his head. "It's really time to pull back though, not expand."

Just then his phone rang, and it was the realtor he'd been in conflict with for some time, all over the price of a building. "I told you what I'm willing to pay," he snapped. "Beyond that, don't bug me."

She snorted. "They're willing to come down $20,000."

"Which is still what? Even at $250,000 that's too high. Don't even call me with ridiculous details like that."

"They are very interested in selling."

"Apparently not. Look. I'm very interested in buying, but we're way too far apart to even begin to contemplate a deal. Coming down $20,000 is pennies on a project like this, so don't bug me again." With that, he shoved the phone back into his pocket. Once he walked down to the next site, he stopped and groaned.

His foreman raised a hand and rushed over to him. "The steel girders didn't make it off the docks."

"Of course they didn't." Simon wanted to pound somebody into the ground for all the delays. "Why this time?"

He shrugged. "What can I say? Apparently it's busy."

"It's busy? It's always busy," Simon muttered. He stared up at the crane—costing him $10,000 a day, and that was a special price—while waiting for these girders. He shook his head. "How much longer?"

"They're hoping to get them delivered by the end of the day."

"*Great.* Now what about the rest of the supplies?"

"Everything else is on the way," the foreman stated. "The girders always cause trouble."

"Of course," Simon muttered. "I want everybody here first thing in the morning to make sure we pick up as much slack as we can and get back on track."

"I actually think that, if we can ever get things running smoothly," the foreman mentioned, "we can make up some time down the road and actually get this back on schedule."

"You say that, then everything blows up"—Simon winced—"so let's not jinx it."

When Simon was finally done here, he headed off to the next job site. This one was almost done, and the work was down to the interior finishing details. He walked inside to see several other business people he'd requested to be here for a meeting. He looked at one of them and smiled. "Barbara, how are you doing?"

She smiled at him. "Well, considering that you've been keeping me busy with all these projects, I'm doing just fine."

He laughed. "I'm a little overwhelmed myself right now

actually. I've got more going on than I'd anticipated."

"I wondered about that," she noted. "Normally you only work on a couple at a time."

He just smiled and didn't say anything because she didn't really know the depth of how much he had going at any given time. "This one is coming along and almost done. How is it going on your end?"

"So far, everything looks good," she replied. "We'll start looking at getting it rented."

He nodded. "This one was always intended to be for low-income families."

She nodded. "And I've got a system in place to start screening applicants. What about the ground floor?" she asked Simon.

"Commercial," he replied. "Something to start paying the way for the building's main purpose."

She laughed. "I do have a couple interested parties, even though we haven't put out any announcements yet. We haven't gotten any figures on lease amounts yet either."

"Have you any idea what you're looking at?"

And that started a discussion of how long it would take to get his money back on this building, and, when he saw the figures, he winced.

She nodded. "This one wasn't cheap."

"No, this is one of the projects that I do because I need to," he stated.

"One of these days you'll have to explain that to me," she said, "because most of the people I work with are motivated by the bottom line. You are that way on some buildings, but, on others, you're not that way at all."

"Nope, on the others I'm not." He didn't go into any further details. By the time he was done, he was over an hour late for another meeting.

He swore, made a quick phone call, pushing everything back, grateful that this time it was just with his contractor, who was there anyway, and headed out. He briefly thought about Kate, wondering how she was doing on the joggers' case. He'd seen the news flash about two more dead runners on the same path and realized the public panic would start setting in. At least the path should end up being mostly empty for a bit. He had to admit it was a hell of a nice place to run, and he'd like to go back there himself.

If it weren't for the drive that would cut into their time so badly, he would put that on a regular run schedule with Kate. Maybe on weekends they could do something like that. He knew that she'd really enjoyed it too. Just the fact that it was in the location where the killer had been active would make it a bigger draw for her, whereas most people would be the opposite. But nothing was normal about Kate. She was all about the bottom line, and it just happened to not be a bottom line that most people understood. She wanted to close cases and to put away killers, but it had nothing to do with numbers for her, unless it was the number of people that she was saving.

As he moved into the foot traffic to get to his next appointment, crossing the street and blending in with the crowd moving with the lunch hour, he thought about giving Kate a quick call, but then realized he was really out of time. As he got nearer to the next location, he stepped into the shadows, feeling a headache coming on—about the only inkling he ever had these days when something was about to blow up in his world.

And he was learning to listen.

He was slow at it, but he was adapting. Somewhat. As he

sat here on a bench in the shade, taking slow deep breaths, he felt the stirring on the inside. He hated that sense, that almost prowling sensation going on. As if something were inside, an animal reaching out, when he didn't want it to.

It was one thing that it was uncontrollable physically, but to think that this was actually something that his body was consciously doing just drove him crazy. And it was a new sensation, something he hadn't really expected to feel before, yet here it was once again, that weird sense of seeking answers. He tried to stop it, tried to still it, but instead it gained power and continued searching.

Simon didn't know whether he was doing the searching or was responding to someone else who was calling out. Almost immediately he was once again flat-out running down the pathway. He swore because, as far as he knew, the victims were all dead, and the last thing he wanted was to relive the final moments of somebody else who'd already died.

It was at least a comfort, knowing that it was beyond him to do anything about it, because this was actually history. At least, he hoped it was. He watched as the same damn running path came through his vision again and again and again, following the trails up and down with the same exhilaration.

"Why are you showing me this?" he murmured.

He heard her calling out to her best friend, the two of them racing, with flat-out joy in every moment. A part of him wanted to say that at least she had been happy in her last moments, that she had thoroughly enjoyed life, and that this activity had made her feel so full of life that she would do almost anything to continue it. Running for him wasn't the same way, but, for her, *Robin*, it was like a drug, and something she couldn't do without. He wondered at that force, that drive. And still she ran and ran and ran. He waited, knowing what was coming, and, just as soon as the girlfriend moved forward ever-so-slightly, taking the lead, the branch came out of nowhere, and she went down hard.

Almost immediately the flash was gone again. He looked at his hands, still trembling, feeling the same adrenaline surge through his body as went through hers. He swore long, deep, and fluently for a couple heavy moments, until he felt his own tension release, slowly moving back down again to a level somewhat doable. Then he straightened up, walked around the building, and came face-to-face with his foreman, an odd look on his face. Simon smiled at him. "You ready?"

The other guy nodded immediately. "Yeah. Are you okay?"

Simon looked at him in surprise. "Yeah, I am. Why?"

"Well, you just took a moment in the shadows."

"Too much heat or something I ate," he replied, patting his stomach. "Not sure what it was. I just needed a few minutes to let everything settle."

Understanding immediately crossed his foreman's face. "Hey, I hear you there, especially when we don't get regular meals, I used to bring my lunch, and then I stopped and started buying it. And you know what? Ever since I started buying food again, damn, I've had more upset stomachs than I can shake a stick at. But since the wife and I split up, it's hard to make lunches anymore. I just don't seem to have the willpower to give a shit, I guess."

"I get it," Simon replied.

"And I tend to do too much purchasing while I'm out because it's convenient."

"Exactly," Simon repeated, "*it's convenient*. But, with all those different foods, sometimes I wonder what's actually in some of what I eat. The street food especially."

"I don't know if we can blame the street food for it," the foreman argued cheerfully. "And you know it won't stop us anyway. Plus, I keep antacids in my pocket," he said, with half a smile.

"Smart," Simon said, looking at the guy as he patted his pocket. "Maybe I should do the same."

"You want a couple?"

"I'm fine now. I don't know what it was, but it's gone."

"Good, because sometimes that can be a bitch, and it hangs around forever."

"I know. I've had a couple bouts like that too. Anyway, let's get down to work." Just as Simon was ready to buckle down to discuss work, his phone buzzed. He looked down at the text coming in and winced because it was Kate, and her words were simple.

You okay?

He pondered that because it seemed that, as soon as he started getting messages or visions nowadays, she could almost sense that something was wrong with him.

He sent a quick response back. **Yeah, I'm okay now. We'll talk later.**

And he put away his phone and got back down to business.

CHAPTER 8

KATE SAT AT her desk, running through all the information she had, setting up some timelines, when the front desk called.

"You've got a witness here," Audrey told Kate in an excited voice.

"What are you talking about? Witness to what?"

"The joggers."

Kate froze.

"You've got somebody who just walked in off the street."

"Yeah, she said that she can't sleep because she's afraid that she saw something important."

"I'll come and get her. We'll see what she's got to say."

As she headed out to greet the new arrival, she saw an older woman, very lean, still wearing her running gear, only now she clutched tissues in her hand, and her face looked like she had been crying heavily.

Kate introduced herself and led the woman into an interview room. "Can I get you anything?"

"Water," she replied, almost in a croaking voice.

Immediately Kate stepped out and brought back a bottle of water for her. "So, tell me what's going on."

"I think I saw him," she said. "I'm sure of it."

"Saw who?"

"The killer," she replied immediately, her voice breaking.

"I think I saw the killer."

"Okay, so start at the beginning, and tell me what you saw."

She took a deep breath. "I always jog around all the time," she explained, speaking in short jerky bursts. "It's how I handle stress."

"Okay. When did you see this?"

"I couldn't sleep, so I went running. I live close to the pathways. In fact, I bought there on purpose. I'm always there because I'm always running."

"And I guess there are a lot of you who know each other by now."

She nodded. "Lots of us, we see each other frequently. We don't talk though," she added. "We often just wave and say hi. Everybody understands because we're all in the same boat."

It was a little hard to understand this woman's version of a conversation because she spoke with such oddness, as if it was all she could do to get the words out. "Okay, good," Kate stated. "It's lucky that you've got a place where you're so happy."

The woman immediately bobbed her head up and down and then started shaking it back and forth.

Confused, Kate asked, "So, you're not happy there?"

"Well, I was, but now there's a killer," she stated.

"Ah, yes, okay. So, you think you saw this killer?"

She immediately nodded again. "Yes, that's what I'm saying. I saw him," she stated eagerly.

"So, can you tell me what he looks like?"

The woman stared at her in shock. "No, I can't."

Kate took a slow deep breath, reaching for that self-control that was getting frayed very quickly and restated her question. "What did you see?"

"I saw him."

Kate reached up, pinched the bridge of her nose. "So, start at the beginning and tell me just what you saw, so I can follow up."

The woman immediately spoke. "I got up at five because I couldn't sleep. I needed to sleep, but I couldn't. I knew I would have to wear myself down in order to go back to sleep again. So, I got dressed and raced out to the running path," she explained. "I ran like crazy. It's stress release for me. It's like life is chasing me, so I run and run and run."

Kate sat here and listened, as the woman went over a description of the route she had used over the past few years. When she ran out of breath, she took a sip of water. Kate asked, "And?"

The witness nodded. "That's when I saw him."

"And what exactly did you see?"

"This man with a rope."

At that, Kate straightened. "Where exactly was he located on the path when you saw him?"

The woman looked at her, her eyes almost glazed, as fear crept over her. "He was off the main path, just standing by one of the trees. I didn't even think anything of it and just lifted my hand and ran past, like I always do when I see someone. But something was so odd about him."

"In what way?"

"There was a stillness to him, as if he was waiting. Like he was waiting for something, but I didn't know what."

"Okay, I've got a map here of the trail," Kate noted, as she unrolled it. "Can you tell me where you saw him?"

The woman pored over the map, her finger running over pathways. "Here," she stated. "He was here." She pointed to a spot just off to the side of the path, exactly where Kate and Dr. Smidge had seen the footprints of somebody who'd been standing there for a while.

"Interesting," Kate murmured.

"Do you think it was him?"

"It's possible, yes," Kate confirmed. "When was this?"

"I said yesterday."

"*Yesterday*." Kate studied her witness. "Are you sure?"

She nodded. "Yes, but why?"

She shook her head. "No reason, I'm just getting a time line."

"I went out this morning but saw no sign of him."

"Were you earlier or later?"

"Earlier," she noted. "I went running at dawn. So, about five o'clock."

At that, Kate's eyebrows went up. "Do you run in the dark too?"

"Sometimes," she said. "It depends."

She wasn't sure what the woman was running from, but obviously there was an issue, and running was her salvation. Kate could hardly blame the woman for finding something that was harmless to help her. So much better than drugs or alcohol to bury whatever it was hurting her so badly. "So, is there any chance I could talk you into finding a different place to run for the next few days?"

The woman looked at her in horror and then immediately shook her head. "No, no, no, that's why I'm here. You need to go pick him up."

Kate looked at her blankly. "You think it's that easy?"

She nodded. "I showed you where he is."

"You also said you saw him there yesterday," she mentioned cautiously, not exactly sure where this sudden turn of events was heading.

"Yes, but he'll be there tomorrow."

"And why is that?"

"I see him almost every second day."

"You didn't mention that," Kate noted, sitting back.

She shrugged. "Well, I do. I've seen him lots."

"And yet you can't identify him?"

"No, he is always in the trees. Originally I thought he was just there, you know, taking a leak. But now that I know somebody is killing people, I assumed it was him."

"Maybe, so what time of day do you typically see him?"

"Morning. Early. Between 5:30 and say 7:00," she stated.

"You could avoid running at that time."

She nodded eagerly. "Yes, yes, I can do that. But you really need to just go and pick him up."

Kate pressed two fingers into her temples, as she studied the woman. "Have you ever spoken to him?"

"No, outside of raising a hand and carrying on."

"And has he ever raised a hand back?"

She frowned, looked at her, and shook her head. "You know what? I'm not so sure whether he has or not."

"Can you tell me about the rope?"

"It was yellow," she stated. "Like one of those bright plastic-looking yellow ropes that everybody has. It's pretty hard to hide."

"Interesting that he has a yellow rope."

"Sure," she agreed, "but you know that not everybody thinks about things like that."

Kate wondered because a killer would definitely think about things like that. "I guess I'll be there tomorrow morning then, won't I?"

The woman immediately stood. "Exactly," she said. "You pick him up early. I'll start my run around six, and we should be good." And, with that, she tried to dash to the door.

"Whoa, whoa, whoa," Kate said. "I need contact information for you."

The woman turned to look at her in shock. "Why?"

"In case I need to contact you again about this."

"I told you what I know. You have it on tape, don't you?"

"Yes, I do. And thank you for coming in, but, in case there's a problem, I need to know how to contact you." She stated it firmly and left no room for argument.

The woman sagged down. "I'm against people knowing where I live," she explained, her voice shaky.

Kate looked at her. "Do you have a restraining order against somebody or something?"

"Not now," she said, "but I did."

"Maybe you should tell me a little bit more about that, so I understand your story."

The woman immediately started shaking her head. "No, no, no. I really don't want that."

Kate sighed. "I need that," she repeated firmly. "So sit back down again."

And what tumbled out of the woman's mouth over the next few minutes was a tale of abuse and then a suicide.

"So, he's dead. Therefore, you don't have to be afraid that he's coming after you anymore, correct?"

She nodded slowly. "Correct."

"Yet you still run, as if he's around every corner."

The woman looked at Kate with a haunted expression. "I feel guilty," she whispered.

"Guilty?"

"Yes, he committed suicide because of me."

"Or he committed suicide because of his own actions and his own thoughts and his own beliefs," Kate explained. "You can't take that on."

The woman stared at her. "That's just what the shrink told me."

"Are you on any medication?" Kate asked.

She nodded slowly. "Yes, but I've had the dose cut way back this last year."

Kate's heart sank because, as far as the courts go, this woman's statement would likely get completely pulverized on the stand, as they broke it apart and made it sound like she was imagining someone around every corner. Kate added, "Please take care of yourself when you're back out there. And maybe find another route to run or choose a different time and maybe not run quite so much."

"It always feels like I have to run," she stated slowly.

"But he's gone, so he can't chase you anymore."

"I know. I know," she agreed, "but the last time he chased me, I wasn't fit enough to keep running," she shared sadly. "So he caught me. Since then, it's all I can do. I run all the time to make sure that, if it ever happens again, I'll be fit enough to get away."

Kate's heart ached with pain, as she realized just how much victimology ran true in this case. "And that in itself can have you just as tied up into this whole pain and terror loop as having this guy in your life did. He's not in your life anymore, and you've done everything you can to be strong and fit," she declared. "You don't have to run constantly in order to get away because it's over."

"Is it?" she asked, with a bitter look. "If it isn't him,

won't it just be somebody else?"

"You mean, like this current killer?"

"Yes, like him. Exactly," she cried out. "The last thing I want to do is get caught by him. I just can't do it," she declared. "I can't be a captive again."

At her wording, Kate's heart went out to her. "And you said he caught you last time?"

She nodded. "He did, and it was terrible. I can't do that again. I just can't." And she hopped to her feet, pacing around the room, as if desperate to get away.

"Calm down," Kate murmured. "When you get anxious, you need to remember he's dead."

"He's dead, yes," she agreed, "but the other assholes in the world aren't. Once you're a victim, it's like they can smell you somehow, and they know. They just know that you've been a victim once, and you'll be an easy victim again."

"Yet that theory doesn't hold," Kate disagreed in a calm manner. "Once you've been a victim, you often make a decision that you'll never be a victim again."

"Yes," she said, turning to look at her. "Exactly. I'll never be a victim again."

"And I think these killers know that you'll fight too hard, that you'll make life too difficult for them. And they're just after easy targets."

The woman stared at her. "Do you think so?"

"Yes, I know so. You've been a victim, and I have in some ways too," she stated. "Not the same as what you've been through. Nobody can ever really know, even if they say they understand. Nobody really ever understands because every situation is different."

She stood still, focused on Kate. "No, but you do."

"To a certain extent, yes," she said, "and I'm sorry for what you've gone through, but you can't let him still have that power over you. Even now, he's destroying your life."

"But running is good for me."

"It is, but not when you're frantic like this. Not when you're still so consumed with terror that you're running to get away from it, even while you're sitting here in my office."

The woman looked around the room. "Oh." She frowned. "I guess that doesn't make sense, does it?"

"Clearly it makes sense to you on some level because that's what you're doing, and you have to understand that's a part of it. You're doing everything in your mind and arriving at the conclusion that it does make sense. But what you want to do now is stop giving this dead crazy man the power to hurt you the way he currently is. By giving him that power, he's still got control over your life, and you don't want that. If he was still alive, you would be looking around every corner, wouldn't you?"

"Yes, I would," she stated quietly.

"Yet you're still doing that. You're still looking for him, even though he's not around to get you anymore."

"What about the other guys?" she asked. "What about all those other crazy people out there? Can you protect me from them? Can you tell me that, by not looking around and not being safe, they won't come after me?"

"There's always a *chance* of somebody coming after you," Kate told her truthfully, "just in the sense that there's an awful lot of assholes out there. But that doesn't mean they *will* come after you."

The woman slowly sagged back into the chair. "I really have been letting him dominate my life, haven't I?" she noted thoughtfully.

"Yes, and it would be really healthy for you to start dealing with that."

The woman gave her a misty smile. "Thank you. I hadn't seen it in that light." She got up and asked, "May I leave now?"

Kate nodded. "Yes, as soon as I get your contact information." And, with that down on paper, she let the woman walk out of the station. She returned to her desk and sat down slowly, shaking her head.

Rodney looked over at her. "Problems?"

She smiled. "No, not really. I just got a reminder of how far-reaching the damage of domestic violence can be to some of these victims."

"Is your witness a victim of a different case?"

"Yeah." Kate sighed. "Sounds like she had been stalked, caught, held, and beaten. She had a restraining order for a time, but eventually the guy committed suicide, so she blames herself."

"Ouch, that'll make it difficult to stand her up in court."

"Almost impossible," Kate agreed. "Even though he's gone, she's still terrified and runs the jogging path frantically all the time, supposedly keeping herself in shape so she can get away. Yet, in reality, she behaves more like she expects someone to jump out and grab her at any second. And you know any defense lawyer would tear her apart on cross."

He nodded. "Well, if we can catch the killer, that's fine. Hopefully we'll have lots of other things to use for evidence."

"I hope so," Kate replied. "I really hate the aspect of the job that requires us to make sure it's a case that can be tried."

"Right, and that's why so many of these cases take so long, since we have to wait until we get the evidence we need to make sure the charges will stick."

She nodded slowly and started to enter the woman's report into the database. She looked down at her phone and frowned, seeing the response from Simon.

"Did she have anything helpful?" Rodney asked.

"She described what sounded like the same guy with the yellow rope. She has seen him there several times. Almost every second day according to her."

"Every second day that she's been there or every second day he's been there?"

"Every second day that she's been there, she has seen him. In this case it's the same thing because she runs constantly, sometimes in the dark, sometimes in the daytime."

"Ouch," Rodney replied.

"Yeah, it's more of an addiction, as she's still running from what happened to her."

"That can be pretty rough."

"Very, and, at the end of the day, even though you come back exhausted, you still haven't resolved or settled anything, so you get up the next morning to run again because the demons are still chasing you," she murmured.

He looked over at her. "Have you ever come to terms with the loss of your brother?"

She looked at him and asked, "Does anybody ever come to terms with something that's not settled?"

He shrugged. "I think some people do. I think some people can realize that it's a done deal and walk away."

"Well, I'm not one of them," she noted, trying to keep the harshness out of her voice and failing miserably.

He nodded. "I didn't think so. You look like somebody who'll search for answers for the rest of your life."

"I will," she declared. "Absolutely I will. Even more so

because of the guilt that was thrown on top of me."

"That was just bullshit," he said. "You were a little kid."

"A kid who'd forgotten her homework at school," she added, "so I ran back inside, and that's all it took."

"That's all it takes for anybody because this was a predator," Rodney stated quietly. "You know—as an adult and as a cop—that these guys only need seconds."

She nodded. "That's what I gave him, and it changed our lives forever. ... Victimology lives on long after the crime, and I just saw another reminder of it."

He nodded. "Which is another reason we do what we do, so these guys are caught and can't keep going out and terrorizing even more people."

She smiled. "Now if only these guys could stay in jail forever."

"That part is out of our hands." Rodney smiled at her. "So don't get yourself caught up in their sentences and whether it makes sense or not. We do our best, and that's all we can do."

With that, she had to be satisfied.

* * *

WHEN SIMON GOT home at the end of the day, Kate was sitting in the lobby of his building. He stopped in surprise, and she looked up and said, "I didn't feel comfortable waiting upstairs."

She looked over at Harry, who immediately turned to Simon. "I thought it would be okay."

"It would have been fine," Simon confirmed, "but I'm not surprised that she could be just as difficult about going up as anything else."

She shrugged. "It's your place. I'll go inside with an invite but not without."

Something was almost abrasive about her tone, as if she expected a fight. Instead of giving her one, he just nodded.

"Wherever you're comfortable," he replied, leaving it up to her. She frowned, as if not liking that answer all that much, but he wasn't up for an argument. "Long day?" he asked, as they took the elevator up.

"Very," she muttered. "And difficult."

"I'm not sure you ever have easy ones," he murmured. "Not given your line of work."

"No, maybe not, when you consider that I deal with murder day in and day out."

He nodded. "Do you want to go for a run?"

"No, I went to my dojo and did a workout already." He looked at her in surprise, and she smiled. "It's just fun for me."

"I get that, and staying fit and alert is a major part of your job, I'm sure."

"It is for me. I don't want to be in the position where I'll be a victim."

Something in her voice was just off. He waited for her to say something else, but she didn't.

Finally she broke down and admitted, "Look, Simon. I'm in an odd mood. I probably shouldn't have come."

"Why is that? Do you think you always have to be in a perfect mood here? That's not how relationships work."

"It should be," she stated. "You don't need my baggage."

"Well, by the same token, you certainly don't need mine," he added, "so we work hard to not dump on each other, and we understand that there's a difference between venting and dumping."

And she laughed. "Only you would say that."

"Nope," he disagreed, "lots of people say that. You still have to be you, and everybody has good days and bad days."

"Right." She stifled a yawn.

He frowned. "You are tired, but did you eat anything?"

She shook her head. "No, I was hoping you had food."

"Meaning, you don't."

She laughed. "No, I really don't."

He nodded. "Well, if nothing else we can order in."

"Ordering in and sitting outside on the balcony sounds perfect," she said.

He pulled out his phone. "What do you feel like eating?"

She stared, fascinated, as he brought up a list of nearby places for quick delivery. "Do you even cook?"

"I do," he replied, "but that means I also must shop."

She winced. "See? I know. And that's why I don't ever have any food at home." She turned as the elevator door opened to let them into his place. "That also means you've been so busy you haven't had time either."

"Exactly," he agreed. "So rather than fussing about it and making plans to do better tomorrow, why don't we just choose something that we can eat today."

She hesitated, and he shook his head. "Now is not the time to say we should be eating healthy."

"We can make healthier food choices here too."

"Yeah, but, when you feel like shit, and you're tired and worn out, you know all you want is heavy carbs."

"Like pizza or pasta?" she asked, with a raised eyebrow.

He laughed. "If Mama had any idea that you hadn't eaten …" He shook his head, and, instead of ordering a delivery online, he made a phone call, ordering in Italian. He smiled into the phone. "I know. Neither of us have eaten all day," he admitted. "We're exhausted and worn out, so we knew you would have a good solution."

Mama's scolding voice came through the phone, but it was in such heavy Italian, he could barely tell what she was saying. But he got the gist of it.

"If you want to package something up for two," he suggested, "I'll send somebody over to pick it up."

"Two or four?" she asked.

"Well, if you send enough for four, we'll have leftovers."

Mama gave a heavy gusty sigh. "You can't keep on like this. It's not healthy."

"That's why we rely on people like you," he said gently, "to try and keep us on track. Some weeks are better than others, and some days are better than others. We're just doing the best we can."

"Okay," she replied, "my son, he will deliver."

"No, that's not a good idea," Simon argued.

"It's a new service. Please, let us help you."

"Fine," he agreed.

"Do you want to know what you're getting?"

"No, I don't. Charge me and send it. We'll be surprised."

She laughed. "Consider it on the way."

He hung up the phone, then turned and looked at Kate to find her crashed on the living room couch, looking sound asleep, her eyes closed. He walked over and studied her carefully.

"I'm not sleeping," she murmured.

"Good, do you want to shower before dinner?"

Her eyes popped open, and she nodded. "That would be a good idea, but it takes energy."

He smiled, reached down, and scooped her up in his arms. Ignoring her squawk of surprise, he carried her into the bathroom.

"If you're too tired for a shower," he noted, "then I'll just have to help you out.'

She snorted at that, but, as soon as his hands went to her shirt to unbutton and take it off, she suddenly had the energy for other things. By the time they had finished their quickie and then had a shower, his security panel beeped.

She looked at him in surprise. He nodded. "That's one of the reasons for the rush," he explained, with a lopsided grin, "not that I ever need an excuse when you're in my arms."

"Well, I wondered, when everything happened so hot and fast."

"I was hungry," he stated, with an impudent smile, waggling his eyebrows.

"Yeah, I was too, but I wasn't thinking about this."

"Yeah, well, I pretty much always am," he declared, with a chuckle. He wrapped a towel around his waist, then walked to the door and accepted the food from Harry. "Thanks, bud."

"One of these days," Harry noted, "you'll have to add in a little healthier food."

"This is from Mama," he said. "She'd be heartbroken if I quit calling her in emergencies, telling her how I haven't eaten."

Harry laughed and laughed. "Well, you've got a point there. That was her son who brought it, I think."

"She told me it was a new service they've just started up, not that I'm sure that's true," he added. "Still, I figured I might as well try it, since it saves somebody having to go out, when we're so tired."

"I'll have to tell my wife about that," Harry stated. "Just

some days when you don't want to leave the place."

"A lot of days I feel that way."

With that, Harry turned and took the elevator back down again. Simon carried the very large heavy bag into the kitchen, put it on the table, then grabbed the pair of shorts he'd dropped there when he answered the door, and pulled them on. Then he opened up the big double glass doors to the balcony and called out to Kate, still in his bedroom, "Dinner is here."

She came out, wearing one of his shirts. He looked at her in surprise. She shrugged. "My clothes were pretty sweaty."

He nodded. "Bring them out, and we'll throw them in the wash."

Her eyes shot up, and then she smiled. "That would be a hell of an idea."

Quickly throwing their clothes into the washer, they got it started, and, with her wearing his shirt that came down just below her butt, he realized she had nothing on underneath, which was guaranteed to keep his mind off the food.

She grabbed the bag and carried it to the outside table. She sat down on the bench with a *plunk* and a happy sigh. "Did I ever tell you how much I love this place?"

"Yes, you have," he said on a dry note. "And yet you still won't come in when I'm not here."

"No, it's your place."

He frowned at that but refused to get into an argument; he felt much too satisfied. By the time he had served her up a large plate, she stared at it with avaricious greed. He smiled. "I'm just waiting for the day you look at me like that."

Startled, she frowned at him, and then burst into laughter. "When it happens, you'll be so invested in what we're doing that you won't even see it."

He had to admit that scenario sounded damn good to him too.

She started eating, and it wasn't long before she stopped to catch her breath. "Want to go for a run in the morning?"

He raised his head from his food and asked, "Same place?"

She nodded; then she finally broke down and told him about her day.

"Ouch." He stared at her in fascination. "So she runs all the time?"

Kate nodded. "It's her way of coping, though I don't know how effective it is."

"No, but it's what works for her."

"Still, it's hard on the body to do that much running, especially since she never really relaxes. She's really, really lean, like a potentially unhealthy lean."

Simon shook his head. "It would be very hard to get enough nutrients in a case like that. I do know lots of long-distance and endurance runners," he noted, "but the stuff they put into their shakes and guzzle back is amazing."

She nodded. "I've heard of that."

"Some of those people who can't just do marathons, they have to do four or five days of running."

She shrugged. "I can't even imagine. What are they called? Ultramarathoners or something?"

He nodded. "They are a class all on their own."

"A scary class all on their own," she said, with a chuckle, as she happily dug into the meatballs in front of her. Soon she sat back, a happy smile on her face. "This has got to be the best Italian food I've ever had."

"You're also starving," he reminded her.

She nodded. "I am, and this hits the spot beautifully."

She looked over at him. "You do know that I'd be very happy to pay my half for all the food I eat here, right?"

"Well, I'm glad to hear that," he replied, "but, if you ever offer, I'll get mad."

She frowned.

He shook his head, one eyebrow raised. "Don't even go there."

"I have money," she stated. "I'm not a charity case."

"That's fine. You're at my house. I'll put on the food."

She obviously didn't like it, but, short of getting into an argument that neither of them had the energy for, she was willing to at least drop the subject for now.

He smiled. "Besides, it really won't break the bank."

"Yes, but I don't want it to become something that I just expect."

"Do you ever think you'll get to that point?"

She looked startled for a moment and then shrugged. "Probably not."

"Good, then calm down." She frowned. He shook his head again. "No, that's not an arguable item. We each have enough issues and problems in our individual worlds that this doesn't need to become an issue."

"I guess," she agreed reluctantly. "I'd invite you to my place but ..."

At that, he broke out laughing. "But no food is there either," he stated, with a chuckle.

"No, but I could have ordered from Mama's too."

"Unless she knew it was you, you would have got probably half the amount," he explained, rolling his eyes.

She looked at the amount of food, snatched the bag from his hand, checked the price, and whistled. "You know that she can't possibly afford to give everybody this deal."

"No, she can't. It's one of the reasons why I had Harry tip her son very well for the delivery."

"Did you?"

"Yep. And besides, it's all good."

She nodded and dug back in again.

"So, back to the run. Do you think he'll be there?"

"I hope so," she said fervently. "This woman seemed to think he was there every second day."

"Seeing that preplanning and then sticking to a plan, that's bothersome."

She nodded. "I know. It is for me too. But, in order to actually see if he's there and to talk to him, I have to find him. I have no idea if we're barking up the wrong tree literally," she quipped, with an eye roll.

"But why would he be so obvious?"

"I don't know," she admitted. "It's just so strange. Although lots of people like to watch sports," she murmured.

He looked at her in surprise.

She shrugged. "You know that lots of people who can't do this stuff like to watch others do it."

"So, like a spectator sport?"

She nodded.

"Is that what this feels like to you?"

"I don't think so, but we don't have a bead on this killer at all," she stated. "It makes no sense."

"Anything you're leaning toward?"

"Well, it's not as if Jenna's ex-husband has an alibi. So he can't be written off. But, so far, I don't know that we have any connection between him and the two newest victims. There is no forensic evidence, so that's no help. And we're starting to wonder if this guy is targeting randomly, which makes it more difficult, because it's just a case of wrong time, wrong place. That's almost impossible to solve because we have to catch him in the act."

"But again, this now should be easier, with the same location."

"Same location but slightly different spot," she noted.

"Sure, but same location still means an awful lot of distance that this guy is traveling on foot, and people will be looking out for him now."

"Yes, and that's another part that I don't quite get. Why continue to stick to the same location?" she asked.

"The killer must have some reason," Simon stated. "Something is keeping him there."

She frowned, as she toyed with the spaghetti on her plate.

"I gather you're almost full," he said.

She pushed her plate back ever-so-slightly. "I think I'll just rest for a little bit. I'll come back and finish it later."

"You can also have it tomorrow," he suggested.

She smiled. "Oh, I'll be hungry again in a little bit. Don't you worry." She got up, walked over to one of the open spaces on his balcony, and slowly started stretching. He wondered why, until she looked over at him. "It helps me think." He smiled, then nodded and got himself a glass of red wine, held out the bottle to her. She smiled. "Yes, please."

As she continued to stretch with the wine waiting beside her, he sat down and let his own food digest. He would have to send Mama another *Thank you* because it was yet another delicious meal. He looked over at Kate to see that she was frozen. He took a couple steps her way, not wanting to interrupt her. She was caught on a train of thought.

She turned, looked at him. "You know something? I

haven't actually checked beyond the last couple years to see if there have been any deaths on that trail in the past."

He looked at her, startled. "Meaning?"

"Meaning," she added, "I wonder if he has chosen this place because someone he cared about died there or something."

"So, what then? He turns around and kills other people, so that their loved ones have to suffer the same way?"

She looked at him in surprise and then slowly nodded. "I realize it doesn't make a whole lot of sense, but sometimes people's motivations are pretty twisted."

"More than pretty twisted," he replied. "How about *very* twisted?"

She smiled. "Well, if you come over here, we can have something very different to talk about."

He grinned, grabbed his wine, and headed toward her. "What did you have in mind?"

She reached up, snagged his ears, and pulled him gently toward her. "I think you better put the wine down," she murmured, "before you spill it."

CHAPTER 9

Wednesday Morning

KATE WOKE UP to Simon thrashing beside her. His hands were at his throat, and his body bucked in the bed, as if fighting an unseen enemy. She immediately rolled over and tried to wake him up, but he seemed to be caught in this nightmare. She hated to think that it was another victim, and, the way he was choking, she really didn't want it to be another one of her victims. Finally she smacked him hard across the face.

He bolted upright and glared at her. "What the hell was that for?" he asked, putting his hand to his cheek, staring at her in shock.

She winced. "I wasn't sure how to wake you out of it."

"Wake me out of what?"

"You were thrashing around and holding your throat, like you were choking to death."

He stared at her and slowly sagged back onto the bed. "Is that what it was?" he asked, his hands automatically at his throat.

"I really wasn't sure what was going on. Do you remember any of it?"

"Nope. When you slapped me, it broke me right out of it. So, if you're looking for information, I don't have anything to give you."

She groaned. "What was I supposed to do?" she asked. "Watching you choke in your own nightmare isn't something I particularly want to see again."

He frowned, hearing that note he'd heard in her voice before but, at the same time, hadn't been able to recognize. Something almost like she was so done with this, didn't want to deal with it, and wanted to be anywhere but here with him. He reached out a hand. "I'm sorry."

She looked at him in surprise. "Can you control it?"

"No, of course not. You know that. You saw it."

She nodded. "Then why are you apologizing?" she asked simply.

He took a deep breath. "Because it seems like you want to be anywhere but here."

"I want to be anywhere but where there is such a reminder that I've failed with this killer," she stated bluntly.

He stared at her. "Seriously?"

"Yes, seriously," she stated. "When I see you choking like that, all I can think of is that it's my runners. And I'm really hoping this isn't indicative of yet another killing."

He lowered his hand from his throat. "I don't think so," he replied slowly, "but I don't know."

She nodded and looked at the clock. "It's almost time to go jogging anyway. Are you still coming?"

"Of course I'm coming."

She cocked an eyebrow at him. "You don't have to. I know you couldn't have gotten much sleep."

"I'm coming," he snapped.

She nodded. "Fine. Any particular reason?"

"Yeah, because, if you're going back to the same place where that damn killer is, I want to be there."

She glared at him. "Remember. This is what I do."

"Remember those dead bodies? Yeah, I'm coming."

She thought about it for a moment and said, "I'll need to go back to my place to get my gear."

"Okay, so get ready, and I will be dressed in a minute."

She nodded, then went to pull her clothes from the dryer, happy that at least they were clean now. By the time she was dressed and had her things collected, he stood at the doorway. She looked at him and frowned. "How can you get ready so fast?"

"Doesn't take much," he noted, "particularly not when we're in a rush."

She didn't say anything, and he drove them over to her place.

As they walked in, he smiled. "I should have brought some of the leftovers here, so at least you'd have something resembling food in this place."

"I was hoping for coffee," she noted, "but we didn't even think of it."

"No, but we can grab a cup afterward."

She nodded. "By then we'll both be racing to get to work."

"We could pick it up on our way, but we can hardly jog with it in our hands."

"Nope, I'll do without until I get to work." She wasn't sure how that would work for her, but, hey, she'd give it a try.

As soon as she was dressed in her running gear, they headed out and drove up to the Stanley Park jogging paths. She got out, stretched her neck, turned to face Simon. "I don't know how you can wake up like you did." She frowned. "Then just act like it's all normal."

He didn't pretend to misunderstand what she said.

"Well, this was a whole lot different than waking up from my usual visions," he stated. "Normally I don't get slapped back into reality."

She glared at him. "Last one there is a rotten egg." Then she bolted down the pathway.

He laughed and took off after her. She seemed to have some plan in mind, as she followed a pathway he hadn't expected. But he kept himself just a hair behind her.

She tried to follow in her head the pathway that the eyewitness she'd spoken to yesterday had given her. Checking the time, she tried to gauge it, slowing down ever-so-slightly, so they wouldn't arrive too early.

Finally she stopped at the top of a hill, her breathing strong and steady.

He stopped beside her and looked at her quizzically.

She whispered, "I'm thinking that, according to the schedule, he should be up and around that corner there."

"And if he isn't?"

"If he isn't, nothing ventured, nothing gained, but it would be really disappointing. If he is there, that's a whole different story."

"And it doesn't mean that he's the guy either."

"No, it doesn't," she admitted. "If it is him, being on a schedule like that would also make it very strange."

"True. ... So, do you want me to go first?"

She frowned. "I'm wondering if whoever is first makes a difference."

"What do you mean?"

"I don't know, just two people. One slightly ahead of each other, one taking a stronger blow than the other, and him having to come up and knock the other one out. I'm wondering if he would consider me in the front to be the worst idea, whereas, if you were in the front, he would potentially knock you out first. And then think that I was the easier victim and come after me."

"Oh, wow. I hadn't considered that."

"He can see us too," she shared.

"And yet, if he's watching us right now, he'll think we're not much in the way of runners at all."

"Maybe not." She laughed. "Let's go then."

She bolted down the pathway first, not giving him a chance to take over. Her gaze kept searching the surrounding area, looking for the man, and when she got to the spot where he should have been, instead of giving any warning, she veered immediately up the hillside, where he should have been waiting. Nobody was there. She stopped, looked around, and then she heard it. Somebody scrambling through the bushes. She took off at a run, Simon right behind her.

"Stop," she roared out, "police."

A shocked gasp filled the air and then footsteps running as far and as fast as they could. She went left. Simon went right. And they came in a circle around where he was. But somehow there were always more pathways and more trees.

"Damn it," she said, when she met Simon in the middle of the pathway. "This place is a bloody maze."

"No way he would have stayed on the path," he reminded her. "When you think about it, it's a maze of pathways, but all roads lead to the same places."

She swore. "Shit, and he's gone."

She raced up to the parking area, looking to see if anyone disappeared or had tried to pull out of the parking lot. Instead, it was complete silence. She turned toward Simon and glared. He held up his hands. "We can go back and wait, or we can sit here and wait," he suggested.

"Nothing's here—no vehicles and no reason for him to come here and wait for us," she noted. "He could just slide out anywhere along the road here."

He nodded. "But at least you know somebody was here."

"I do, and somebody who didn't want to meet the police."

"Honest to God," Simon said, "coming out of the dark woods like that, I'm not sure anybody would have stayed nearby."

"Catching them by surprise is usually the best, but now he's likely alerted that we're on his trail, so now he probably won't show."

"I don't know about that," Simon countered. "He might change the time, the location, but, if you think about it, his pattern is pretty set. For whatever reason he's doing this, it's probably like he feels he has to."

She nodded slowly. "Yeah, that's true, but I wonder. I just wonder how much any or all of this is just for show."

"Just for show?" He stopped and stared at her in shock.

She nodded. "Yeah, just for show, and how much of it is to cover up the first murder?"

"Are you saying that somebody is killing other people, just to throw you guys off the scent?"

She nodded slowly. "As stupid as that may sound," she noted, "there are multiple instances where people kill more than one in order to hide their actual true target among a few others."

"And that brings you back to the first ones, doesn't it?"

"Yes, it does—though again there's still no good reason for it. At least, not that we know of yet." She turned and glared into the woods.

"You know he's long gone," Simon stated at her side. "Otherwise we would have found him."

"I'm not so sure about that. Yes, I think he is gone, but still it makes me wonder." And, with that, she started to slowly walk back down the pathway.

"Wonder what?" Simon called out.

"If he has a way to hide in here somewhere." She worked her way up toward the same spot where she had bolted to find this guy. As she studied the area, she walked over to a tree that had branches low enough to climb.

She looked up and swore. "What do you want to bet that he went up there, when the couple came through here? And they didn't see him due to the heavy foliage. The entire middle and top of this tree has enough greenery to hide a man."

"And that would probably be a good guess," Simon agreed, as he swung up onto the bottom branch. "I'll let you know if he's here now in a minute though."

She didn't have a chance to say anything, and Simon was already well on his way scampering up the tree. She swore. "Simon, you shouldn't even be involved in any of this."

"I'm involved already, so let's not argue about that now, okay?"

She had to agree it was too late for arguing, because, dammit, he was already well and truly up into the tree. He called down a few moments later. "It's empty."

"Of course. Now get down here, for God's sake."

He came back down, but he had something in his hand.

"What's that?"

"I don't know, but it was caught on a branch," he noted. "So I think somebody just ruined his shirt."

"If it's even the same person," she replied.

He gave her a fierce look. "How many people do you think are climbing around in these trees?"

She frowned. "No, you're right," she admitted grudgingly. "I don't imagine there are too many. But still, we can't completely rule it out." She grabbed the piece of material. "I'll send this to forensics."

"Do you think there'd be anything on it?"

She shrugged. "If he's been out running, it could have skin or sweat. But again we still wouldn't have any DNA to match this to. So we'd have to place him on this pathway at some point in time in the last God-only-knows how long. Even if it rained in here," she noted, "there's no guarantee that he couldn't have been here. There are all kinds of reasons for sitting up there. I mean, I'd imagine the view up there is pretty incredible, isn't it?"

He nodded slowly. "Actually, it is. Anybody who's a bird-watcher or any number of photography buffs or even landscape artists and the like could have gone up there, thinking that everything was better from up there."

She nodded slowly. "And you know what? That view could also be how he found these runners in the first place."

He looked at her in surprise.

"Well, unless you're actually here to target runners, how else would you see them?"

He looked at her, and his face lit up. "I get it. You're wondering whether or not he was a bird-watcher."

"Well I don't know too many bird-watchers who would climb up a tree like that."

"So maybe he's just a photographer, looking for sunsets and sunrises. Because that's a perfect place for it, you know?"

She frowned at his comment. "That could be quite true. He also may have come at an earlier hour and had waited longer. Then, suddenly seeing the runners, maybe he started taking pictures of that too."

"I wonder if at some point it could have just been their behavior that set him off, if maybe they were disrespectful to the wildlife around here or something. Maybe they were disrespectful to each other, and maybe he thought there was a natural order, and they weren't following it." Simon raised both hands in frustration. "I don't know, but the two women, maybe he saw something more than what was there."

"What do you mean? Thinking that they were lesbians, maybe?"

"I don't know about that. Maybe they were swearing at each other in a way that pissed him off. Maybe he has this idea of how women should act."

"Okay, and the next couple?"

"I don't know," he admitted, "but it isn't a stretch to think that maybe she was disrespecting him."

"Well"—she stopped, then frowned—"it's a theory," she grudgingly noted.

"Gee, thank you," he said, with a mocking tone. "I appreciate that."

She smiled. "No, it's a good theory. I don't know that it'll have any legs, but it is definitely something I need to check out."

"To check out as long as you actually have man-hours available."

"We have two new victims," she stated. "So believe me. I'll get all the time I need right now, particularly if it means stopping a third set of victims from showing up."

"I get it," he said. "Nothing like having the potential for public outcry, like what will be happening here to make the police add more manpower to a case."

"And yet you can understand that, when there's nothing for us to go on, we soon get assigned to other cases," she explained.

"Wouldn't it be nice if we all had the ability to do what we needed to do? But, with killers coming out of the woodwork on a regular basis, sometimes there's just no time for any of this."

"We have to make the time," she declared, "and believe me. Right now? I'm making the time."

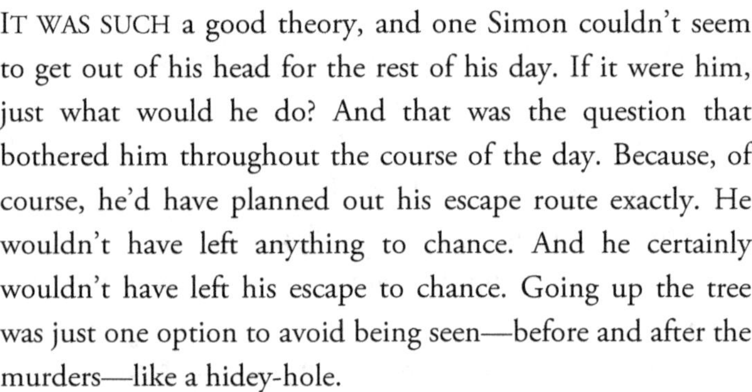

IT WAS SUCH a good theory, and one Simon couldn't seem to get out of his head for the rest of his day. If it were him, just what would he do? And that was the question that bothered him throughout the course of the day. Because, of course, he'd have planned out his escape route exactly. He wouldn't have left anything to chance. And he certainly wouldn't have left his escape to chance. Going up the tree was just one option to avoid being seen—before and after the murders—like a hidey-hole.

If anyone found out where he was, then he would be in a worse place. But the chances of anybody finding out that he had gone as far up into the tree as he had would most likely rule out somebody coming after him. If he played his cards right, that tree would be the killer's bolt-hole—a place to go when nothing else was working.

Simon still didn't understand why these particular victims were targeted, and he knew that that was something Kate was mulling over constantly too. Motive was everything.

Why would somebody do this to these people? He understood the first two better because of his vision but the next two? Not so much. And he also knew that no way in hell he wanted another phone call, saying Kate was on a third case that was exactly the same.

The public outcry would be expected, yet he could hardly blame her. She was working the case as hard as she could. If there wasn't a whole lot there, what was she supposed to do? That problem was something that he had never really considered before. Like what was she supposed to do if there were no other leads? He frowned at that, wishing he could do something to help her.

He also worried that she would head back there to the running paths again today. The cases just haunted him, and he had been absolutely no help so far. He had nothing here to give her any assistance.

He kept looking for visions with numbers, looking for anything that might help. In the past, there had always been a little bit of something that came through his psychic senses, even if it wasn't much help. But it's not as if this case had safes to open or a numbers game to follow. It just seemed like his related visions were completely useless. How the hell was that something he or Kate could use? He also wondered if maybe his connection was too tenuous because he couldn't relate to this crime or to its victims.

He didn't understand what the connection was to the other woman in his nightmares and visions—kissing her partner, going back to bed—but obviously she was a runner. The fact that she hadn't died yet was huge. The fact that she didn't even appear to be a victim was remarkable.

Simon didn't want her to become one, but he still didn't see what his connection to her was. Like how do these people reach out and just snap onto his psyche? From his perspective, it seemed like, *Hey there. Let me just sit here and fill your mind with this shit. I know you've got nothing better to do.*

If he could figure out what the connection was to this woman in his nightmares and his visions, then maybe he could develop a better understanding of why this kept happening. He understood his connection to that very first case—the pedophiles' case—where he'd met Kate. That was easy, a given even. Pedophiles victimizing children was something directly related to Simon's own life. But the murders of runners? No, that didn't make any sense. So why the hell was he connecting to this one woman, the one who leaves her bed to run but goes back to her lover?

He shook his head, wishing that the answers would come as easily as the damn visions did. Had to be some reason for them, and it just got him more depressed than anything to realize that all of this was happening and was beyond his control. However, being shown these uncontrollable visions, he wanted to know why? What for? Sure, he had a logical mind, but that wasn't necessarily what he needed to figure out these psychic messages.

If nothing else, it caused him more stress to realize that, somewhere along the line, this person in his latest vision was attracted to him or was reaching out to him. At least that's what he thought was happening. Maybe she wasn't doing it consciously; maybe it was her subconscious. Maybe the guy that she was with had the same name as him. Maybe that was the only connection there. He frowned at that. Was it really that simple? Could it be something that simple? He didn't know, and he didn't know because there was obviously no way to prove it. One way or another he was stuck in this same damn limbo.

"Hey, Simon."

He shook himself out of his reverie and turned to see his foreman walking toward him.

The foreman stopped and said, "Whoa, man. You okay?"

He nodded slowly. "I gather I don't look okay. Is that it?"

"You look like you're ready to murder somebody, actually," he admitted. "In which case, I think I'll talk to you later."

Simon gave a snort of laughter at that. "Well, considering we've worked together for a very long time, I highly doubt you're my target."

"Well, I would hope I'm never your target, especially if you get that look when you're just busy thinking about something randomly."

"Yeah, well, I'd like to get something in my life cleaned up."

"Yeah, it seems like, one way or another, we all have something like that." He shook his head. "I'm not so sure we're all as active about it as you are, though."

"Probably not," he replied, with a solid attempt at levity. "So, what's the problem around here today?" And, with that, they got back down to work, and that kept Simon busy for the next three hours because plenty of problems were here to mull over and to find solutions for. As always, delayed products and staffing issues topped the list. But the foreman mentioned how they also needed to bring the engineers in on something.

Simon swore at that. "Those engineers are costing me more money."

"Yeah, these kinds of changes involve bigger money outlays," the foreman noted. "We might want to remember that for later projects."

"I know," Simon replied, raising his hands. "Still, it's a shitty deal."

"It is. I'll get him down here as soon as I can."

"Yeah, and you tell him that this one's on him because this one is his fault," Simon declared.

The foreman laughed at that. "You know that, by the time he gets here, he'll have worked out how it isn't his fault."

"They always have an excuse," Simon noted. "I'm used to it."

"I know, but we'll get this done and fixed as soon as we can."

With that, Simon had to be content. He checked his watch and swore because it was already well after three o'clock. He'd missed his two o'clock appointment, and no way in hell would he make his three o'clock. Plus, the four o'clock appointment remained, still sitting there, waiting. He hated having anybody wait for him. But today he'd completely glossed over several of his meetings and hadn't even had a chance to deal with any of them. He quickly sent messages of apology to the two o'clock that he'd missed and to the three o'clock, saying he wouldn't make it. Then quickly raced ahead so he could salvage his four o'clock.

When he realized it was with the damn realtor, he almost swore at that too. He'd have been better off rescheduling the three o'clock to let him know that he was available now, if they still were. This realtor meeting was just enough to piss him off, but he still wanted that property. He walked the last of the blocks, heading up to the place in question.

When he got there, she was stamping her feet impatiently. He just raised an eyebrow, perversely delighted that she'd been forced to wait for him. "What's your problem?" he asked.

She declared, "My time is important too, you know?"

"So is mine," he snapped, "and you keep wasting it with these ridiculous counters, when I've been very clear in my position."

She snorted at that. "Well, if you could just come up in price a little, you'd have a done deal."

"I'm not interested in coming up. It'll cost way too much money to fix up this building."

"And yet that's what you're doing with all these old places," she noted. "Do you think we haven't noticed?"

"I don't care if you've noticed or not," he stated. "This one is overpriced, which is why you haven't sold it."

She frowned. "All I have left is to finalize the paperwork. My clients are actually prepared to come down a little bit," she announced, as if that tidbit were gold.

"A little bit won't be enough, which you know very well," he snapped. "Stop wasting my time."

"Well, my time apparently doesn't matter to you," she said in a snide tone.

He just crossed his arms and waited. "So, have you got any news or not?"

She frowned. "They are interested."

"Don't give me that. I told you what my price is. Yes or no?"

She hesitated.

"So that's a no then, I presume, and we're done here." He raised an eyebrow. "As I've told you too many times before, don't bother calling me again. My price is my price. I'm not interested in any other deal." He turned to walk away.

"Wait."

He stopped, placed his hands at his hips, and slowly pivoted, so that he could glare at her. "What?" he snapped.

"Fine, they're prepared to drop the price."

"All the way?"

She nodded slowly. "And against my better judgment, I'll have you know."

"I don't give a damn about your judgment," he declared. "It obviously sucks if you're defending the price for this property like you are."

"It's worth a lot."

"*Fixed up* it's worth a lot. In the shape it's in right now, it needs to be dropped."

She stopped, looked at him, and asked, "You'll actually drop it?"

He shrugged. "I don't know. I'll do that cost analysis later." He glared at her. "So, is that a yes or no?"

"It's a yes," she snapped. "I just said so."

"Fine. Draw up the paperwork then."

"You know, you could do this a nicer way."

"My lawyer will contact theirs, if they're paying you a fee, that's up to them." He turned to face her. "And I'm not, so don't even go there."

"We'd get along much better if you paid for my time," she noted. "I could go out looking for these properties for you."

"Why would I bother? That I can do myself."

She just glared at him.

He shrugged. "I don't understand why we all think real estate agents are even necessary," he growled. "Even when you do bring certain products to the market, you get in the way of us closing them."

"Well, that's because my clients get the best prices," she explained. "However, if I were on your side, I could get you the best price."

He shook his head. "It'll still be the same rule. They're paying you, not me."

"Unless you hire me to go hunt out some of these properties."

"No way. Not interested." He had his reasons, and at the top of the list was the fact that he didn't trust this woman at all. "If this is a go, send me something in an email," he told her, "and I'll contact my lawyers." He turned to walk away.

"Don't you want to take another look at it?"

"Nope, I sure don't. I know very well what it looks like."

"You didn't go in there without my permission, did you?"

He stopped and just glared at her. "Are you done wasting my time?" She pouted. He shook his head. "That's not a nice look on you," he said, and, with that, he turned. He heard her screaming at him in the background, and it made him perversely happy. There was just something about dealing with realtors, particularly the pushy ones. So, if he had a chance to shove their noses in it, he was happy to do so. It should be a decent business relationship, but it didn't take long before they could turn it sour. He was all for getting help and helping others, but not when it came to this bullshit industry.

For that reason, he bought most of his properties without realtors. Yet this one seemed to capture some properties, either knowing what he wanted ahead of time and contacting him, or somehow managing to get the listings. Otherwise he would have preferred to deal with the owners or their attorneys directly. He wondered if it was a case of her understanding more about what he was doing than he wanted her to, possibly reaching out to contact these people before the properties were even listed in the first place, jacking up their expectations on the value, resulting in unrealistic pricing.

It would be a smart business move on her part, but it also meant that he wound up continuously dealing with her, and that had proved not worth the aggravation.

CHAPTER 10

KATE STARED AT the trees surrounding her; she was back here yet again because she couldn't get it out of her head. She'd already walked several of the other pathways, looking to see other angles, other ways of catching sight of who was running. And unfortunately she had found way too many. With the hillsides adjacent to the trees, now that Simon had pointed that out, there were just way too many areas to cover. She slowly walked back toward the area where her car was parked. Her phone rang, and she looked down to see it was Rodney. "What's up?" she asked, when she got to her car.

"Where are you?"

"I'm back at the damn scene," she replied. "Just way too damn many areas for somebody to have watched for whoever was coming. I've been trying to determine whether these two sets of victims were targeted or random."

"The coroner just called about the second couple."

"Good, I'll call him back."

"No need. I just talked to him, and he told me absolutely nothing is there, outside of two very healthy individuals, cut down in the prime of their lives."

"Which really sucks." She let out a slow breath. "They were out here, fit and healthy, exercising and looking after themselves, enjoying life, and some asshole had to stop it."

Running her hand through her hair in frustration, she added, "Oh, I was thinking about running a search, looking for anybody else who may have died out in this area, beyond that last two years."

"You mean, on the trails?"

"Yeah, I was wondering about that," she shared. "I did run a search on any criminal history for any of the four victims, and, so far, nothing major showed up. The one woman was in a car accident quite a few years ago, but there didn't appear to be any charges or any major injuries to it."

"Yeah, I did the same thing," Rodney confirmed. "Nothing popped in my case either. I haven't looked for any deaths on the pathway though. Do you want me to follow up on that?"

"Sure, I just don't know where to go from here." The frustration was evident in her voice. "Sorry, I don't mean to be taking it out on you."

"No problem. The death notices have been done, regarding the two latest victims," he stated. "And, of course, it's the same deal. Everybody is in shock. The couple had no enemies, and nobody knows why anybody would do this to them."

"You know what I keep coming back to?" she began. "And I know it's a horrible thought, but I keep coming back to this second case being some cover-up."

There was silence on the other end. "You actually think somebody killed these two in order to make the first two look random?" he asked slowly.

"I don't know," she admitted. "It's a big deal because it means the killer is taking a lot more chances to do this again, without being seen or leaving evidence."

"Not only taking a lot more chances of getting caught

but also showing a complete disregard for life."

"Or a super-sensitized regard for his own," she clarified. "When you think about it, that's an awful lot of people dying in order to get whatever he wanted out of it."

"Yet we haven't really got anything—outside of too few witnesses and the two husbands' word for any of this."

"I know," she agreed, "and that just adds to my headache."

"Of course it does," he murmured, "but let me see if I can come up with anything on the crime history in that area."

"You know that, if nothing else breaks," she said, "the worst part is feeling like we're just waiting for another victim."

"And yet what good will that do, another death with no forensic evidence? Surely he wouldn't kill a third time at that same general area?"

"The second kills were just a tad removed from the first," she noted, "which makes sense, in case we staked out that initial crime scene. So that also tends to mean any third kill would likely be over a little bit more."

"Or in a completely different area," he warned.

"I sure as hell wish we could get surveillance out here."

"You can ask the sergeant for it, but you know what they say about public spaces like that."

"I know. I know." She groaned. "And honestly, there'd be no good way to hide the cameras. And too many locations where we need eyes to even get started."

"Not well enough anyway."

"And you know, chances are, we'll be hiding them in one area, and it'll happen in another."

"Always," Rodney replied. "These guys aren't stupid."

"Yet I wonder just how smart they really are," she murmured. She hung up and walked back toward her car.

The trails were vast paths all over the place, and some of them even connected through blocks of townhomes and came back around again to hook up to other spots.

She shook her head at all of it because it was such a beautiful place to run, and obviously it was very popular. It was one of those things that she herself would do if there was that opportunity. Again she thought about it—*opportunity*. She could drive over here, but chances are most people were coming here because they were local and lived nearby. Just as she would prefer to do. She had to wonder though, if the killer was local.

At that, she frowned and turned to look around. Not very much in the way of public spaces either. They were all part of the runs. And that brought up another thing. Maybe that was the problem—that someone had taken over the area for running paths. Was there another purpose to this area before? Was it like a bird-watching area or something of the kind?

Frowning, she went through her phone and found the number she was looking for.

When the professor answered the phone, she smiled and said, "It's Kate Morgan. I have a couple questions, if you have a moment."

"Only if I get to see you in person," he noted in a jovial voice. "Previous students are always nice to see."

She laughed. "All right, I'm about fifteen minutes out. Well, it depends where you are, though."

"I'm down at Second Beach at the moment."

"Oh, in that case, I'll be right there."

He laughed. "As long as you don't mind if I'm tanning."

"You go ahead and do you." With that set, she drove down to the beach, laughing at the thought that this was where she'd really wanted to come in the first place. It didn't take long to find him, although he definitely looked different in just bathing trunks. He raised a hand when he saw her.

She smiled, walked over, and admitted, "Not exactly where I see my favorite professor in my mind."

"Why not though?" he asked.

She smiled. "So you're part of a bird-watching group around here, aren't you?"

"Yeah, past president of it, actually," he noted proudly.

"Not anymore?"

"Nah, too much politics." He shook his head. "You get tired of that crap after a while."

She nodded. "Makes sense to me. Any bird-watching areas around here?"

He stared at her. "Well, all of Vancouver is a huge bird-watching area—being coastal is one thing, warm weather is another. We have some very unique species here."

"What about like right here?" She motioned toward the hills around her. "Specifically thinking about the Stanley Park area, with the running paths."

He stopped and stared at her, as his gaze clouded. "You mean, related to the recent murders?"

She nodded slowly. "I'm trying to figure out what the draw is for the killer there."

"You mean, outside of convenience?"

"Yes, exactly," she noted. "Outside of convenience. Obviously, if you're looking for random people to kill, where there are a lot of people, that would be anywhere. But why would you choose to kill runners? What would you have against them?" she asked.

He shook his head. "That's one of the things I don't do, the psychology of psychopaths," he murmured.

"Well, I guess I'm wondering whether he's holding a grudge against some of the runners or organizers, or maybe that he used to be a runner, or a bird-watcher, and his area was taken away."

He laughed. "Well, bird-watching isn't exactly something that they can take away," he corrected. "An area might have become busier." He frowned, as he thought about it, and then nodded. "Although that would make sense in a way, because becoming busier might have chased away his birds. But you know that I hate to even think we'd be dealing with something like that here."

"But it's possible?"

"Of course it's definitely possible, and we see people doing the stupidest darn things here, all in the name of whatever it is that's behind it for them," he replied. "When people want to be assholes, they'll be assholes, without needing too much of a reason."

"So you don't know of any particular bird-watching area around Stanley Park that would have been impacted by this becoming a very popular running area?"

He shook his head. "Not offhand, no." He paused. "I can think about it for a bit, but you know that it's not like that. I don't know of any species specific to this particular area that's protected. And besides, the birds would be mostly nesting higher up, unless you've got some of the ground nesters." At that, he quieted, thinking thoughtfully. And then he shook his head. "No, I don't see it."

She didn't either, but she was grasping at anything. "Okay, I'm still trying to come up with motive."

"Nothing on the individual victims?"

"Not enough to provide any evidence."

"That's always the worst, isn't it?"

"Often it is, though frequently we have a suspicion of what's going on, or a suspicion of who it might be, but this time we just don't have any suspects."

"Well, you do, but you just don't want to tell me."

She smiled. "Let's just say, I don't have any *good* suspects."

"That's a different story," he agreed. "That goes back to that whole evidence thing again."

Kate nodded. "Still, I don't suppose you know of any major accidents or anything that happened in or around Stanley Park in the past?"

"Nope, not really." He frowned. "I know this area pretty well, but no."

She nodded again. "It was a hope."

"Keep hoping, just keep pushing too."

"I hear you," she said. "I'm working on it, and really that was a long shot anyway." She sat and visited with her former professor for a little bit longer. As she got up to go, he turned to look at her and said, "I know you've probably already thought about this, but most people kill for only a few reasons."

She nodded. "Yeah, power, sex, money."

"Revenge," he added.

She nodded. "True, something else to think about."

She slowly walked back to the car. "Revenge, *hmm*." She headed back to the office with that thought uppermost in her mind. As she got back in the bullpen, she looked over at Rodney. "Did you come up with anything in the past?"

He shook his head. "No, nothing at all."

She nodded. "If somebody was doing this out of revenge,

what would that look like to you?"

He stopped and stared at her. "If it was revenge, I would think it would be for specific victims, and it would be for something that they've done or had failed to do. And, if it weren't for specific victims, it would be for the whole group of them."

"So what are you thinking? Like targeting groups of healthy young individuals, if he's no longer a healthy young individual?"

"Something like that is quite possible. Or against a running group, if he can't run anymore or had some other grudge against them."

She frowned at that. Her next phone call was to one of the largest running clubs, asking if they had specific group leaders for running groups in specific areas.

"We have a large running group that goes out every Saturday morning," Charlie answered cautiously. "What do you mean?"

And she explained what was going on.

"We heard about the murders," he said, with shock in his voice. "It's so horrific to think about."

"I'm just wondering if you had any trouble with anybody or if someone in your group maybe was kicked out or otherwise disenfranchised somehow."

"We've had several disputes with various people over time," he noted, "but we haven't had a problem lately."

"What does *lately* mean?" she asked, as she sat up, looking at her phone in surprise.

"I mean, there are always people who think that somebody should do something better or different. You know? Even the clothing envy—there's always somebody who looks more dashing. Then somebody else takes offense because someone stepped closer or cut them off on the path, or the ones who have always got to win, even when not a formal race. Some personalities just don't get along with each other, when you get them in a group, and there'll always be one or two who will set things off."

"Right, and you do a lot of volunteer runs for charity as well, don't you?"

"We do all kinds of events," he confirmed. "We do sun runs in the spring for training to get new runners out. We do marathon runs. We do trail runs. We do a running-for-money thing," he noted, "and then we generally give it to injured runners or some of the training camps that need extra funds. We're really quite busy in a socially responsible sense."

"Did you ever have anybody make threats or anything like that? Or has anyone ever attempted to hurt somebody and had to be kicked out of the group or anything major like that?"

He replied, "We did have a couple get into an argument in the parking lot."

"Did they come to blows or anything?"

"The woman tried to run him over with a car," he stated.

Kate stopped. "Seriously?"

"Yeah," he said. "They solved it amicably, and they were running afterward, so it wasn't that bad, but it was shocking for most of us."

"You want to tell me some more of those details, please?"

He explained, "They'd gotten into a dispute on the trail, and she had accused him of jumping in front of her. She was really popular and very competitive," he noted. "You understand that some runners are, and some aren't. In this particular case, she was quite competitive."

"And beyond that?"

"Well, she went to get in her vehicle and drove forward. He wouldn't get out of the way, and he kept saying, 'Go ahead. Hit me. Hit me. Is this what you're really all about?' And she surged forward in her car and actually hit him. He was pretty shocked that she would do something like that, and I think she was shocked that she had actually done it. She hopped out immediately, apologizing like crazy, saying she hadn't done it on purpose."

"Did he believe her?"

"I don't know. They weren't ever what I would call friends again, but they certainly managed to continue to run."

"Do they still?"

"I haven't seen him in a long time," he mentioned. "I thought he moved to Alberta or something. He just drifted away eventually. He wasn't nearly as mouthy right afterward, which maybe was a good thing."

"Was he before?"

"Oh yeah, he was one of those guys who knew everything and who generally grated on the nerves of a lot of the members, but you can't really mow him down based on his personality," he protested.

"No, of course not," she said. "That's not why I'm even asking. I'm just trying to figure out if any of these recent murders has something to do with disgruntled past runners."

"I can't see it," he replied. "We're all about health, and, you know, being the best people that we can be physically."

"I get that, but physically healthy doesn't always mean emotionally healthy."

He snorted. "No, you've got that right. Sometimes

they've got the most immature attitudes of anybody I know."

"So, I know it probably sounds like an imposition, but I just need to check out that this guy is in the clear. What was the name of the woman, by the way?" When he gave the name, she stopped and said, "Pardon?" He repeated the woman's name. "*Jenna?* That's one of my dead victims."

"Oh my God."

"Yeah, *oh my God* is right," she snapped. "Was she alone in the whole thing?"

"Yes—and no," he replied slowly. "That best friend of hers was involved too. Egging her on, you know? She was good at that. The both of them were. If one wasn't egging the other on, it was in reverse. The two of them had this weird relationship."

"How much did you interact with them afterward?"

"Well, they came for quite a while, and then they distanced themselves. They haven't been part of the club for a long time."

"And what about him?"

"Same thing. All parties involved were disciplined for their behaviors. I mean, that's not exactly the stuff we as a club want to get a name for."

"No, of course not," she said. "I need the name of the man involved in the altercation."

"His name was Kirby. I've got his number, but I'll have to find it."

"Yeah, I'll wait," she replied. Sure enough, he came back with it just a few minutes later. "Here it is."

"Do you have an address?"

"No, we don't keep that information, only cell phones."

And, with that, she thanked him and hung up.

She turned, looked at Rodney. "Finally a decent lead."

KIRBY, SHE REPEATED the name in her mind, over and over again. "Have I heard that name before?" She paused, then looked through all her notes on the case and shook her head. "Yet it sounds a little familiar, and I don't know why."

"Just let it roll around in the back of your head," Rodney suggested, standing beside her now. "You never know what might come up."

"I'm bringing up his Facebook page right now."

"Yeah, I've been tracking everybody involved in this to see if anybody posted anything."

"I never understood that whole thing about posting about killing someone."

"I think the percentage is pretty small too."

"Neither woman posted anything beforehand, saying they were aware, afraid, or had any premonition of what was happening," she murmured. "The other couple didn't either."

"I get it," he agreed. "Social media for some isn't very interesting. For others it's a lifeline."

"Oh my God." Kate rolled her eyes at him. "Some people post everything, including the underwear they put on that day."

"Are you kidding? Some people start with that?"

She shook her head. "It's nobody else's business, as far as I'm concerned."

"Are you sure about that?" he asked, wiggling his eyebrows. "Are you sure Simon doesn't have any say in it?"

"He has no say in it at all, thank you very much," she stated firmly. She quickly sifted through the various Facebook pages, checking to see posts from the husbands of both of the dead women. And yet nothing was there. "Neither husband was involved on Facebook."

"I think that's fairly common too," Rodney noted, "for them, the grieving."

She nodded. "The one has kids, but they're pretty young, so I doubt they're on Facebook."

"I would hope not," Rodney huffed, "but you know that stranger things have happened. But these really young kids can't handle keyboards yet, so I think we're safe."

Yet, just to be sure, she punched in the names; thankfully nothing was there. Of the husband and wife who had been recently taken down, the wife was much more into fashion and constantly posted photos of the clothing that she made. Kate had to admire somebody who had the perseverance and style and know-how in order to make some of the outfits this woman had designed. "What a freaking waste." She shook her head. This was so senseless because she really, in her heart of hearts, now believed that couple may have just been collateral damage. The killer's real goal was the first two.

Kate knew just enough to dislike both Jenna and Robin, so she saw them being specifically chosen as targets. Kate hadn't uncovered anything negative on the second couple yet. He worked at home at his own graphic design business. Forensics had already gone through his computer and found no threatening emails or letters, nothing in there to say he was anything but what he appeared to be. The woman had been in the process of setting up her own clothing design company.

As Kate looked at their Facebook pages, it read true and yet very sad. The last post on both was that they were heading out for a run. And, of course, nothing else had been updated. She didn't even know what to do about that. Like, how did one handle that? Did family members go in and post about their deaths, or did you have to contact Facebook to have something posted to say they were now deceased?

She frowned, wondering what the protocol was. Was there even such a protocol? And considering it was social media, did the protocol change every day of the week, depending on who was in charge? She kept checking through the sites she had bookmarked to see if anything was new or different, but nothing stood out. She sat back, tossed her pen on her desk, and said, "I need to set up a meeting with this Kirby guy."

"Yeah, make sure you choose a time when I can come with you."

She looked over at Rodney in surprise.

"You know this is heating up, if you've got a name and if we've got somebody with good reason to hate this woman."

"Sounds like they pretty well hated each other," she murmured. She picked up her cell phone and dialed the number she'd been given, and, when a man answered, she asked if it was Kirby.

"Yes, who's this?" he asked, his voice deep.

"This is Detective Kate Morgan," she said smoothly. "I need to ask you a few questions."

"Oh, doesn't that just figure? The stupid bitch gets herself murdered, and, of course, you come after me."

"Well, anybody who had an antagonistic encounter with her is almost guaranteed to have us come knocking."

"It was hardly antagonistic," he argued. "As a matter of fact, it was all in good fun, until she took it too far."

"By hitting you with the car."

"She was way out of line doing that," he stated in outrage. "Okay, so I was being an ass, but you know that's the way I was back then. I'm not like that now."

She changed her tone. "You want to tell me exactly what happened?"

He gave a shortened version, but it was along the same lines as what the chairman of the running club had given her.

"Have you seen her since?"

"A couple times, and then I finally realized that it took too much effort to avoid trouble with her, when all I really wanted to do was just go out there and run," he explained. "I did move away for a time. Then I ended up back in Vancouver again."

"Why?"

"Work," he said. "I work for a tech company, and I did try Alberta for a while, but it wasn't for me. I asked to come back and eventually was given a transfer here again. It's that simple."

"Do you still run in that same area?"

"Not very often," he stated, "bad memories and all. It's not exactly a place I would want to go back to."

"Anybody else have a problem with her?"

"You should have asked if there's anybody who *didn't* have a problem with her," he quipped. "She was a very difficult woman."

"What about her friend Robin?"

"They both were very difficult," he declared. "If you gave them a wide berth, it was fine, but they were very over-the-top, very loud, and very assertive personalities. Two peas in a pod. And, if one ever started to calm down, the other one would egg them back on again."

"Sounds lovely."

"No, not really. Their husbands are bloody saints to have put up with that," he said in disgust.

She stayed silent on that because one had a much worse relationship than the other, although it wasn't that great for either of the husbands. At least that's the way it looked right now. As she sat down to update her notes, she asked Kirby, "Have you seen them anytime in the last six months?"

"Only on the front page of the news when it reported they had been murdered," he replied. "I'd be a hypocrite to say that I'm sorry because I really can't drum up too much sympathy. For their families, yes, of course, especially the kids. However, honestly, both women were very difficult to be around."

"Any idea who might have done this?"

"Seriously?" he asked. "Okay, they were irritating as hell, but that doesn't mean that anybody would be upset with them enough to go through the trouble of trying to kill them."

"Right," she said. "Anyway, if you think of anything else, please let me know."

"Will do."

Then she stopped and asked, "By the way, where were you on the day that they were killed?"

"Really?"

"Yes, really."

He replied, "On that Saturday morning, I was in bed with my partner, and, yes, you can talk to her."

"Anybody other than your partner?"

"Well, I was still in bed later that morning because I was pissed off that I had a video conference meeting at nine in the morning with Europe. You can easily check that out too."

He quickly gave her the details, and she jotted them down. "What about on Tuesday?"

"What happened on Tuesday?" he asked curiously.

"Just answer the question."

"Okay," he said, "let me check my schedule here. Ah, I had a team meeting at eight in the morning on Zoom. There would have been at least eight people there who can confirm my presence."

"And before that?"

"I went for a run over at Stanley Park. It's a huge place and lots of running trails."

"Alone?"

"No," he replied, "actually two guys run with me on a regular basis these days." He quickly gave her those names. "You can confirm that."

"Will do."

She hung up, and, because it needed to be done, she quickly made the phone calls and confirmed his alibi for each murder. When she tossed down her phone, she glared at it.

"Not what you wanted to hear?" Rodney asked.

"Well, that lead just got shot down," she said. "He offered an alibi for both times, and both alibis checked out."

He nodded slowly. "It does make sense. I mean, if it was a place where I'd had such a negative confrontation, I'd always be afraid of seeing the same women again. And, if just the sight of them would drive me batty or ruin my running experience, which is a highlight of my day, I wouldn't want to go there. Maybe if the guys were together…"

She looked over at him in surprise. "Would you really let somebody like that ruin what had been your favorite run?"

"Well, I can't stand running anyway," he noted, "but, if it was a favorite place that I really liked, and I felt myself pulling inward to avoid seeing them, then, yeah, I'd find another place to run because that's not why I want to go anywhere."

"I get it." She sank back into her chair, pondering the whole thing. "We really don't have anything, you know?"

"That's not what I want to hear," a man spoke from the doorway, his voice harsh.

She looked up and glared at her sergeant. "Well, I won't manufacture evidence to make you happy," she snapped back.

At that, her sergeant glared back at her, putting his hands on his hips.

She raised both hands, palms up. "I don't know what else to do. We have very little forensic evidence, and, in fact, there's very little anything. Somebody took a rope and pulled back a branch enough that, when he let it go, it knocked them down at least, and then he followed up with a stick if they weren't out already. Then he strangled them or rather used a garrote. The second time he went right for the garrote, no need to strangle them with the rope because he already knew it wouldn't work. He took the garrote with him both times. No forensic evidence around. Used gloves and probably tossed them to boot."

Colby nodded slowly. "I get it. So what do you want to do?"

"Well, we don't know if this guy will act a third time. God help us if he does. But my thought would be," she hesitated and then said, "give him some bait."

Immediately he shook his head. "Hell no. You know too many places are on that trail for us to accurately pick his next attack point. We can't have that many people out there. He'll know something is up."

Colby was correct there. "I also don't want to just sit

here and wait for him to make a move. I do have a few threads to chase. Other than that, I'm out of ideas."

"Tie up as many loose ends as you can. Write down all the potential theories you've got, and then you move on," Colby ordered, his voice sharp. "We got two more murders last night, both down on the east end. So these other deaths are accumulating, and your jogging murders may be dormant."

She sagged back in her chair. It was always this way; you ran a case as long and as hard as you could, until you ran out of things to do. Then that case would go to the back burner, while you carried on with other cases, until hopefully something broke. What she could still do was check up a little bit more on the two husbands. She'd already checked their social media accounts, so next she did a Google search and checked at their offices. Neither had mentioned that they were great friends, but they obviously knew each other because their wives were great friends.

But how did she find out anything more about that? It was starting to feel too much like this one would go cold.

She finished off the report she was supposed to do, and, by the time she closed the file and set it off to the side of her desk, she realized she was alone in the office. Groaning, she stood, grabbed her keys and her wallet, and headed outside. She'd gone home after her earlier trip to the park and had walked back to work this afternoon, an impulse that she regretted right now. But, as she stood outside, catching her breath, a sports car drove up beside her. She stared in surprise as Simon hopped out. "Is this yours?" she asked.

He nodded. "Get in."

She got in and said, "I should go home and get some extra sleep tonight."

"Sounds fine to me," he noted. "I'm all for it."

She laughed. "But?"

"I just thought maybe we could go for a picnic at the beach first."

She looked at him, smiling, then twisted around to see a large hamper in the back seat. Almost on cue her stomach growled.

He laughed. "So, was that a yes?"

"Sure. Whereabouts though?"

"How about Second Beach over at Stanley Park?"

"Perfect." She was enormously pleased at the thought of something different. "Otherwise I would go home, grab some toast, and crash." She checked her watch and winced. "I'm not sure how it got to be six-thirty, but that's just the way it is. Have you been waiting for me very long?"

"No. I checked at the front desk, and they told me that you were still in, so I just sat in the car out here. The meter was actually running but whatever."

She smiled. "I'm very happy that you did. Thank you."

"You've got to look after yourself better than this," he noted.

"I do look after myself," she stated. "There's no *better* about it."

At that, he let out a bark of laughter. Then he asked, "Any progress?"

"Hell no," she said. "I thought I had a lead today, only it turned out to not be a lead at all."

"Explain."

She quietly told him about the confrontation between Jenna and a man named Kirby in the parking lot, and the end result of getting a hold of the Kirby guy.

"Interesting, so those women seem to have been quite

aggressive."

"Apparently the pair of them together was not great because they really egged each other on."

"I've seen that a couple times before," he stated. "The dynamic may be great for the two involved, but they aren't better together in the sense that all friendships and relationships should be. They may, in fact, have brought out the worse in each other, and together they gave each other permission to behave badly. That's the opposite of how it should be."

"Do you believe that?"

He gave her a quick frown, as he maneuvered through the traffic and over the bridge to Stanley Park. "Of course I do."

As soon as they arrived near Stanley Park, he pulled into a parking lot and slowly rolled down to the far end. He asked, "How about here?"

She nodded. "This looks great." As they got out, he reached into the back seat and lifted the big picnic basket and a blanket. She smiled. "You at least thought ahead."

"One of us has to," he teased, with a smile. As they walked toward a nice grassy spot with picnic tables, he added, "And, yes, to answer your question again. I do succumb to that theory."

She looked at him in surprise. "What? About two people together need to be better than they are apart?"

He nodded. "Yeah."

"But how often does that happen?" she asked.

"Well, for this couple of women, they probably thought that was exactly what happened—because together they made each other stronger and better in all ways, at least in their minds. But I'm sure everybody else wondered if they had pushed it too far, if they were just being too aggressive. I'm sure the husbands probably have a lot to say."

"They may have a lot to say, but neither of them is talking, although that's not uncommon under the circumstances."

"Any way to find out if they're talking to shrinks?"

"Well, I hope they are. They've just lost their wives."

"But maybe before that because of the abuse?"

She frowned. "Well, even if I knew that, what good would it do?"

"Maybe *both* husbands were considering a divorce."

She thought about it slowly and wondered. "The one couple was divorced and already lived apart. I guess I could check with their family members."

"Not that they'll help, mind you."

"No, they probably won't," she agreed, pondering it. At the picnic table, she sat down and smiled. "We should have brought bathing suits."

At that, he pulled out his bathing shorts. "Done, though I wasn't sure if you'd wear these though." And he held up what looked like a tankini and some boy shorts.

She looked at it and frowned. "Where did these come from?" He just shrugged. She pressed him deeper. "Come on. Where are they from?"

"Okay, I picked them up for you," he admitted, with a nonchalant attitude that she found interesting. It was almost like he was trying to hide what he'd done.

She held it out, checked the size, and whistled. "So, did you check out my clothing, or are you just that good?"

He flashed her a brilliant smile and stated, "Pretty sure I'm just that good."

She burst out laughing and turned to see changing

rooms. "I'll go pop these on then and see *just* how good you are." With that, she got up and dashed over to the changing rooms. A few minutes later she had her answer. He was damn good. The boy shorts were something she would never have chosen for herself, but they were actually really cute. They were similar to runner's shorts but much shorter, almost like something that she'd wear to sleep in, and the tankini fit her like a glove and exposed a whole lot of skin.

She packed up her other clothes and walked outside, barefoot across the grass. He took one look and whistled. She shook her head. "I would never have chosen these."

"Maybe not," he agreed, "but they look really good on you."

She admitted, with a soft voice, "I agree. Thank you."

He asked, "Food first or swim?"

She gazed at the water, rippling back at her in the sun, and said, "You know something? I think a swim first."

"Good, let's have a go at it," he stated. They put all their stuff—their clothing, watches, phones, and whatnot—in the basket and carried it down close to the shore, leaving it all to the side.

Once there, she walked straight in and dove under the water. As soon as the cold water closed over her head, she felt the stress just slipping away into the waves around her. By the time she broke the surface again, she was lively and yet at peace. She swam out as far as she could with a hard front crawl, did a flip, turned around, and came back toward shore. Only as she came up in the last twenty feet did she realize Simon swam steadily at her side. When she came back to the shallow part and stood up again, she brushed her hair off her face, flipped backward, and just floated.

"Oh my God," she moaned. "Every time I come to the

water, I wonder why I just can't live in it all the time. It's always so calming and decompressing for me."

"You should have a pool at your place."

"That would be fun," she agreed, "but I don't, and I'm not prepared to move to a place that does."

"Why not?" he asked.

She looked over at him, her head just barely rolling in the water, so she saw him from the corner of her eye. "Because it costs a lot of money." He just nodded and didn't say anything. "Besides, it's not the same thing being in a pool, where everybody has access to the space that you want."

"A lot of homes to rent have pools in their backyards," he noted.

"Sure. And have you checked out the real estate prices in Vancouver lately?"

"Yes, actually." He laughed. "I just bought a building yesterday," he shared.

She rolled her eyes and asked, "Another dilapidated one that you felt sorry for?"

"Absolutely."

She stood up and looked at him seriously. "Do you just keep throwing money away or are these actually decent investments?"

"They are investments," he stated, "but not short-term. They take a while to earn back out again," he admitted.

"Like a long while?"

He shrugged. "I'm okay with the five-to-ten-year mark," he replied, "though some of them will be twenty years because they cost more and won't rent or lease out at the prices I could hope for, but that's just business and the housing market."

She nodded and slowly worked her way up toward the shore, sad to feel the water slipping off her skin. "I am getting hungry, are you?" she asked.

"Perfect, and, yeah, I was hungry before we went in the water."

"You could have said something," she protested.

"Hell no, it's way too much fun to be in the water with you."

"Well, we're getting back in again after we eat," she threatened.

"Perfect, I'm up for it."

As they walked back to the picnic table area, still dripping and carrying the basket with their belongings and the food, he pulled two towels from the folded blanket.

She looked at him in surprise. "You really did think of everything."

"Well, let's hope so."

She sat down at the picnic table and stared at the food. She shook her head. "Wow, where did you get all this?"

"It wasn't too much," he noted, "and it's from the deli around the corner."

She opened up a tinfoil pack and found meat pies, still warm, several of them. "*Yum.* We could have eaten right away, if I'd known you had something that was hot."

"They were hot to begin with, but they're meant to be eaten either warm or cool." He handed her a pie and opened up another big tub, which was a big Greek salad, and she immediately lit up.

"I love Greek salad," she cried out and scooped up a large serving.

"There's also fresh buns, sliced meats, and cheeses." He pointed off to the side.

She immediately cut open a bun and ladened it with meat and cheese too.

He grinned. "I really do like the fact that you know how to eat."

"How does anybody not know how to eat?" she asked, sending him a sideways glance. "We learn it as children."

"And a lot of women worry and carry on about their weight to the point that you can't even have a decent meal with them."

"Yeah, well, I've burned a ton of calories today," she said, "not to mention, after picking up running again, I can't seem to get full."

He nodded. "Are you getting lots of oils and carbs?"

"I am," she stated, "and you're doing a bang-up job of helping me." She noted another container off to the side and nodded toward it. "What's in that?" she asked curiously.

He grinned and pointed to another box she had missed off to the side. "Coffee and dessert."

At that, she looked at him with a fat smile. "You really do know me, don't you?"

"I do. I could have picked up wine, but, in your case, coffee is preferred."

"Wine is always nice, but it feels like it's too early for wine," she noted. He looked at her askance. She burst out laughing, absolutely loving the joyful playfulness of the evening, after such a hard series of days. "You know this is just what I needed, right?"

"Well, I hope so," he replied, "but there's really no guarantee from one moment to the next what you need because I never really know what kind of day you've had."

She nodded slowly. "It's been pretty tough because, as of today, I don't really have any other avenues to explore."

"Ouch," he murmured.

She nodded. "And we caught two more cases last night—unrelated to the jogging murders—so our plates are all overwhelmed. Therefore, I'll have to park these until something else breaks.

He nodded. "Sometimes there's nothing you can do but just do the best that you can do, and then you have to step away."

She frowned. "I know, but for the four families affected, … walking away just doesn't seem like an answer."

"But you aren't really walking away though, are you?" he asked. "That was just a turn of phrase."

"I know. I get it." She picked up the meat pie and bit into it, and immediately her mouth was filled with the taste of hot beef gravy and onion. "Oh my God." She licked the gravy, dripping down her fingers. "Where did you get these?"

"Same deli," he said. "They make them there." She shot him a look, and he nodded. "You can get anything in Vancouver. You know that, right?"

She smiled. "I do know. It just seems odd that you would have picked some of these things."

"Not at all. I have eclectic tastes. I knew Mama would be more than interested in packing us up a big basketful, but that wouldn't likely stay hot and isn't as delicious cold."

"Maybe not," she agreed, "but just the thought of it makes my mouth water." She took another bite of the meat pie. "This is beautiful."

He nodded. "I'm glad to hear that."

Before long, her plate was empty, and she sat back, patting her tummy. "And I suppose I now have to wait half an hour to go back into the water?"

He looked over at her, then smiled and asked, "How

about coffee?"

After that suggestion, she studied the box. "This is one of those take-out boxes, isn't it?"

"It is," he confirmed. "It's probably way more coffee than we needed, but I figured, *What the hell?* This way you could at least have all you wanted."

There were take-out cups for them too. She tilted the box off to the side, noting the pour spout at the end, and carefully poured two cups of coffee. As she sat back, she saw a meat pie left too. She studied it, looked at him. Then she looked at the meat pie, looked back at him, and grinned.

"Go for it," he said.

She didn't need any second urgings and snatched it up in her fingers and bit into it, almost swooning in delight as her mouth filled with the rich gravy taste. "I can't even believe how good this is," she whispered.

Finally, with that finished and a cup of coffee to top things off, she sat with her knees tucked up against her chest and just watched the area. A few other people were around, some people running, others out with their families. She said, "It's just beautiful here, isn't it?"

"It's one of the most gorgeous cities in the world," he stated.

"I have to keep reminding myself of that, since I'm in a job that highlights the ugliness instead."

He reached over and gently picked up her hand. "You are dealing with the ugly parts of life, but it's a very important job that you do."

"Is it?" she asked. "The families hate it when we don't make any progress. The killers hate it when we pick them up, and then there are all the people in the media who hound us constantly for updates."

"None of which is your problem," he noted. "Your focus is on finding out who did this."

"Somebody has to stand up for the victims," she declared. "It seems too often that, once you die, everybody else just moves on and forgets about you. You go to your slab in the morgue, and then you're either burned all to hell or you get buried." She shook her head. "Everybody picks up the pieces and moves on, as if these people never existed."

"I don't think that's quite true," he disagreed quietly. "But it is true that everybody else is left in a position of having to deal with the aftermath of that person being gone, so it isn't as if they can do anything for them or to help them anymore."

"Which is why it's my job," she stated, with a nod. "And some days it's rewarding, and some days it's just plain frustrating." After her second cup of coffee, she smiled and added, "It's been at least thirty minutes."

He grinned like a kid and said, "Let's go."

And they carried their coffee a little closer to the shore; she stuck hers in the sand and walked straight out into the water. Almost immediately she sank beneath the waves and just let the current carry her. After a few moments she paddled her way back to the shore again and sat in the shallow part of the ocean, the water lapping up over her, crashing up over her shoulders, as she now held her coffee.

When one particular wave dumped into her coffee, she realized she had lost the last little bit. She moaned and cried out but was laughing too hard to worry about it.

Simon immediately snatched the cup from her hand, and she watched as he walked back to their table and refilled them both. He came back down with a big smile and suggested, "Now move maybe just a little bit up the shore, and that won't happen again."

She scooched backward, accepted the cup, and sat here, a big smile on her face. As far as evenings went, this one was perfect.

* * *

SIMON DIDN'T WANT to drop Kate off on her own, and, when he took her back to her place, she looked at him, raised an eyebrow, and asked, "Are you coming in?"

He felt a spark of hope inside. "I was hoping so," he replied. "But, if you're really tired and need extra sleep, I don't have to."

"I am really tired, and I do need extra sleep, but it's been such a beautiful evening," she noted, "and I really don't want it to end."

On that note they headed up to her apartment. Every time he stepped in, the comparison to his own place made him wince. Hers was clean but almost sterile in a way, as if she didn't even live here. Boxes were still parked off to the side that he contemplated every time he visited.

She caught his gaze once again, shrugged, and said, "I haven't had time."

"What's even in them?"

"You know what? At this point I don't know," she admitted. "I could probably just pack them into the car, take them down to Goodwill, and never even miss that stuff because, if I haven't opened the damn boxes in the last year, I'm pretty sure I don't need whatever's in them."

"Isn't there somebody who's making a killing out of cleaning things out of closets and such?"

"Somebody is always making a killing off the latest fad, but, in this case, you're not far wrong. I mean, if I haven't even opened them—"

"But you never know. Maybe mementos of your mother or your brother are in there."

She nodded. "That's what the second-to-the-bottom one is, I think," she noted slowly. "And you're right. I do need to at least take a look at them, before I just get rid of them."

"Or you could just move them to the next place as is," he suggested.

She paused, then smiled. "I'm heading for a shower."

"Is that an invitation?"

She looked at him, then grinned. "Beat you there."

And, with that, she raced ahead. He burst out laughing and followed her. The sex was hot, perhaps the hottest he'd ever had, but tonight she was molten lava in his arms— whether it was the evening at the beach, feeling full, or just being completely relaxed for the first time in a very long while. She surged to his touch and melted all over him.

By the time they came out of the shower, he felt shaky and barely able to walk. He collapsed on the bed. "You nearly killed me, woman."

"Good," she whispered, as she took a towel and dried herself vigorously and then tossed it his way. "Roll over."

He rolled over, and, to his surprise, she crawled in under the covers. "Just like that?"

She mumbled, "Just like that. When I said I was tired, I really meant it."

It was almost like she pulled a switch, and, moments later, she was out. He sat up, grabbed the same towel, and realized it was too wet to do the job. He headed to the bathroom, searching for a drier one, and ended up pulling out one of the beach towels that was drier than hers.

Once he was dry, he quickly dressed in boxers and wandered around the apartment. He wasn't ready to sleep just yet. But neither did he have his laptop with him, though he did have his cell phone. He sat for a little bit, checking out things on the internet, checking his email. Then he figured he should probably clean up the picnic basket, and he quickly washed up all the dishes.

With the kitchen spick-and-span, he headed back to the bedroom, only to find her tossing and turning, caught up in a nightmare. He raced to her side and tried to wake her up.

She cried out, "No, no, don't." Then the part that hurt him the most was when she cried out, "Timmy, please don't go."

And, with that, he gathered her up in his arms, still asleep, and crawled back into bed with her. "It's all right," he whispered against her hair. "I'm here. It's okay."

Almost instantly her shivers calmed down, and she slid into a deep sleep. He held her for the longest time, before falling asleep himself.

⚬⚬⚬

Thursday Morning

WHEN HE WOKE the next morning, he was alone. He stayed here, feeling hurt inside. He knew that she had to get up to head off on her own to go to work. As he checked his phone, he winced because it was damn late. He was normally out between 5:30 and 6:00 a.m., yet it was already one-quarter to eight. How the hell had he fallen asleep so deeply that he hadn't even heard her getting up and leaving?

He got out of bed, headed for the shower, and then dressed. With a last look around the place, he headed down to his car. Once there, he made his way back to the penthouse.

Harry looked up and grinned at him. "Rough night?"

"It wouldn't be so bad if she'd just come here," Simon admitted, "but staying at her place is never quite the same."

"You'd think she'd be happy to move in with you."

"Well, I'm not sure we've gotten that far yet," he noted, "but I can't say that I'd be against it."

"She won't do it if you don't push it. That one is particularly independent."

He smiled. "That she is. And I have to admit that I actually really love that part about her."

"I disagree on your earlier comment," Harry stated. "I've seen the two of you together. If you aren't there yet, you're damn close to being all the way in love with her. You'll just have to make sure that she's in love with you."

"Isn't that the truth?" Simon shook his head. "It shouldn't be that hard but somehow …"

"I've seen them fall all over you for the last few years. Maybe it's a good thing that this one's a little more hesitant."

"A good thing how?" he protested. "How on earth do you see that as a positive?"

"Makes you work for it a little bit more."

He rolled his eyes at that. "I could do with a little less work in that department."

Harry burst out laughing. And, for Simon's part, at least he was finally smiling again.

CHAPTER 11

E VER SINCE THE phone call came, and Kate had crept out of her bedroom, she'd wished that she could have woken up slowly in Simon's arms. Just something about the two of them together that made her feel like she was home. But she didn't tell him about it. They were a long way from that level of a relationship—weren't they?

She walked into the hospital and looked over at Rodney. "What's going on?"

"One of the husbands tried to commit suicide."

"Oh no. Which one?"

"The one with the kids. Agnew."

She winced at that. "That really sucks. Who'll look after the kids if he's gone?"

"I don't know," Rodney replied heavily. "He didn't succeed, and the doctors are just now saying that he's likely to make it."

"I'm surprised you woke me then."

"It was already seven-thirty," he noted, "and I didn't exactly think I would be waking you anyway."

"Point taken," she said and yawned.

He asked, "Late night?"

"Actually a really good night. Simon picked me up with a picnic basket and took me to Second Beach. I haven't been swimming there in years."

"Me either. What was it like?"

"Perfect. … It was just perfect. And I guess I finally destressed."

"That is good," he agreed. "You needed it."

She nodded. "I didn't need this though."

"I know, none of us do. The kids? I just can't imagine."

"No, can't imagine." She thought about it and asked, "Are we really thinking he did this out of grief?"

"I don't know." Rodney looked over at her. "What are you thinking?"

"How about guilt?"

At that, one of the doctors stepped out of Agnew's room. He looked at her and asked, "Guilt over what?"

She stared at him, lifted her badge, and then replied, "His wife was murdered."

He shook his head. "I don't think there's guilt here as much as grief in this. But what do I know? I'm not a shrink."

She nodded. "Do we know what happened?"

"He slit his wrists," the doctor stated. "One of the kids saw it and called Grandma to tell her that he was bleeding. Instead of trying to come over, she called for an ambulance."

"That was smart."

"Very," he agreed. "The family is here. I need to talk with them now."

"And we'll talk to them afterward."

He nodded. "Good enough. Looks like he'll survive, but he's not conscious yet."

"How long before he comes to?" she asked.

He shook his head. "I don't know but likely at least a few hours."

"Okay," Kate said, "I might sit here and wait."

The doc studied her and asked, "Are you really thinking

he had something to do with his wife's murder?"

"I don't know what I'm thinking," she admitted, "but what I can tell you is that I'll stay here and talk to him."

He frowned, and he seemed to want to argue with her but didn't. Finally he nodded and left.

She looked over at Rodney. "He really doesn't want me to stay, does he?"

"Nope. Any particular reason why you will?"

"Yeah," she said, "I need to talk to him about the suicide attempt. I need to know exactly what's going on in that mind of his."

"Most people won't take that kindly."

"Yeah, well, this is a whole different deal. Suicide isn't illegal in Canada, but you've got to wonder where his head is at when he'll leave the kids behind with no living parents."

"I know. That's tough." Rodney frowned, and just then his phone rang. He groaned. "I've got to go."

She waved him off. "I'll stay here and wait."

The family came and walked in to see the patient. She frowned at the doctor, and he said, "Family first."

She just raised her eyebrows at that. Because, if she had any reason to suspect that he was actually a party to the murder of his wife, then Kate would have been pretty aggressive about making sure the family didn't even get in there. But no point in upsetting the apple cart at this point.

She didn't really have any reason to object, outside of the fact that she didn't like that he had tried to commit suicide. Just because he might be depressed and more concerned about his own world than that of his children, although that's totally shitty, it didn't mean he was a criminal.

When the family finally came out, teary and clearly upset, Kate called out to the woman—Agnew's mother—who looked over at her. She identified herself. "I'm Detective Kate Morgan."

Immediately her husband wrapped an arm around her shoulders. "This is our son," he stated. "It's really not a good time."

"I know perfectly well what time it is," she noted. "I just need to ask a few questions."

Immediately Agnew's father shook his head, "No, it's because of your questions that he's like this anyway."

Kate stopped. "Sorry?"

Agnew's mom immediately rushed forward. "He was really upset about all the questioning, thinking you might have thought he was involved. We think that's why he tried to take his own life."

"Interesting," she replied. "I still need to talk to him, and I would like to talk to you guys too, if you have a moment." She tried to make it friendly, but it was obvious that she was determined to talk to them, and they were equally determined that they wanted nothing to do with it.

Finally Agnew's mom agreed. "If you can make it quick, okay—as I'm really exhausted and need to go home."

"I just wonder about the state of their marriage."

"It was fine," Agnew's father snapped. "All you people ever think to do is get into people's faces and make their lives miserable."

"Agnew's wife was murdered," Kate declared. "I understand it wasn't your daughter, and I won't be shocked to learn something less than love was between you, but Robin also had a family and has somebody who really cares about what happened to her."

Immediately he stiffened and glared at her. Agnew's mom rushed in to soothe the situation. "We do understand.

We do. She was …"

Kate stopped. "Yes?"

"She wasn't the easiest person to get along with," she murmured. "And I don't want to say anything bad about the dead, but it was hard when you weren't part of the inner circle."

"Meaning that you were kept at a distance?"

She nodded. "That does happen though a lot with sons." Agnew's father snorted at that. The mother nodded. "That's true, and you know I have seen it happen with some friends, and I did go speak to some people about it, but Agnew just seemed to never be himself. When they got married, he just suddenly seemed to do everything that she said, without any question or discussion."

"And maybe right now he's really grieving his loss," Kate murmured, studying both people. The husband turned to look in a different direction, while the woman looked at the floor. "Or not?"

The mother looked up at her. "Again, I don't want to say anything bad, and obviously he's very traumatized over this whole thing. My son is a good person. I don't know how tough these last few years were for him, but I can tell you with certainty that he's much better off without her."

"I have heard some other murmurings to that effect."

Agnew's mom nodded. "Damn right you have. But that's it. Some people tell the truth, but too often everybody lies for their own sake."

"Which isn't what I'm doing here," Kate clarified, hoping to keep the conversation going. "I just need to know what state of mind Agnew was in, when this suicide attempt happened."

"I don't know," she whispered, "but I wouldn't have said

that this was normal behavior for him at all."

"Meaning?"

"He would never commit suicide."

"And was he alone? Outside of being with your grand-children?"

Agnew's mom looked at her in surprise and then slowly nodded. "As far as I know, yes."

"What was it your grandson said when he called you?"

"Just that Daddy was bleeding everywhere and that he couldn't wake him."

"It's good that you phoned for an ambulance first."

"Yes, yes, I know." She put her hand on her chest. "I can't imagine what it would have been like if I hadn't." A sob escaped. "We're taking the grandkids home with us. Agnew's not in any shape to deal with them at the moment."

"No, of course not," Kate agreed.

And, with a warming smile, Agnew's mom added, "Now we'll go spend some time with them. We'll come back and see our son later today."

Kate watched as the couple walked away. Agnew's father was still bristly and upset that anybody would be talking to his son about this whole mess. Just then another thought entered the back of her mind, but it would necessitate talking to Agnew first. She poked her head inside his hospital room and saw that he was awake, staring at the door.

When he saw her, his gaze hardened.

"Glad to see you made it," she said quietly.

He closed his eyes. "Stupidest thing—trying to take your own life, I mean. Some people would say that it was stupid, but I just got really depressed. Couldn't handle it."

"And what were you doing?"

"What do you think I was doing?" he snapped. "I was

drinking, and I don't do well with booze."

"Yet I think it's probably an understandable reaction, given your life right now."

"I hadn't expected to be in this scenario. Ever."

"And I'm sorry. Obviously your wife's death has been hard on you."

"Not just her death," he stated, "her murder, and there's something so much worse about that."

She had to admit she'd heard that a few times before. She wanted to tell people that losing somebody and not having any answers ranked right up there too. But this wasn't a case of who had it worse, it was about how all of these things sucked.

She nodded. "Your parents will be back this afternoon. They were heading out to spend some time with your kids."

He sighed. "Good. That's probably for the best."

"You know your kids need you, right?"

He turned and looked at her and asked, "Do they?"

"Yes, they do."

He stared at her for a long moment and then shrugged. "I didn't think I was suicidal when I started drinking that booze—but, man, sometimes it just brings out the worst in me."

"So maybe, *uh*, don't drink?"

"Ha, ha, ha. As if that's even funny."

"It's not funny," she stated, "but I do mean it. This could have gone a completely different way."

He nodded, acknowledging her point.

"But this doesn't have anything to do with your wife's death, I presume?"

"You mean, did I kill her and decide to kill myself?" He snorted. "I figured that'd be the first thing you'd think of, when I saw you pop in here."

"Since we haven't had any luck finding a good suspect for this case," she noted, "it makes it difficult."

"Of course it does," he agreed, "and that's just frustrating too. Because the questions of who and why and what's really going on, they just drive into my brain and stay there."

"It's always the *why* for me," she murmured.

He nodded and started to look really tired. Just on cue, a nurse walked in. Kate hopped to her feet. "I'll see you again soon, Agnew. Remember to stay strong and to get better."

He gave her a half wave, and she took that as a request to leave, and she turned and walked out of the room. She walked down the hallway, her hands in her pockets, pondering the scenario. By the time, she got back to the office, she was even more confused than ever, but a kernel of a suspicion brewed in the back of her mind.

Owen looked up. "Hey, did you get a chance to talk to him?"

"I did—and his parents. Sad deal all around."

"What did he have to say?"

"That he got drunk, and booze is always an unhappy friend for him."

"Well, you'd think, in that case, you wouldn't drink."

"I think in his case," she replied, with the wry look, "*not* drinking was a much harder option than giving a shit about what might happen if he did."

"Well, considering his wife was just murdered, I would think so."

"I'm not necessarily getting the vibe that he's in much grief over Robin at all. More like he feels like he should be grieving but is almost maybe feeling guilty because he isn't."

"That can be pretty twisted up too," Lilliana stated

calmly from the back corner of the squad room. "Relationships tie us up in knots. We have this expectation from everybody else about how we're supposed to feel, but they aren't part of the core relationship. So, was he really happy in his marriage or was he just expected to be happy? And, if he wasn't really happy, is he now really expected to actually grieve? Was she a good friend, or was she becoming a pain in the ass? Was she somebody who bossed him, bullied him, and possibly even abused him, or was she somebody who was his partner and tried to meet his every need out of love?"

Kate looked at her team member in surprise and nodded.

Lilliana continued. "So much of this is just part of the private relationships that publicly nobody knows or understands, until we get in there and start tugging away at the curtains. Everybody is happy with the status quo, until that status quo gets changed, and then people get pretty pissy about everything."

Kate nodded slowly. "I hadn't really looked at it that way, but there is a weird vibe about Agnew. Maybe I'll go talk to him again this afternoon," she suggested. "And maybe he'll have had a chance to think about it a little bit more."

"Maybe," Lilliana replied. "Of course the other issue is, he might have firmed up how he'll handle this publicly and be even less helpful."

"That's something we need to know too," Kate said, "because, if they won't be helpful, the next question is, will they actively hinder us instead?"

"I've not seen so much hindering but definitely plenty of not helping," Lilliana noted, as she sat down. "It's all something to think about."

"Exactly, and nothing quite like a death to shake people

up and to make you wonder just how much they're actually even playing a part."

"And how much they were always playing a part but didn't even really know it."

"Sounds like you've had some experience with that," Kate suggested.

"We've had some cases that were pretty interesting," Lilliana replied. "The bottom line is that, with something like this, you just don't know what you're dealing with. Sometimes the individual people don't know what they're dealing with, until actual horror hits. Some people rise above it really well, prepared to honor and love and cherish. Other people realize just how much they hated the person, and, now that they're gone, they'll start to really live again."

"Ouch," Kate noted. "That sounds pretty rough."

"Maybe, but it's also not necessarily a bad thing in this case," Rodney added. "We know perfectly well what's being revealed about these two women."

"I know." Kate nodded. "I was thinking of that. It still feels pretty rough to consider that Agnew wouldn't know exactly who and what Robin was."

"Oh," Lilliana explained, "it doesn't mean he doesn't know. It's just, in a relationship like that, you put up blinders, so you can continue to live but without having to deal with unintentional side effects of the bad relationship. So you block it off. You push down your feelings, and you don't allow yourself to think about it. You convince yourself that it's all just fine, perfectly normal, and you just don't worry about it." Lilliana shrugged. "When you go back and see him this afternoon, think about it and see which way he is going. It could be either or a little of both."

Kate nodded. "I'll do that."

And, in fact, as she walked back into the hospital and down the hallway to his room, that's exactly what was on her mind. As she turned the corner to walk into his room, he was sitting up, staring out the window, a tic working his jaw, looking pissed off. She tapped on the open door.

He looked over, saw her, and immediately a frown crossed his face.

"I know," she admitted. "I'm a pain in the ass until I solve this case. Sorry, but I just wanted to come back and see if you had any other impressions over what happened."

He looked at her in surprise. "What do you mean, *what happened?*"

She shrugged. "Like if you wanted to clarify what happened to you last night."

He stared down at the bandages on his wrist. "Apparently I've signed up for a lot of shrink visits right now."

"Standard policy for anybody who tries to commit suicide," she shared apologetically.

He nodded. "Still, I guess it is what it is."

"It is, unless you didn't do it," she stated, just tossing that out there.

He stared at her for a long moment and shook his head. "I was the only one there."

"Good enough." She realized it wasn't exactly an admission of guilt.

"Have you found out any more about my wife's murder?"

"Unfortunately not yet," she confirmed quietly. "Are you always there at the house early in the morning?"

He nodded. "Yes, my kids don't leave for school until eight. Then I usually walk with them."

"Do you ever go out running?"

"No, I used to run all the time, but then I ended up with a tendon injury and messed up ankles, and I can't run anymore."

"Ah, shit, I'm sorry about that," she said sympathetically because, in truth, a tendon injury was damn painful and could have even really hindered his ability to walk again.

"It took me a long time to get past it," he shared. "I really loved running."

"Sounds like that was a bond between you and your wife."

"Yeah, we used to run all the time," he said, with a gentle smile. "It was a lot of fun."

She noted his change in tone, like this was long ago. She smiled. "I'm happy for you. At least you had those years."

He looked down at his legs. "I had those years, until I got injured, and then I couldn't run anymore."

"What happened?"

"Oh, it was just a stupid thing," he explained, "a trip on the trail, and I ended up going down part of a cliff and getting more of an injury than I expected. Just one of those freak accidents."

"Were you alone?"

"No, I was with my wife and several other runners. We belonged to a club," he added. "It was really heartbreaking at the time. We didn't know how bad it would be until I got to the hospital, and that's when they gave me the news." His smile was grim. "But, as you can see, I've healed and am much better now. And I'm fully capable of at least walking and carrying on my duties, as need be."

"Good. I'm glad it's not part of the reason for the suicide attempt."

"No. ... I won't do that again." She gave him a questioning look, and he raised both hands. "It was a mistake, and I know it. I won't do it again," he stated.

"Good," she murmured. "And I get it. I know that it's easy to try and drown your sorrows, but you can see what happens and how it impacts everybody else around you."

He sobered at that. "Honestly, I can't believe that I even got to that point mentally. I would have sworn that I would never do anything to hurt my kids."

"Especially when they're already suffering," she noted. "You know perfectly well that they need a parent, and you can't even begin to think that your parents, no matter how committed, would make a good substitute."

He shook his head vehemently. "Oh no, not at all. I guess that it scared me—more than I expected something like this would—because I couldn't have imagined such a thing would ever happen. Now I have to do a lot of work to make sure it doesn't happen again."

"And realize that you can't handle booze. So don't go there."

He nodded slowly.

As she went to walk to the door, she asked, "By the way, when you were running and had that injury, who all was with you?"

"Just some runners from the club. Charlie was there," he offered, with a smile. "We've stayed friends all these years."

"Did he run with your wife afterward?"

"*Nah*, he's a runner, but he's not crazy like she was," he replied, with a smile.

She nodded. "I'm glad to hear that. Please take care of yourself."

He looked over at her. "Honest, I won't do that again."

There was enough belief in his tone for her to realize

that he at least meant it. It didn't mean that she actually believed it would hold him through times of trouble in the future, but she had to believe that maybe he could get through this. She wished him well and walked out of the hospital.

As soon as she got outside, she phoned Charlie. "Hey, Charlie," she greeted him, as she identified herself. "I just came from the hospital, where I spoke with Agnew."

"Shit," he said, "I heard about that."

"What did you hear?"

"That he tried to kill himself. Man, that kid just can't get a break," he stated.

"I'm hoping that he'll get what he needs now. Obviously this was just a little more than he could handle."

"Well, wouldn't it be for everybody?" Charlie stated, disgust in his tone. "Jesus, you lose your wife like that, and it all just comes crashing in."

"No, I hear you," she said. "Were you there when he had his accident?"

"Yeah, I sure was," he confirmed. "He and that crazy-ass wife of his were out running, chasing each other, instead of being safe on the uneven trail. He went ass over teakettle off the trail, snapped a tendon, and did some other muscle and ligament damage, bad on one foot but terrible on the other. He could never run after that. I mean, obviously he could do a little bit of running, more like hobbling, but nothing like he could before."

"Yeah, that's what he was telling me. Did he get really depressed back then?"

"Oh yeah, big-time. It was part of the bonding with his wife," he stated. "And that made for a lot of difficulties in their marriage, up until she hooked up with her running buddy. Then those two women together were nuts. Nobody would run with them."

"Some people are always after the adrenaline," Kate noted.

"Well, that's what these two were, adrenaline junkies like you wouldn't believe. The harder, the faster, the steeper the trail, the better, and, if it was a flat run, then it was always about who could beat the other," he said, an odd note in his tone. "But still, it's not them that bothers me. Yeah, of course, they were young and in the prime of life, and somebody took them out, but I am sorry for the people who are left behind. That's just so sad." He sounded genuinely sincere. "Like, who'd have thought this guy would have ever tried to take his own life?"

"No, I hear you there, not with his two kids," she added quietly. "Yet I'm pretty confident that he'll get some help now."

"And I'll be there for him too. I would have been right there with him, if I'd known," he said sadly. "I didn't even know it was that bad. I guess, when we lose somebody, we don't know quite what to do."

Kate suggested, "You can share your condolences directly with Agnew, then offer any help you can actually provide, you know?"

"But what help can we really give him and his kids? What could I do for a guy who lost his wife that way?" he asked. "It just sucks all the way around."

"At least his wife had a lot of good running years afterward," she murmured. "You hate to think of people dying without actually having a chance to live. Sounds like they all had a chance to really enjoy life."

"There is that," he agreed cheerfully. "At least I'm hanging on to that theory. Because anything else just sucks." And, with that, he hung up.

She stared at her phone and shoved it in her pocket, thinking it really did suck. But it also brought back that whole premise that she had pondered earlier. About whether somebody who had really loved the game had hated these women enough to actually take them down. She quickly sent Charlie a text. **Was there anybody to blame for Agnew's accident?**

He responded immediately. **Yeah, his wife tripped him. Bitch that she was, she couldn't stand to lose, so she tripped him, just so she'd win.**

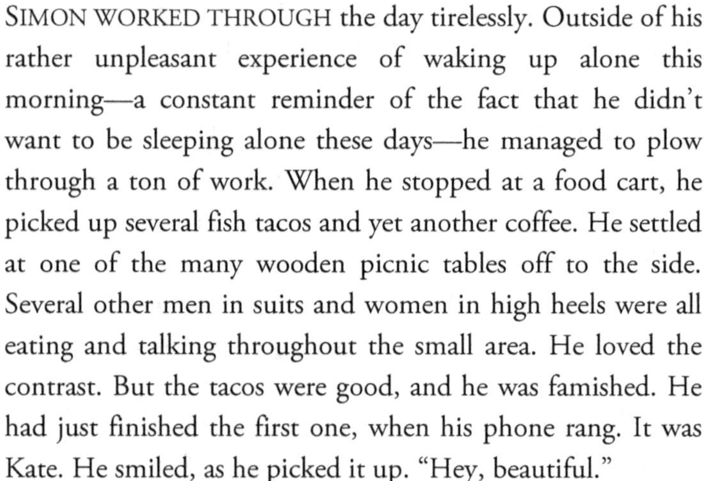

SIMON WORKED THROUGH the day tirelessly. Outside of his rather unpleasant experience of waking up alone this morning—a constant reminder of the fact that he didn't want to be sleeping alone these days—he managed to plow through a ton of work. When he stopped at a food cart, he picked up several fish tacos and yet another coffee. He settled at one of the many wooden picnic tables off to the side. Several other men in suits and women in high heels were all eating and talking throughout the small area. He loved the contrast. But the tacos were good, and he was famished. He had just finished the first one, when his phone rang. It was Kate. He smiled, as he picked it up. "Hey, beautiful."

There was a moment of pause on the other side. "What's wrong with you?" she asked.

"What? I can't give you a compliment?"

"I guess," she replied slowly.

He snorted. "You don't have to sound quite so shocked about it." That just reminded him that he obviously didn't give her nearly enough compliments.

"Whatever," she said dismissively. "Where are you?"

"I am at a fish taco stand downtown."

"Oh."

Such disinterest filled her voice that he knew she wasn't even thinking about food. "Where are you?" he asked her.

"Just heading back to the office."

"That must have been quite the call you went out on this morning."

"Did I wake you?"

"No, I wish you had," he noted. "It's such a weird feeling going from never having anybody sneak out on me, to you, who can apparently sneak out all the time."

"That's because you know I'm no threat," she explained immediately.

"Maybe," he agreed. "It's still a discomforting feeling."

"Well, deal with it," she stated, "or the alternative is not sleeping over."

"I'll deal with it," he said instantly.

She snorted at that.

"Did you have a reason for calling? Are you okay?" he asked, staring down at the fish tacos still on his plate.

"No, I'm fine. Just checking to see that all is well."

He frowned at that. "Is there a reason for it not to be?"

She hesitated. "No reason for it to be anything. I was just wondering."

"Wondering if I had picked up anything else?" he guessed, pinching the bridge of his nose. "You know that I'd tell you, right?"

"I know. ... I'm just frustrated."

"You also don't sound like you believe me."

"I know how it works with your visions, but they do give

me something for my mind to work on," she shared, with a half laugh. They talked for another moment and then hung up. He wasn't even sure what to think about that.

She was such an example of contrast. On the one hand, she absolutely detested that anything possibly psychic was an option in this world, and yet she couldn't stop herself from asking if he'd gotten anything new. And he understood because, when you were desperate to find a solution to a problem, particularly when people were dying, you would do almost anything. He knew that. He'd been there, and he'd played the same game, time and time again.

But, at this point in time, he really didn't want too many more of these psychic visions, particularly when he hadn't asked for them. He could almost hear his gran's voice in the background again, but he was happy to ignore it. Instead he picked up another taco and spoke directly to the voices in the back of his head. *Stop. I'll eat now. I need the nourishment.*

Then he took a big bite. It was delicious, and, in no time, he had polished them off. Nobody took their time eating these things. They were small, and he could probably even eat a half dozen more, if he applied himself, but he also knew that wasn't the best answer right now. Thankfully the voices in the back of his head were a whole lot calmer. He wasn't sure what that meant, and he also felt guilty trying to still those voices, just so that he could get a meal eaten in peace.

With that thought, he closed his mind and intentionally pushed open the door. *Okay, so what was the message?*

There was a moment of silence, and then the voices just slammed him. He immediately slammed the door closed, seeing his hands shaking in reaction. He looked around, but everybody else seemed to be busy on their own stuff and weren't concerned in the least about him. But he also knew it wouldn't be long before somebody would notice.

He got up, hurriedly wiped off his hands, and tossed all his garbage, then quickly strode down the street. A couple alleyways were up ahead that crisscrossed over. He needed some privacy, and he darted inside one of them. He leaned up against the wall, his hands still shaking even now, and whispered, "You'll want to do this calmly and quietly," he told the voices. "I'll try to help, but, if you'll just slam me all at once and make my life very difficult, screw you guys."

An almost shocking silence followed for a moment on the other end. He didn't know who the hell he was talking to, and he probably shouldn't be speaking to them this way, but how in the hell was he even supposed to function if they would just keep screaming? When he opened the door to his mind ever-so-slightly again, he heard some semblance of calm.

He smiled at that. "Good. Now did you have a message?" But there was no verbal message. People were around, and he could sense ghostly energies. But, as far as words, nothing was spoken. The "messages" were more about emotions, primarily fear and panic. He frowned at that. He spent a moment sorting through what he sensed, but nothing seemed to be related to the runners. The fact that maybe these were people related to other cases was enough to drive him crazy.

"I can only focus on the priorities," he stated. "So, if there's any priority here, let me know." Almost immediately, an image slammed into his head. Once again, he was running down the path. It was so clear and crisp. He reached up to smack a branch, feeling it hit the palm of his hand as he ran. It was such a great feeling, and he looked over to his side, where he could sense and then see a man running beside him. He winced because now he realized what was coming. He was in the woman's viewpoint. This would be the other couple. Found dead already.

Almost instantly a branch smacked up hard against her face and down she went, stunned by the shock and the force of the blow. He didn't want to see what came next, but no way to do anything else but wait because, waiting, when you were in a cold dead body, didn't give you any answers. It just made the sensations that much more horrific because Simon already knew what was coming. This couple was dead, and then he froze. Or were they? Dragging himself free of the vision, he quickly texted Kate and asked if there had been new victims.

She called him instead of texting. "No, why?"

"I just had a vision of a couple on the pathway," he said, his voice heavy and dark. "I was in the woman's point of view."

"Can you describe the man?"

"Maybe." He gave as brief a description as he could. There was almost relief in her voice when she confirmed, "That's the couple from before."

He stopped for a moment. "The woman was taken down first."

"Interesting," she noted. "I wouldn't have thought that would be the smartest of the choices. Generally, when couples are attacked, the males are taken out first because they're the ones who provide the most resistance."

"True enough," he agreed, "but I think, at the last moment, she darted ahead of him and slammed right into the branch."

"So, it was a branch again?"

"Yes." Then he stopped. "You already knew that though, didn't you?"

"I did. Just confirming."

"Just don't play games with me."

"Never games," she replied, with a gentleness he had never heard before. "But listen. There will always be a certain amount of fact-checking because I deal in the world of facts," she explained. "And I still have to get evidence for the courts, regardless of what woo-woo magic you may have at your fingertips."

"I don't have anything at my fingertips," he snapped. "Otherwise I would be giving you answers that would stop this madness."

"I would happily take them too," she replied, "but then I'd still have to turn around and prove to the rest of the world that this is what happened."

He thought about that, then nodded. "I guess that's the thing about the two of us, isn't it? I can only give you visions, and you still have to lock the information down to something much more concrete."

"I do," she agreed, "because the end result is not only to just stop this guy but to make sure we take him off the street so that he can't ever do it again." And, with that, she hung up.

He walked out of the alley and stood for a moment in the sunshine, the warmth slowly seeping into his pores. Something was so cold and chilling about this psychic work, and he had never expected to end up involved in this. It certainly wasn't where he wanted to be. In fact, this was not the work he would ever have chosen to do at all, but then he had to question why he was doing it then. Why was he helping Kate? The answer was one he couldn't even begin to argue with. Not now, not before.

He was doing it because he had no choice.

CHAPTER 12

K ATE WALKED INTO her office, poured herself some coffee, and made some calls. She knew Agnew wouldn't be happy, but, when she found out he was being released from the hospital, she wanted him to come into the station for questioning. Rodney sat beside her in the bullpen, sipping his own coffee. She looked at him. "Any luck with your case?"

"Yep, the two on Hastings Street are taken care of."

"What was it?"

"A dispute over drugs."

She winced. "That sounds very familiar."

"We never run out of reasons to kill each other in this world," he quipped. "Particularly when drugs are involved."

She nodded.

"What about you?"

She filled him in on what she'd found out from Charlie.

"Wow." Rodney stared at her for a long moment. "Now *that* is one hell of a motive."

"Well, it's a motive, and, of course, the attempted suicide also adds a potential look of guilt," she noted, "but I want him to come in for a more formal questioning phase."

"Sounds good to me. I'd like to watch, if you don't mind."

"That would be great," she said, "since our impressions

will be huge here."

"Because you don't have any evidence?"

"What evidence can I have? We have nothing forensically. He tried to commit suicide, but a lot of people would put that down to grief or any number of other confused emotions."

He nodded. "You really need a confession."

"And I don't know that I'll get it," she stated, facing him. "Agnew couldn't even talk about the suicide."

Rodney winced at that.

"I know, right? And, with my luck, he'll come in with a lawyer in tow."

"I wouldn't be at all surprised. If he talks to anybody at all, you know that'll be the first thing they recommend."

"Since when did the public become so aware?"

He stood, laughter bursting out. "Cop shows of course."

"But they get it wrong all the time," she said good-naturedly.

"Yeah, but they don't get all of it wrong, and those are the things that the public seems to pick up on pretty fast."

She groaned. "I know."

"Still, it's minor compared to the rest of the things you'll need in order to lock down the case."

"I know," she agreed, "but, somewhere along the line, things are supposed to start going our way."

"Only when we have a way to prove it."

"And that's what I'm up against," she declared.

"I just don't get why he would kill the two of them?"

"I think it was just the fact that they were both there," she noted quietly, "to make it look like it wasn't just his wife."

"Do you really think he's the killer?"

"Well, I think he has things he needs to answer for," she stated. "Does that make him the killer? I don't know. I know that, at the moment, he's looking like the best lead I've got." Staring into the air for a moment, she shook her head, looking glum. "Honestly," she added, looking up at Rodney, "Agnew's the only lead I've got."

Two hours later she got a call from the front desk, saying that Agnew had arrived for his interview. She let Rodney know, so he could watch from the observation room, if he chose to. Then she got up and headed into interview room B. As she walked in, she found that Agnew had arrived with his lawyer. She smiled at Agnew, and he just looked at her nervously.

The lawyer frowned and asked, "What is this all about?"

"I just need him to answer a few questions," she replied easily.

"You were at the hospital, so surely you could have asked your questions there."

"And I did," she noted, as she sat down. "Yet I'd like to get an interview on the record," she stated, then started the recorder, identifying the occupants of the room, including herself, handling the interview. She looked over at Agnew. "Now can you tell me again how you injured your tendon?"

He looked at her in complete surprise. "What the devil does that have to do with anything?"

The lawyer immediately said, "You're just fishing."

"I asked a simple question," she stated firmly, "and I'd like an answer."

Agnew raised both hands. "Fine." And he went through the process of what had happened.

She nodded. "How did the accident happen?"

"We were running," he repeated. "I tripped and fell."

She looked at him steadily. "Well, I have somebody else who says it didn't happen quite that way."

He shook his head. "I don't care what anybody else says. That's what happened." Then he stopped for a moment, before asking, "What else could have happened anyway?"

"According to the person who saw it happen, your wife tripped you."

Agnew stared at Kate for a long moment, and the color rapidly faded from his face. "Who told you that?"

She stared at him steadily. "Do you want to confirm or deny that, please?"

He shook his head. "It's news to me."

She looked at him in surprise. "Are you saying that you didn't know your wife intentionally tripped you?"

He shook his head slowly, and she saw the reality of it setting in. He looked at his lawyer, back at her again, and added, "No, but that's something the goddamn bitch would do."

Immediately the lawyer tried to shush him up.

Kate leaned forward and asked, "Why is that, Agnew?"

"Because she could never lose. It didn't matter what it was, but she could never lose. She had to always win, no matter what, even if it meant cheating."

"I'm sorry," she said. "That appears to have been a problem in your relationship."

"Well, it wasn't after that, was it?" he asked, with an ugly snort. He sat back, then scrubbed his face. "Jesus, please tell me that's not true."

"Are you really unaware of what actually happened?" He nodded slowly, and unfortunately she had to believe him. She looked at him and asked, "You really thought you tripped on a branch or something?"

He nodded. "Yes, of course I did. I'm not the kind of person who would look at my wife and blame her for it. Not to mention the fact that I had to get packed out of there on a stretcher."

"And yet I presume you would have forgiven her if she had accidentally tripped you. If it would have been done in play or on the spur of the moment."

He nodded. "Absolutely I would have come around," he said. "I wasn't anywhere near as competitive as she was, and it didn't matter to me if I won or not."

"And yet," she noted calmly, "if that were the case, you wouldn't have been winning in this instance—because you would have realized it would have pissed her off."

He laughed. "Just because I didn't care about winning didn't mean I didn't enjoy poking at her for fun. She had quite the temper, especially about getting beat, and sometimes it was pretty fun to watch." He shook his head. "Listen," he admitted. "I know it sounds childish, but, sometimes in relationships, you play a game that ends up being quite satisfying later in the day," he admitted.

"Apparently it could also be quite dangerous," she added, studying him.

"Absolutely, and apparently it was more dangerous than I knew." He shook his head. "Christ, I still can't believe I didn't know she did it."

"*If* you didn't know ..." she began.

He looked at her and frowned. "What difference does it make whether or not I knew anyway? Why bring this up now? She's dead and gone, and it's not as if I can sit here and accuse her of it now. It just seems mean to even bring it up now, when she's not even here to defend herself." He glared at Kate in irritation.

"Yeah, I get it," she said, "but it does lend itself to motive."

"Motive?" He stared at her in surprise, then turned and looked at his lawyer. "I don't understand." Then his lawyer leaned forward and whispered in his ear.

"Seriously?" He twisted to face Kate in shock. "You actually think I'd kill my wife over something like that?"

"People have been killed over lesser things," she noted quietly, but, in her heart, she started to doubt what had looked like a promising avenue.

"I feel sorry for you, Detective," Agnew said. "Sorry that you have to deal with people who would make you even think such a thing. Our marriage wasn't perfect by a long shot, but I loved my wife."

He declared those words with such sincerity that she found herself believing him.

Agnew continued. "What she did—if she even did it, and I'm not yet convinced of that—was petty, small, and absolutely true to her inability to lose a competition," he stated. "But that was a flaw in her own personality, not something to be killed over." He shook his head again. "I can't even believe that's why you brought me in here."

"We're looking for a killer," she stated. "And killers will kill for any number of reasons, and revenge is definitely one of them."

He shook his head. "Well, that's not the case with me," he murmured. "I couldn't have done that—and surely not for such a petty reason."

"So what reason *would* you kill over?" she asked curiously.

His jaw opened, then closed. "I'm not even sure I can answer that because I don't know of any instance that would cause me to kill."

"And yet you were prepared to take your own life. Over what?" she asked.

He frowned. "I already told you that it was the booze talking at the time." His back stiffened, as if talking about his drunken attempt at ending his life were even more of an affront than her accusing him of killing his wife.

"I get that," she murmured. "And I'm glad to see that you survived whatever turmoil was in your mind at the time."

"Me too," he said, seemingly understanding what she'd been thinking. "So, have we put to rest the idea that what I recently did, however stupid, was most definitely not an admission or evidence of guilt regarding the death of my wife? Which, for the record, I'll state again that I had nothing to do with."

"Well, it certainly wouldn't have been the first time this had ever happened," she stated.

Agnew stood and stated, "Not this time, Detective. Not this time. Now, can I leave?"

She let them go, watching as they walked down the hall and out of the station. As she headed back to her office, the same old frustration ate away at her.

Rodney stood there, waiting for her. "Hey, it was a really good theory."

"And it still is, as far as theories go," she noted. "But proving it? That's another story. He has no way to prove he wasn't out on the trails, but that would have meant he left the kids home alone for that time."

"Right, and somebody surely would have seen him to place him at the scene of the crime at the hour of the murders."

She nodded. "I can go knock on doors," she suggested. "And I might just have to because nothing else, and I mean *nothing else*, is breaking."

"And you're running out of time."

She nodded. "More than just time and patience, I'm running out of avenues to look at." And, with that, she added, "I'll head down and check with the neighbors. If nothing else, I need to write it right off."

"Got it," Rodney agreed, "and, if you're lucky, you won't catch another case in the meantime."

She winced. "I would hope not."

But she also knew that, as far as that murder time frame went in Vancouver, there was always an average of one or two a week, if not three times that. She didn't have much time, before something else would require her attention.

And she could fight it all she wanted, but the next victim deserved her attention just as much as these did.

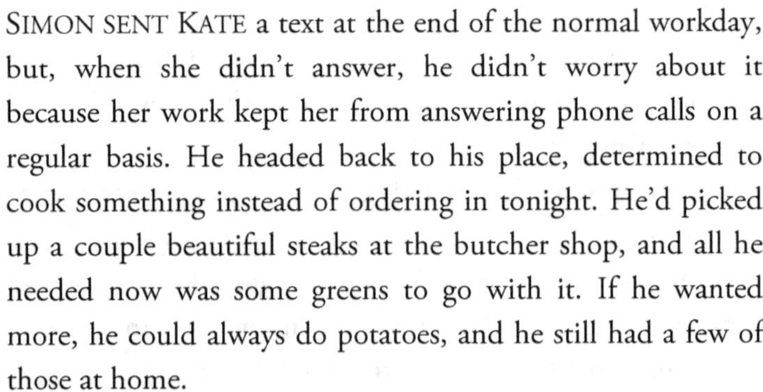

SIMON SENT KATE a text at the end of the normal workday, but, when she didn't answer, he didn't worry about it because her work kept her from answering phone calls on a regular basis. He headed back to his place, determined to cook something instead of ordering in tonight. He'd picked up a couple beautiful steaks at the butcher shop, and all he needed now was some greens to go with it. If he wanted more, he could always do potatoes, and he still had a few of those at home.

Stopping off at one of his favorite produce stores, he picked up a few items and then headed outside and walked back to his place. It was a long walk, and, by the time he got there, he was tired and more than ready for a glass of wine outside on the balcony. Harry was at his usual post, and Simon lifted a hand, as he headed to the elevator. "Don't you ever take time off?" Simon called out.

"I get my days off," Harry confirmed. "It just seems that I'm usually off when you're spending time with your little chickadee."

"Well, that doesn't seem like enough downtime for you," Simon noted, "And I sure don't get to spend nearly enough time with her."

He laughed. "She's the only one I know who's resisted your charms as much as she has."

"I don't know how much she's resisting, but she's definitely not like the others."

"And that's a good thing," Harry noted. "No insult intended, but the others weren't keepers."

At that, Simon burst out laughing, as the elevator doors closed in front of him. That was a very true analysis. The others weren't keepers, and even his ex fiancée Caitlin ended up being a freaking nightmare. That they were now capable of speaking to each other said a lot about how far they had moved forward. Yet it was not as if he would make the mistake of going back down that pathway, not now and not ever. Caitlin wasn't somebody he wanted a do-over with. Particularly now that he had Kate in his life, revealing how lacking his other relationships had been. And Kate was a completely different animal. Independent, feisty, refusing to fall into line just because he wanted her to. And sometimes refusing precisely because he wanted her to. He shook his head at that.

"Trust you, Simon, to find somebody who would complicate your life more than you ever thought possible."

The trouble was, at the same time, she had also brought

him more joy and peace than he'd ever thought possible. How could he argue with that?

Upstairs in his penthouse, he quickly traded his blazer and slacks for a pair of shorts and a tank. Pouring himself a cold beer, he sat outside on the balcony. He was uptight and stressed, and it was one of those days when even walking miles hadn't been enough to loosen it up. He hated being that uncomfortable in his own home. He did a simple workout and then moved into a yoga stretch, loosening up his back and lower legs.

With that done, he opened up the package of steaks, quickly seasoned them, and left them sitting on a plate, while he prepped the potatoes. He layered potato slices in between cheese and onions and butter, then wrapped them up in tinfoil and had that ready to go into his preheated oven, and then quickly tossed a Caesar salad. After that, he turned on the barbecue and oiled up the grill. As he waited for that to heat up, he realized he'd made enough for two. Frowning, he studied the meal, then decided he might as well find out for sure. He picked up the phone and called Kate. This time she answered. "Any chance you're coming my way for dinner?"

She burst out laughing. "So, is that an invitation?"

"Well, I just finished prepping everything and realized I'd made enough for two." He heard the smile in her voice when she spoke next.

"You know something? A home-cooked meal sounds pretty damn nice. Depends on the timing though."

"When are you off?"

"Now," she replied, "but I'm down by the beach, making a few quick visits to some neighbors here."

"So, you'll be at least forty minutes?"

She thought about it and said, "Yeah, forty minutes is

probably pretty close."

"Good," he replied. "If you'll be any later than that, give me a shout."

"Will do," she stated.

He hung up, a grin on his face. It was a roundabout way of making an invitation, but he honestly hadn't thought about it when he was shopping or prepping the food; he'd just naturally made enough for her too. Because, in his heart of hearts, this is where she belonged. He found that because there was just no *belonging* with her, she would go and do whatever she felt she needed to do. Sometimes he wondered if it wasn't fear keeping her from committing to something more.

He'd been reticent about pushing the issue because she really wasn't yet open to the discussion. It's not that she was shutting it down; it's just that, any time it came up, there seemed to be another reason for her to talk about something completely different. So, either she was really good at changing the conversation or she was really good at avoiding the conversation. And, in this case, both scenarios were probably very true.

He had plenty of work to do, so he sat down at his laptop, with a pad and pencil, and got after it. He started writing down some notes about what he needed to fix up and change on his projects, but, as he was writing, his hand kept going around and around in a circle. He stared at it. "What the hell is that?" he muttered. He didn't want to think of the spirits talking to him in this way, but his grandmother had told him that, if they needed to talk, and he wasn't prepared to listen, they would find different avenues to get to him. He remembered her doing some crazy things with a pencil and paper as well, at various times.

He'd never really considered that it would be something coming his way though—because who the hell wanted to consider any of that shit? As he sat here, studying the drawing, he noted that his hand continued to go around and around. He wasn't sure what to do about it, but, when he tried to stop and put down the pencil, he was almost subconsciously forced to pick it back up again. He shook his head.

"I don't know what this is," he muttered, "but it needs to stop."

And, of course, stopping was something that he thought he was doing, but his hand wasn't paying any attention to him. And then, understanding that he needed to address the spirit, he looked at his hands and asked, "What is it you need to do? What is it I need to know that I'm not getting?"

Almost immediately his hand started to write a name. Shivers went down his back, as his hand wrote, "Kate, Kate, Kate," over and over and over again. Finally it stopped, and he stared down at the message on the notepad. But it wasn't very much of a message; it was just her name, over and over again.

"What the hell," he cried out. "What is it you want me to know about this? What am I supposed to do?"

He picked up the pencil and waited for an answer. But there was nothing.

Absolutely nothing.

CHAPTER 13

K ATE KNOCKED ON the second door. When the woman answered, Kate smiled, identified herself, and stated, "We're just checking around the neighborhood and asking a few questions about whether you saw any of your neighbors out and about early in the morning on these dates." Then she gave the dates of the four recent murders.

The woman looked at her in surprise. "Oh my, this is about those poor women, isn't it?"

Kate nodded. "Yes, we're just confirming some times and dates of people coming and going."

"Well," she began, "being runners, of course, they're up early."

"So you know they are runners, *huh*?"

"Everybody knows they are runners," she stated, with an eye roll. "And, if you weren't into running, you just weren't on their radar. It's not that they were mean or anything," she hurriedly added. "It's just that their whole focus was running."

Kate nodded slowly. "And that's an interesting thing, isn't it? I've never met anybody who was quite so obsessive about running."

"Me either," she agreed. "I've never liked exercising, and thankfully I'm skinny, so it's not as if I have to do it for weight loss or anything. Yet I know that my husband in particular always wanted me to do more to get fit."

"Right," she noted. "So, have you ever seen any of your neighbors head out for their runs?"

"In the morning, no," she replied, "I like sleep too much."

"Nothing ever wakes you? You haven't heard or seen any signs of anybody at all?"

"Nope," she said, "they used to go running in the afternoon, or the evening every once in a while, but I haven't seen that very much either. Honestly, when you see something over and over again, you just block it out. It's like it's a normal thing, so you don't even register that it's happening."

"That is very true," Kate admitted, as she nodded. "If you do happen to remember anything," she added, "could you give me a call?" She handed over her card.

The woman nodded. "I can. I just don't know that I can be of any help."

"Well, at this point in time," Kate stated, "we have very limited suspects, and we're just crossing our *T*s and dotting our *I*s just to make sure we don't miss anything."

"I know the husbands used to run," she noted suddenly.

"I know the one did," Kate murmured. "Did the other one run too?"

"They used to run together every once in a while."

Kate stopped and stared at her. "Are you saying that the husbands of the two women who were murdered used to run together?"

She nodded. "They did. Not so much early in the morning. I don't think at least"—she paused—"but then what do I know? Because honestly I'm not kidding when I said I don't do mornings. So, I don't really know what anybody was doing in the morning, but I used to see the husbands sometimes going out in the afternoon."

"But not for a long time?"

"I presume no, not for a long time," she replied, "not since Agnew's accident."

"I heard about the accident," Kate mentioned. "And that's got to be tough for any runner."

"Right. I can't imagine. It's like a painter losing a hand. It just wouldn't work so much for me."

"Well, I don't think it works for anybody in that situation, but you do the best you can do with it."

"I get it," she noted, with a delicate tone. "I'm just grateful it's not my life."

"And what about the other husband? Did he continue to run afterward?"

"I don't know. I didn't see much of him running at all. I think he did some solo running afterward, but yet I don't really remember seeing him."

"And the husbands never ran with the wives, did they?"

"Again I don't know about the morning time," she repeated, 'but it seemed like, once the two women hooked up as running partners, they seemed to be a match made in heaven. So everybody else just backed off and let them go at it."

"Yeah, they were pretty crazy about it all, weren't they?"

"That's one word for it," she said. "Man, they were really fierce competitors."

"But not against each other, right?"

"No, I don't think so." Then she stopped and thought for a moment. "You know though, some of that competitiveness fed into other things too."

"Like what?"

"About their clothing, their makeup, just all of it really.

It seems like, once they became that competitive, everything became open for a contest."

"Interesting," Kate replied. She wasn't sure how that helped her or if it helped in any way, but it was an opinion at least. "Thank you for your time," she said. "I appreciate it very much."

The woman shrugged. "I'm sure I've not been much help at all."

"Do you live here alone?"

"Well, I do now," she murmured. "I divorced two years ago, and I ended up getting the house out of the deal," she shared, with a bright smile.

"Good for you," Kate replied. "It's a gorgeous location."

"It seriously is." Someone called from inside the house just then. A male.

Kate laughed. "You don't appear to be suffering too much."

The woman winked. "Nope, not at all. I like my men with a little more backbone than those two you're asking about. Neither of them had much of a spine," she said, then she shook her head. "Honest to God, I wouldn't be at all surprised if things weren't pretty abusive in the opposite direction—if you know what I mean," she added. "I used to hear this couple pretty frequently." She pointed to the house beside her. "They used to fight all the time. It actually got pretty loud, and sometimes I heard blows being delivered and cries. I did ask at one point in time if she needed me to contact the police, and she just laughed at me. She said something about *Why would I need to do that because her husband was far too spineless to ever actually hit her.*"

"Interesting."

"Again I think it's just, you know, the more competitive

the women got, the more aggressive Jenna got too. Not exactly my kind of person." She stepped back from the doorway, with a shrug, "But both women are dead now."

"Exactly," Kate murmured.

"That makes me feel terrible for talking about her in a negative light," she said, curling up her lip. "You're a bad influence, Detective."

"No," Kate disagreed. "Unfortunately talking about people after they are dead is what I have to do for a living."

She winced at that. "I could never do your job. Have a good day now." She stepped back inside and closed the door in front of Kate.

Armed with all of that not necessarily helpful information, Kate wandered to the next couple townhomes. She talked to everybody on the block, and, when she got to the very last one, she found an older lady, sitting on a rocking chair, out on the front porch.

"I wondered if you were coming my way," the woman noted, with almost a cackling laugh.

"Well, if there was something you wanted to say to me," Kate stated, "I'd hope that you would have called out to me before I left."

"Depends on what you're talking about," she quipped, "but, with a double murder of those two women in the neighborhood, it's not hard to guess."

"Isn't that the truth," Kate murmured. "I was just wondering if you saw the women's husbands or anybody else out during the early hours of the morning on the day the women were murdered." Then she also gave her the other date.

"Nope, can't say I did," she replied, "at least not on those mornings. I did see a couple people out after that. But, of course, the two women were gone."

"What hours and what days?"

"God only knows," she declared. "My memory is not exactly what it used to be. I was only up because, well, it's a known fact that old people don't sleep much." She snorted. "I thought all those rumors were lies, until I got old myself, but now I realize we really don't sleep much anymore. But nothing goes on in the world between four and seven in the morning that we can really talk about."

"What do you do at those hours?"

"I usually get up, have tea, maybe work on a puzzle. Nothing much is on TV at all. I get on my computer, doodle around on the internet a bit," she said, "but, other than that, it's books. I read, lots and lots of books, mostly on my Kindle."

"Interesting," Kate noted, "so you wouldn't have seen anybody anyway because, chances were, you were inside the house."

"Oh no, I sit out here a lot in the summertime."

"Do you remember seeing anybody?"

"I saw the two women leave on the morning they were murdered," she stated.

"Did you see anybody else around?"

She shrugged. "Nope, I didn't, but I did go in and have tea when they left."

"Why is that?"

"Because they always reminded me of a time when I wasn't old," she explained. "That gets distressing after a while, so I just got up and went inside, rather than have the constant reminders."

"And yet they would have left the area already, right?"

"That doesn't mean that just because they're out of sight that the reminder is gone, Detective. I get that you're young enough to not be concerned about getting old, but you might want to remember that it catches up with you pretty damn fast. Then you do your darndest to make every day count. But most of the time people forget about that mantra, and they just carry on, so busy with their lives that they don't even enjoy their youth plus don't give a fuck about the future."

Since Kate was equally guilty of that, she nodded slowly. "I think it's always a good thing to remember to live in the moment," she agreed. "Unfortunately, because of the field that I'm in, I get reminders on a daily basis of how short life can be."

At that, the older woman stopped, looked at her in surprise. "You know what? Maybe that's a good thing about what you do," she suggested. "I could never do it myself, just too much evil out there in the world. I wouldn't want to be reminded of it daily, but you should take time to smell the roses. You should take time to find that partner, to have the kids, to go on holidays, and to sit outside, watching the sunsets, while the ocean rolls onto the beach," she stated. "Because, before you know it, your number of sunsets is limited, and those rolling waves are hard to get to because it's hard to walk in the sand. And then you can't take holidays anymore because the travel insurance is so damn much, and your kids are long gone and don't even give a shit about you anymore." She shook her head. "And all those years I've put in, you could almost divide it into parts that started and ended. And now I sit here, in the last part, the twilight section, wondering when this one will end."

Her tone wasn't sad exactly but more pragmatic, as if expecting to see the end coming soon.

Kate murmured, "This has been a good reminder, but I

don't necessarily think that, because you're in your twilight years, that it should be sad either."

"Maybe not, but it's really hard to find much to look forward to when you're counting your pills and making sure you've had enough fiber to take a crap. All things that nobody in their younger years even contemplates." She shrugged. "And why would you?"

At that, Kate laughed. "There is something to be said about *Why would you?* because, when it happens, then you have to deal with it. So worrying about it ahead of time won't really make it any easier."

The older woman grinned. "No, and that's one of the reasons why I make sure I get my red wine at night, so my morning is a little easier."

"The red wine at night is a good idea too," she agreed, "and, so far, I think the research still supports that."

"You know what? There's something about all that research." The older woman leaned forward in a confidential manner. "It'll change every couple years anyway, and I've been around long enough that nothing surprises me anymore."

Kate looked at her and asked, "What about the murders? Did anything about that surprise you?"

She shook her head. "No, not really. But I heard about the two people killed after that, and those ones surprised me."

"Why?" Kate asked.

"Because these women here, I saw them getting murdered anytime," she stated. "They were the kind who lived large and aggressively, and, if a killer was around, those two women were the kind to attract that attention. The couple after that, I don't know anything about them, but it just seemed off to me."

Kate studied the older woman. "*Off?*"

"Yeah, *off*, like I clearly knew these two women would get taken out. Hell, if I'd been a little younger, I might have done it myself. They were that obnoxious."

Kate wanted to laugh, but it wasn't very appropriate. It was all she could do to hold back her chuckles.

But the other woman nodded, seeing her reaction. "Those people in our world who are like that, they get your goat going, you know? It doesn't matter if you're supposed to be nice or not. You don't want to be anything but honest about those two women because they're just bitches."

"Did you ever see them actually do anything that was bitchy?"

"Well, that Jenna, that one for sure," she stated. "She degraded her husband all the time. It made me feel terrible. I mean, I was raised in a time period where you deferred to your husband. However, by the time I got rid of husband number three, I had ditched that philosophy too." She giggled. "But never in all my years have I contemplated intentionally humiliating any person, man or woman, and never somebody I supposedly loved."

"And that's a truth, isn't it?" Kate murmured. "When you love somebody, that's not how you treat them."

"Exactly," she declared. "So, when I heard those two bitches were murdered, my first thought was the husbands. Yet they're still walking around, free and clear."

"Both husbands?" Kate asked.

"Hell, maybe not both," she corrected herself, "but, I mean, the one for sure. I never saw that other woman humiliate her husband. Yet I figured that, if those two women were two peas in a pod—which is what I've always seen them to be—that there was a damn good chance that the other bitch treated her husband the same way as that Jenna did."

"Well, I would hope not," Kate murmured, as she studied Jenna's house, right in-between these two women Kate had been talking to.

"Well, this one was bad news here," she stated. "So, no matter what you say, I'll never think of Jenna in a nice way."

"Well, the thing is, even though we're supposed to be nice about it, death doesn't exactly change who they were or our view of who they were."

"Exactly, which is why my opinion won't ever change," she claimed. "Jenna was a bitch in this world, and, chances are, she's a bitch in the other world too." And, with that, she stood up and said, "Now, if you'll excuse me, I have to go in and take my fiber pills."

Such disgust filled her tone as she headed inside that Kate burst out laughing.

The old woman turned and looked at her, then grinned and added, "See? Find the humor in the moment. The fiber pills await. Even you."

With that, the older woman turned and slammed the front door.

Still chuckling, Kate headed back to her car. And honestly she was still laughing about it by the time she made it to Simon's. She lifted her hand in greeting to Harry and smiled at him.

"There you are," he said. "About time you got here to put him out of his misery."

"I'm hardly the person to do that," she replied, with a bubbling laugh. "But he is cooking dinner, so that's a good reason to come."

"Hopefully you're coming for more than just dinner," he replied, a frown forming on his face.

"Well, don't you worry about it," she said. "That's between Simon and me."

And giving him a laughing look, she headed up the elevator.

⚊⚊⚊⚋⚊⚊⚊

"SHE'S ON HER way and seems to be in a bit of an odd mood tonight. Laughing, yet not."

"That'll be fine," Simon replied, waiting for the elevator to open.

She smiled at him. "Hey."

"Hey," he said, opening his arms.

She stepped into them, and he kissed her ever-so-gently.

"There's an odd look to you today."

"I just met a character, just came away from her place. She was an older woman, somebody who makes you think a little bit more about life. But sometimes maybe we shouldn't be thinking a little bit more about life, at least not according to what I heard from her."

He raised his eyebrows, and she still smiled. As he listened to Kate talk about the older lady, he started to laugh along with her. "Oh boy, it's not exactly *fiber* we want to think about. But you know something? I remember my old gran talking about it too."

"I think it becomes something they almost hover over," she murmured.

He chuckled. "And she's right. We should be doing more to live each day, shouldn't we?"

"Well, I thought yesterday was pretty darn good living," she murmured.

255

He smiled. "I'm glad that held you over for a while."

"It was great," she murmured. "I wouldn't mind doing it again."

"We can do it again," he stated instantly.

When he looked around, she added, "We don't have to do it today by any means."

"Good, because I don't even know how I would manage to move any of this."

That's when she lifted her nose in the air. "Oh my God, is that steak?"

He laughed. "I love that you're a red meat eater."

"I think everybody should be," she declared, and then she frowned. "Yet I also understand the philosophy behind the vegetarians and vegans."

"It's just that you don't love it enough to become one."

"No, I really love my protein," she murmured.

"Well, protein can be gotten in a whole lot of other ways."

"Yeah, and a whole lot of *fiber*," she added, with an eye roll.

He burst out laughing. "Come on. It's almost ready."

He poured her a glass of red wine, then handed it to her and said, "Everything is out at the barbecue."

He led the way onto the balcony, and she immediately crashed onto one of the big lounges. "You know what? If you had a pool here, it would be absolutely perfect."

"I know. I was thinking about that. You've mentioned a pool a couple times."

"This is still pretty special. You won't get this view just anywhere."

"No, but a lot of good view locations are in Vancouver," he murmured.

She nodded. "Still, it'll be a lot of money."

"Yeah, it is. That's what real estate is all about though." She nodded and closed her eyes. He watched her for a few moments. "Tough day?"

"Yeah, tough day," she agreed, "and a shitty day and still not getting anywhere. What do you think about what she said about the husbands and their wives?"

"I think she's right. I think it's about them. Apparently plenty of people hated those women individually—or at least were disgruntled by their behavior."

"Yeah. I can see motive, but I haven't been able to lock down any suspect. I mean, both husbands were the obvious suspects, right? Barry admitted to having no alibi. And Agnew would have had to leave his kids alone to do the deed. And he didn't even know that his wife had caused his accident way back then, not until I talked to him today."

"What do you mean, he didn't know?"

She filled him in on what Charlie, the running buddy, had said.

"What? Well, that's pretty shitty."

"I feel bad now because I'm the one who told Agnew, even though she's no longer here. So he can't even ask questions and vent or whatever. Of course he doesn't want to think poorly of her. But how do you not think poorly of her, if that's what happened?"

"And she didn't tell him or apologize, so at no point in time was telling the truth and clearing it up an issue for her?"

"No," she said, looking over at him.

"That bothers me too. But it does screw up the whole motive thing, right?"

"Exactly." She shook her head. "And then, what's with the other two, the dead couple afterward?"

"Yeah, I wondered about that," Simon noted, looking over at her. "What about the other two?"

"Nothing. That's the problem—absolutely nothing, and that makes me even more irritated. A really nice young couple, with absolutely nothing wrong with them, as far as anybody is willing to say. Nobody saw them there. Nobody looks even remotely good for it."

Simon nodded. "Why don't you park it for now, and let's deal with dinner?"

"I can do that," she agreed, as she hopped up and walked inside, around the dining table. She stopped when she saw a pad of paper in front of his laptop. "What's this?"

He just looked over at it. "Oh, I was trying to get some work done before dinner."

She tapped the pad of paper. "What work has my name written over and over again?" she asked curiously, as she looked up at him, with one eyebrow raised.

He frowned, didn't know what to say, so he said nothing.

She nudged him. "Simon?"

He groaned. "I don't know what to tell you about that."

"Well, why don't you just explain what it is?"

"It's not that easy," he replied.

She looked at the paper and over at him. "Okay." She collected all of his material and moved it off to the side, so that they had room for dinner. When she was done, she sat down at the table. Then she asked, "Were you going to call me or were you wondering whether you should talk to me about something?"

And he realized that she was completely misreading the scenario. And in a way it made it worse on her because he didn't know what she was thinking, but chances were, she would be wrong about it.

"No," he stated. "I was basically trying to contact and control whatever messages I was getting."

She looked at him in surprise and asked, "Messages about my name?"

"I'll explain," he promised, "but let me get dinner off first."

He quickly finished serving up dinner, and, with large platters in hand, he sat down, then passed one over to her. She accepted the plate, inhaled the aroma, and grinned. "This smells divine. There's something about steak, and there's something even more about barbecued steak."

"Well, I was always of the opinion that it should always be barbecued," he murmured, "but one can't always make that happen. However, today we did, and you're right. It looks divine."

He reached for a steak knife, but she reached over and touched his hand. "Please tell me."

He looked up, caught the worried look in her gaze, and sighed. "Okay. … But just in case you don't believe me, remember. *You* asked."

He told her about the psychic messages and how it just seemed like there was nothing but screaming on the other side, so he slammed the door and then tried to open it on his own time.

She looked at him and then reached for her own steak knife, dropping her gaze to the plate in front of her. "But there was nothing about my name necessarily?"

He shook his head. "No, and it's frustrating. I know because I was just trying an exercise to see if I could get some control."

"I understand that," she murmured. "I think the biggest

thing that bothers you about this whole vision thing is the fact that it doesn't appear you have any control over these messages."

He nodded. "Exactly, and who the hell needs that?"

She smiled, gently stroked his fingers, and spoke. "You've come a long way."

He stared at her, fascinated. "How can you say that?"

"Because I remember when you walked into the police station, all those months ago," she began. "I know you were angry and frustrated, but you were also scared back then, about the kids."

He nodded. "It's the only reason I went to the cops."

"And I get that," she noted. "I know it took a lot out of you, and I really appreciate the fact that you made that first step."

He snorted. "You're thankful now. You weren't so happy at the time."

She grinned at him.

"But that's true enough. You're right, and I get it. I mean, I wouldn't have normally done it, but it was a step that needed to happen for those kids."

"And because of it," she noted, "you know things are definitely moving along."

"Maybe," he replied, "but not enough."

"Meaning that you still don't have control when you think you should have?"

"Yeah. Don't you think I should have some control?" he asked in a challenging voice. "I look like a complete idiot when this shit hits me in the middle of the street or when I'm out on a job. If you're me, a little control would go a long way."

"I don't know because I don't know how much control

one can have over these psychic images," she admitted. "So, it's like a sliding scale, with no ends."

He stared at her for a moment and then slowly nodded. "I think that's the thing I'm judging it by, the reality of what our current world is," he explained, "but I don't know if it's appropriate to even look at it that way."

"I wouldn't imagine so," she stated, "because nothing about what you're doing is normal. So, you can't judge it by the normal scale. And, of course, judging isn't the easiest or best way, but, even if you measure it by a normal scale, I can't imagine that'll work very well."

"Then how do I measure whether I'm doing okay or not?"

"Well, by what you were doing today," she stated simply. "Don't use anybody else's yardstick. Just go by your own improvements on a day-to-day basis. And the fact that you could do what you did today, that sounds like—to me—that you have made huge progress."

He sat back, looked at her in surprise. "You know something? I think you're right."

She frowned. "What do you mean, you *think* I'm right?" she said in a teasing voice. "Of course I'm right. I'm always right."

At that, he burst out laughing. "Well, I don't know about that," he replied, a big grin on his face.

"At least we don't compete over it," she noted. "People who have told me things about these two dead joggers and their relationships just blows me away. Everybody seems to have been aware of the two bitchy women, but nobody could do anything to change them because they weren't inside the relationship. They were all on the outside, watching, just shaking their heads."

"I would think you would too, wouldn't you?" he asked curiously.

"It's not something anyone else can really stop, is it? I mean, how would those two women have taken it if somebody were to interfere? If they were that aggressive with their husbands, who would want to interfere? It sounds like the two women were just as bad competing between the two of them as well, and it wasn't just over running."

He nodded. "I get it, and there's no peace in that kind of relationship, if you're always trying to one-up each other. That's not a nice way to live. So, I wonder if the marital relationships were competitive in that way too."

Kate shrugged. "Unless they just saved it for the friendship. And how long can a friendship like that have lasted?" she murmured.

He looked at her. "You know what? That's a really good question because you mentioned how they had been running for like five years together? Yet I can't imagine their relationship lasting that long. Pretty soon somebody will have won too often, or one of them would have assumed somebody cheated, and all that friendship would dissolve almost instantly."

She frowned at that. "You would certainly think so. If the relationship's not competitive and if they both have to win even though there can only ever be but one winner, surely trouble comes eventually."

"Exactly," he stated. "I highly suspect the friendship could even have been already starting to turn."

"But that doesn't help me," she murmured. "They didn't kill themselves."

"No," he agreed, "I don't imagine that would be possible, given the scenario." He thought about it and added, "I wonder if there was another friend trying to get in on the action that they were keeping out."

"Why would anybody want to?" she murmured, with a headshake.

"I don't know." Simon shrugged. "We're back to that thing where a certain person draws a certain audience. In this case, they seem to have had a pretty major audience all to themselves, with the rest of the world just watching, not really in shock though."

"More like disgust, if you ask me," she replied immediately.

He nodded. "That could very well be true. Maybe people were fed up with it. Maybe the husbands were fed up with it and wanted the wives to break up."

"It is a relationship of the sort that would require a breakup, isn't it?" she murmured.

He nodded. "I would think so. I know it sounds strange, but, when you think about it, there was nothing healthy about their friendship. So, if anybody tried to interfere, it might have made them even tighter and closer together."

"I can see that more than a breakup," she murmured. "I don't think breaking up was part of their psychological pattern."

"Maybe not yet, but you can see that long-term it would have been very hard to maintain that intense competition over time. I mean, if the one would trip her husband on a rocky downgrade to keep him from winning, what else was she capable of?"

"Agreed." Kate took another bite of steak. "God, this is good."

"Glad to hear it. I do actually know how to cook. I just rarely do it."

"*Time*," she said dismissively.

"Yes and no," he replied. "Sometimes I think that's just an excuse."

"Effort?" she asked, raising an eyebrow.

"Yes, that's probably true too," he agreed. "Yet today I was just thinking about it and looking for something different. I passed the butcher shop, saw the steaks, and that was it. I was in."

She laughed. "Well, I'm glad because I'm definitely reaping the benefits."

"Well, some days it's just perfect," he noted, "but other days? It doesn't work out so well."

"Which is why you have awesome places to go and get food from," she noted, "like Mama's."

"Indeed."

She continued to eat, then looked over at him. "Maybe we could do the beach again sometime."

He nodded. "Pick a day," he said instantly.

She thought about it. "Today is Thursday. How about Saturday?"

"You'll get the weekend off?"

She nodded. "If I don't have anything else to chase down, then yes. That's exactly what I'm hoping for."

"Sounds good to me," Simon declared. "So, late afternoon, early afternoon, or do you want to make a whole day of it?"

She stared at him in delight. "You know the bulk of the day sounds awesome. Would that not be absolutely perfect?" Then she nodded and said, "I think that would be ideal. Noon it is."

CHAPTER 14

Friday Morning

THE NEXT MORNING found Kate driving once again up to the site of the double murders. She stood at the edge of the parking lot, watching as vehicles came and went. A couple she vaguely remembered, but most of them were different. She checked her watch. It was similar to a time she'd been here on other days, but there was just enough time variance today that it could bring about different results. A lot of people were here. It was also way later than the time frame for the previous murders, according to the coroner.

He'd estimated between five and seven in the morning for both couples. Which hit the running time the two women were well known for. Kate had been able to confirm with their husbands the set time that the women had always left, as both husbands had very conveniently been asleep, well used to the time frame and schedule that their wives followed. And, of course, one husband no longer lived in the same household.

Kate walked up and down the parking lot and then, on instinct, headed back down the pathway to where the first murders had occurred. She walked up into the hills and all the way around, watching the runners come and go, also people walking with their dogs, others just out for a stroll with cameras around their necks. Making a mental note to contact the bird-watching societies in the local area, she stopped one older gentleman and asked him how often he came with his binoculars and his camera.

He laughed. "Every chance I get, my dear, every chance I get. The more I head down this retirement path, the less I find that I want to be home, and the more I want to be out here, enjoying nature," he said, with a big smile, his white mustache twinkling in delight at the opportunity to talk about his favorite topic.

"Do you ever meet other people with the same interests here?"

"Oh yes," he agreed, "very much so. Early mornings are best—or late in the afternoon, when it's just about to hit sunset," he murmured. "But it can get busy here too. You can see runners up and down here always."

She nodded. "Have you ever been concerned, you know, considering the fact that several people were murdered on this trail? Have you ever been afraid or seen anybody who worried you?"

He immediately shook his head. "No, not at all, and I'm hardly part of the group that would cause trouble. I'm older. I'm obviously not as strong as these other people. I'm not here to compete or to wreck anybody's exercise time. I'm just here to take pictures of birds if I can."

"Do the runners ever disturb the birds that you're looking at?"

He nodded. "All the time. But I'm okay with that."

"But what about other bird-watchers?"

He frowned, thinking about it. "You know what? I hadn't realized that runners were quite so cutthroat, but bird-watchers can be really bad too."

Her interest perked up. "Meaning?"

"Meaning," he explained, "that some people will stay out all night for an opportunity to see the bird that they're looking for at a specific time of day. And, if anybody disturbs them at the precise hour that they've been waiting for, you can get quite a ruckus. I'm not typically a traditional bird-watcher in the sense that I won't sit camped out all night long, waiting for a bird to get out of its nest in the morning. I'm here for the unstaged photographs." He held up his camera.

She admired the camera and the long lens on it. "And there's a certain amount of money that goes into this to make it worthwhile, isn't there?"

"It's not even so much about the money," he noted, "but it is one area that the more you spend on equipment, the better the value is. And I have the money, so I like to spend it on my toys, such as quality camera equipment. I was a teacher for many, many years, and I always held on to the belief that one day I'd reap the benefits of all those evenings, working late, marking homework, and all those days, dealing with cranky kids in the classroom," he said, with a belly laugh. "And I have to tell you that I'm loving life right now."

"I'm happy to hear that," she replied, with a bright smile. "I'm investigating the killings and trying to figure out motive, and I've been wondering if bird-watchers or photographers would have been pissed off by these runners."

He looked at her in surprise. "That is possible," he agreed, "because, you know, well, *people*. But I can't imagine that it would be something that would go on all the time." He turned to look around. "I've been walking these trails for years, and this is the first time I've ever heard of any nastiness like this."

She nodded. "I did check for crimes around this area and found a couple rapes, but they were many years ago."

He nodded. "Yes, and they were university students too, as I recall." He frowned. "I think they were specifically targeted by a boyfriend or something of that nature, if memory serves."

She nodded. "Yes, that's what I understand as well. There doesn't seem to be much of a clear motivation for these recent murders, at least that I've been able to see so far."

"Well, I won't try and tell you how to do your job, young lady. However, I'm sure, by the time you figure it out, the motive will be clear."

"Oh, I agree with you there," she murmured. "Now if only I had some insight into why and how."

"And here I thought you'd be right after the husbands or the partners," he noted, with a jovial smile. "Aren't they always the first ones you look at?"

"Yes, and they've been looked at already," she confirmed, "for the first two women killed, that is. And the second set of murders was an apparently happy couple." Not that she would get into it with this guy though. "I just saw you with the camera there and wondered what it was like in this area, with so many competing interests occupying the same space."

He nodded. "Honestly, most of us bird-watchers are pretty easygoing," he noted. "There is a certain amount of patience a person must have to be successful at it to begin with. But still, you will find people who get very irritated. You know, somebody who's planned ahead, maybe even taken a day off work, and this is their one chance to find this specific bird. So they are all set up to see or to catch that one perfect shot, then somebody comes thundering along or chattering away at just the wrong time and potentially blows the opportunity they worked so hard to set up. You know what? I can almost see that happening."

"I get it." And Kate listened as he carried on. It was possible; it certainly was. But, in that case, the killings would be completely random, and those were even harder to pin down. Of course, if they were random, then it wouldn't matter to the victims.

She thanked him for his time, then frowned, as she walked around the area a little bit longer. Frustration and not wanting to go back and admit defeat at the office pushed her to continue. With that, she slowly walked the path once more, looking around the area, wishing there was some way to set herself up as bait, even knowing the rest of the department would be completely against it.

But she had no way to know when this guy would actually jump up and do something. It was sad, but, as she headed back to her car, dragging her ass, she knew—as soon as she got to the office—she'd have to turn her attention to the other cases. But she also knew that she could do very little else with this joggers' case. She would further check social media as soon as she got in to see if there was any belated mention of any of the victims or any of the suspects. But, other than that, she was pretty well out of trails to follow.

Once back in the office, the others looked up at her.

She shrugged. "Nothing new."

She sat down and spent the next hour on social media, and then finally she got a cup of coffee and sat down beside Rodney. "So, what else have we got?"

He looked over at her and winced. "Sorry."

"Has to be something more," she moaned. "I've been racking my brain on what else I can do, but I'm out of ideas."

"Well, we've got two people dead from last night, where a vehicle ran into a crowd and ran them down."

"Targeted?"

"I don't think so. He just had broken up with his wife. Apparently she had asked for a divorce."

"Sounds pretty open-and-shut."

"It does, and you know what? In some ways that's a good thing. We just have to cross all the *T*s."

"Good, give me a bunch of the names or whatever you have, and I'll do some research on them." She sat back down at her desk and ran through as much as she could. It really did appear to be open-and-shut.

In a mad rage the guy had flown out of the restaurant, got into his vehicle, and used it as a weapon against a group of young people standing around outside, laughing and joking, just enjoying being together. Two of them died, and four of them were injured. The driver took off, leaving his vehicle, and ran, but that made absolutely no difference because he left the vehicle behind. So the local authorities had the registration, license plate, insurance, and all. The cops had already picked him up at home, and he was even now waiting in an interview room. She thought about going in with Rodney, or at least watching from the observation room, but decided against it.

When her phone rang, and it was Simon, she looked down and smiled.

He asked, "Do I make plans for tomorrow?"

"I hadn't realized it was almost four," she noted, "but absolutely. Yes."

He asked, "You'll be off?"

"Yes," she confirmed. "Unfortunately that means I have absolutely nothing to go on with my runners' case."

"Sorry," he said. "Sometimes life is like that."

"Isn't that the truth," she murmured. "I'll go to the dojo and work out tonight, catch an early night. I was actually thinking about maybe going for a run in the morning."

"I can go with you," he offered.

"*Nah*, I don't even know if I'm really all that dedicated to the idea."

"Well, why don't you come here after work," he suggested, "and we'll see if I can get you dedicated to something else."

She burst out laughing at that. "You do know that that's a really cheesy line?" she asked. "Yet it sounds fun."

"Hey, I aim to please. I'll see you here in a couple hours."

"And you'll have dinner?" she asked, with interest.

"With you, always," he declared. "It's one way to your heart."

"Wow, that sounds terrible," she replied.

"Nope, I just know that it's a necessity, and one that you tend to slide on." Without saying anything else, he hung up.

As she turned, Rodney stared at her. "You two are really getting into this, aren't you?"

She shrugged. "It's nice for a while."

"For a while?" he repeated. "Does this guy Simon know it's only *for a while*?"

She glared at him. "Hey, I'm not rushing into anything. You know as well as I do that it only leads to chaos and dashed hopes."

He nodded. "Well, that's true enough, and I'm happy to

see that you won't go crazy with it, but you know? He, on the other hand, seems pretty serious," he stated cautiously.

"He is. Tomorrow we'll head to the beach."

"Good, with any luck, you'll get the weekend off."

"I'm supposed to get the weekend off regardless," she stated, looking at him.

He laughed. "You know that only works *until* we get called."

"But I am not on call this weekend," she stated, with a big grin.

"Oh, shit, how did you manage that?" he muttered.

"Well, unless it's a big case, and then we're all called."

"Exactly," he noted, "but here's hoping you get the weekend off."

She nodded, then stood, so she could stack and box up the jogger-related files on her desk, then looked around the bullpen. "It feels odd, dissatisfying in a way, because I couldn't do anything with the joggers' case."

"Let it go for a while," Rodney said. "As soon as more information comes in, we'll jump back on it."

"Got it." And, with that, she headed out.

Rather than heading straight home, she walked outside for a bit, just to clear her head and to enjoy the fresh air. She walked over to her workout gym, and, once inside, she quickly changed and walked in for her training. An hour and a half later, she was on the floor, staring up at the ceiling. "Why do I keep paying for this?"

He laughed. "You keep paying for it because it's good for you."

"You keep saying that," she murmured, as she slowly got to her feet.

"You're getting better. I'm glad to see you coming back

in for more regular workouts."

"I need it," she admitted. "It does tend to be something that slides, and I don't mean for it to, but circumstances in life can be hell on schedules."

"Especially in your job," he noted.

She nodded. "Isn't that the truth." Standing up now, she walked over, grabbed her towel, and wiped her face down. "And sometimes the stress is what really gets me worked up," she murmured.

"For you, I imagine that's a constant thing."

"It can be, though it's not something that I'm particularly happy about. But how do you stop stress when it eats away at you or your subconscious?"

"And again, there's not always anything you can do about it," he admitted. "You can only protect yourself so much."

"I know, and then, at some point in time, it just feels like you're a failure." He winced at that, and she shrugged. "It's a case that I just can't get anywhere on."

"I'm sorry," he murmured.

"Me too." She tossed him a smile and headed out. She was sorry, but it was also about what Rodney had said—as soon as new information came in, she could jump right back on it. In the meantime, there were other cases. As she got back to her vehicle, she hopped in and drove slowly and carefully down to Simon's place. She wondered if a vehicle was following her, as she headed into his last block. She frowned and carefully drove on for a few more blocks to see if she could shake him. When she did manage to, it just kept her guessing. She parked outside and got out slowly, keeping an eye on what was going on around her and then walked carefully up to Simon's. She stopped just inside the doors and looked back out.

At the lobby desk, Harry asked, "Problems?"

"I hope not," she murmured, "but I did wonder if I was being followed."

He immediately walked to her side. "Do you know what vehicle?"

She replied, "An older two-door hatchback, dark blue. Other than that, I couldn't catch it."

"Well, I can keep an eye out in case anything like that drives by."

Just then, a vehicle did drive by, almost identical. She raced out the door, and it took off. She swore as she called it in, asking for a BOLO on the car. She couldn't give a license plate or any description of the driver.

As she walked back inside, she was pissed. "Dammit, that could have been the one lead I needed."

"But do you know what case it's even related to?" Harry asked her. "I imagine your life is one dangerous job all the time."

"Well, it is," she agreed, "and that adds to the frustration too."

"Of course," he murmured.

No way she could get back to her vehicle and chase him by now. He'd be long gone. She wished to hell she knew what the license plate was on that. "Do you have any cameras here?" She turned in austerity.

He nodded. "We sure do." He walked back to his circular workstation and started tapping on the keyboard and the big monitors sprang to life. She waited on the one side, and he finally motioned at her. "Come take a look."

And looking at the view from in front of the building, she saw the vehicle as it drove past. He brought it up as close as he could, but at no point in time did it capture the license plate. And she realized that was because something covered part of it. "Damn it."

"It's definitely an old Toyota," Harry confirmed, "but I'm not sure that helps much."

"Not a whole lot." She frowned and said, "Be alert though, *huh*?"

"Always," he replied, "though you do keep life more interesting."

She snorted at that. "Trust me. Not really what I'm trying to do."

He laughed. "That's okay. It can get a little boring here at times."

"Well, if that vehicle comes around again," she stated, "I want to know. And, if you see it at any point in time, call the cops, would you please?"

He nodded. "You going up now?"

She nodded. "I am. I need to talk to Simon."

"I know he's got some dinner planned for you up there," he noted, with a grin.

She laughed. "I don't think he likes anything better than feeding me," she murmured.

"Oh, I bet he does."

She snorted with laughter and headed over to the elevator and on up. When the door opened, she was surprised to see Simon standing there, waiting for her.

He opened his arms, and she walked right into them. When she was calm enough to step back and look up at him, he leaned over and kissed her gently on the head.

"Did Harry call you?"

"He did."

"And did he tell you about the vehicle?"

He nodded. "He sounded pretty excited. Anything that breaks up his day is always good."

She chuckled at that. "Lord love anybody who is bored in this world because there's a shit ton of stuff to be done around here."

"Always"—Simon laughed—"and that's okay too."

"Says you," she murmured. Then she sniffed the air. "Oh my, what is that?"

"Curry," he replied.

She looked at him in surprise. "And here I figured we'd be barbecuing again."

"I figured I would make some curry."

"You're making it?" she asked in surprise. He looked at her with an overly injured expression on his face, and she burst out laughing. "Hey, I'm all for it. I just hadn't expected a home-cooked curry."

"Well, I do like to cook," he noted, "and some of these recipes have been in the family for a long time."

"Sign me up," she said immediately.

"That's not exactly a compliment," he murmured, "because you are always starving and would be happy with nearly anything you can get."

She grinned, then gave him a fat smile and nodded. "Absolutely. Food is what makes the world go around."

"Well, I won't argue with you there," he agreed. "At least in this instance you'll get a whole lot more than you would if you were to buy it."

"*Nah*," she disagreed, "because, if you're always hungry after buying takeout, you're just not ordering enough."

He burst out laughing at that. "Such logic," he murmured, shaking his head.

She sighed. "Everybody seems to think I look at the

world very oddly."

"Well, you do," he stated.

"I don't think so. I think the rest of you guys just don't really get the world."

"And you do?"

She stared at him in surprise. "Sure, I do," she declared. "I live and work and function in it very easily."

"To a certain extent, yes," he agreed cautiously, "but there's an awful lot more to life than just functioning."

She shrugged. "Sure there is. There's eating."

At that, he burst out laughing and led her to the kitchen. "While we're getting this prepped and ready, tell me about the car."

She told him about the sensation of being followed. "That's it."

"So, just a concern got your attention. Then, all of a sudden, you saw him."

"Something like that," she murmured.

"Any idea who it was?"

She shook her head. "Neither of the husbands have that vehicle, and I don't know anybody else with one."

"So, you'll go back to the office and set up a database search?"

She frowned and shook her head. "I think what I'll do—while you're still cooking—is bring in my laptop up here. I'll see if I can come up with however many vehicles. Harry confirmed it was a Toyota Camry."

"Interesting," Simon noted.

"And it was an older version, but I don't know how old."

"So, there could be quite a few of them."

She nodded. "Didn't see the sides of the car. So, just

because it was blue doesn't mean that it started out blue."

"No, not at all," he agreed. "And nothing else to distinguish it?"

"Not that I saw. Just looked like a small hatchback car."

"Of which there are literally thousands on the road."

She nodded. "I couldn't see the driver, and the license plate was partially covered, so it was hard to identify as well."

"On purpose then."

"I assume." She shrugged. "If I wanted to follow somebody, I wouldn't want to be too easily identified."

"Any idea what he was up to?"

"No," she said, as she came up short as she thought about it. "No idea."

"You've been rattling cages," he reminded her.

"I have. That's just, you know, part of what I do," she noted, as if that was an explanation. When he sighed, she added, "It's part of being a cop, you know?"

"How often do you get followed?"

She looked at him and frowned. "Not all that often, but enough that it's not really a big surprise anymore. It's not a problem."

His eyebrows shot up. "Unless they're trying to catch you at a time where they can run you over."

"That's a whole different story," she stated, "and I did cross the road very carefully, looking both ways a couple times, to ensure that nobody was close enough to attempt an attack. But I never really know if someone will come after me, can't be constantly on guard, and not a whole lot I can do about it."

He stopped whatever he was doing and slowly turned to look at her, incredulous.

She replied impatiently, "You know that's true. You can

be as prepared as you want, but, if somebody is determined to come after you, what are you supposed to do about it? You can be vigilant and try hard to stay out of trouble, but trouble will find you if someone is after you."

He slammed down the spoon but kept working, not saying anything.

She winced. "I guess you didn't want to hear any of that, *huh*?"

He turned, stared at her. "Just tell me you'll be careful," he asked, his voice sounding hoarse.

"I'll be careful," she replied instantly.

He frowned.

"What? Too fast now?" she asked.

"I don't know. It's just a disconcerting thought to think that you're a target."

"Anybody in law enforcement is always a target," she stated. "At any point in time we can be taken down by somebody who has got something against us, or not just us personally but against the whole division, against law enforcement as a whole. People often target those of us in the industry, even though they don't have a beef against us."

"It sucks," he said, "It's just upsetting to know you're always potentially under attack."

"Well, hopefully I'm not *always* under attack. Hopefully I'll never actually be under attack. I consider the fact that this vehicle is driving around, watching to see whether it was me or not, is a very interesting turn of events," she revealed. "I'm pretty glad he did that, actually."

He stared at her.

"Somebody is getting nervous," she explained, "and that makes me happy."

"I can see that," he noted. "But you have so many cases

going all the time, you don't know if this is connected to a new case, an old case, or a current case. Who the hell knows where this guy is coming from?"

"Nobody knows," she admitted, "but, as you said, I have rattled a lot of cages lately, and I've done it on purpose, hoping that I could shake something loose. Even today I was back up there at the site, wondering about bird-watchers and photographers. It was pretty interesting to speak to one older guy, who told me that some of the bird-watching community can be incredibly competitive. Who knows where any of this will go?

"The fact of the matter is, I don't have enough to go on in any direction right now. I like the look of a couple suspects, but I have nothing in the way of proof. The joggers' case will sit until something else happens, until I get another lead, with something else to go on," she shared. "It's frustrating, and it's making me angry. I didn't even want to go back to the office because of it. And that's stupid because that's where I belong, but knowing that somebody is out there, waiting for me to catch them, and me not having the knowledge and the proof to actually go get them, is what drives me forward all the time."

"Sure," Simon said, "but it also drives you crazy."

She laughed. "It does," she murmured. "It does, indeed. So, you just hope that you can do the best you can do and that, at one point in time, this will all come out in the wash and be okay again."

"But, in the meantime," he added, "there's not a whole lot you can do."

"Exactly." She smiled and asked him, "So what do you want me to do to help you with dinner?"

He stared at her for a long moment, muttered under his

breath, then turned back to his curry. "How about you set the table? That should keep you out of trouble for at least five minutes."

And for five minutes it did. After dinner they went for a walk and then sat outside on his balcony, with a bottle of wine.

She took a sip, relaxed into her lounger, and said, "I brought my work and running clothes for tomorrow, I think I'll go for a run first. The workout tonight was good, but I'm feeling rusty."

"Sounds good. I'll go with you." As he got up to pour more wine, his knee joint gave way, and he swore as he caught himself.

She looked at his knee and frowned. "How long has that been a problem?"

"For years," he replied. "It's fine, and then it's not so fine. It's one of the reasons I used to run and why I haven't done a whole lot of it lately."

"Makes sense. I don't want you running with me tomorrow. You know that, right?"

"It'll be fine," he said dismissively.

"Nope," she disagreed. "I don't want anything to mess up our plans for tomorrow."

He laughed at that. "So, now this will mess up our day?" he asked in astonishment.

She shrugged. "Feels like it."

He smirked. "We'll talk about it tomorrow."

"Good enough," she agreed, then kissed him gently. "Just looking after you too."

"I'm fine," he repeated.

"No," she countered. "If I've got to look after me, then you've got to look after you."

He laughed, grabbed her in his arms, and said, "Deal."

CHAPTER 15

Saturday Morning

KATE WOKE EARLY in the morning and stretched—her muscles, her body, all still humming from the lovemaking of the night before. Something was absolutely wonderful about rolling over to see him, tucked up against her. Something comforting, something about being at home. She knew that other people would think she was crazy, but that's what it felt like, like her heart had finally found a resting place. And wasn't that a whole lot of romantic garbage?

Sighing, she slipped out from underneath his arms, but he grabbed her tight and pulled her back again.

She chuckled. "Let me go."

He murmured. "As long as you're not going running."

"Nope, have to go to the bathroom."

His hold immediately eased back, and she slipped out of bed and headed to the bathroom. After using the facilities, she looked over at the bed, checking that Simon was asleep, then quietly grabbed her clothes from her bag and quickly changed into her running gear. If he knew, he'd be pissed, but she was willing to let him be pissed about some things. She'd seen that knee slip out from under him last night.

He needed to do some rehab work to get it back into shape, and the last thing she wanted to do was ruin their plans for later today. She meant what she had said about that. Days off were a treat, and days off spending most of the day at the beach were an even bigger treat, and they didn't come around very often.

She didn't want anything to mess it up.

Right now she would warm up a bit. She did a few stretches in the living room, careful not to disturb him, then she walked out to her vehicle. She stopped as she looked around and thought, *I could just run here.* "Really no reason to go anywhere else," she murmured. *Except for the guy driving the Toyota Camry,* she added as an afterthought.

Plus, running on pavement wasn't her thing, and running in a cement city really wasn't her favorite thing either, and she didn't know of any running trails here. There should be some, but she didn't know about them. She frowned as she considered that, then got into her vehicle and—almost without thinking—headed toward the running path out by the beach. She knew that, as long as Simon didn't know about it, she'd be fine.

And as long as that asshole who had followed her last night didn't know about it, better still. She thought about that, wondering if she was being foolish, but, so far, the murders had happened to couples, definitely not to singles, and there was no real reason for her to be targeted.

She checked her watch and noted that it was a bit later than when the murders had happened, so that helped ease her worry at the same time. Not enough maybe. At least that's what Simon would say. Not nearly enough to make him happy. Still, by the time she finally got out to the pathway, she almost didn't even want to go for a run anymore.

"No wonder people find places to live close by where they want to run because this driving to a different location sucks." On a whim, she drove around through the blocks where the two women had lived, studying the vehicles and looking to see if anything here was like the vehicle that had followed her to Simon's last night.

But she saw absolutely no sign of it. She frowned at that. She'd already checked the DMV and found no record of either of the husbands owning that vehicle. That didn't mean that they didn't have access to one through siblings, friends, or even stealing one, but they didn't own one personally. That was a little more reassuring, and they returned to their positions a step farther down the suspect list.

As she drove up to the running paths, she smiled to see other vehicles parked here. She got out and stretched for a few minutes and watched another couple come by, wave at her, and then head off. She waited a moment and then headed off behind them. At least if she was close to other people, she wouldn't be a target either. Nobody was idiotic enough to try and take down three of them. It still bothered her, as she moved through the heavily vegetated pathway, that somebody would actually take out two at a time. That was just greedy. The word *greedy* wasn't exactly what she meant, but it's what her mind offered in the moment.

She thought about it, pondering it back and forth. Was somebody really just being greedy? Was this more about a challenge? Was this more about what somebody *could* do versus what they *should* do? That didn't even make sense to her. She was still mulling it over when she finally got loosened up enough that she felt her muscles starting to hum along nicely. The first mile in a run was always hard for her. She didn't run enough for it to actually be something her body started to crave, but, once she got enough miles under her belt, then she felt like everything was starting to move the way it should. At least she thought so.

Something about the freedom of running that she absolutely loved. It had never occurred to her to join a club though. She was more of a loner than a team player, even though she was finally finding ways to settle in with her coworkers. Yet still not necessarily her preferred way to work. If she had her way, they'd all be off working their own cases, and she'd have hers.

As she thought about it, that was the way she had it set up now. Whether it was good or bad, she didn't know, because she wasn't exactly getting anywhere on this jogger case, and that point was being driven home further every day, as she struggled to find a way to bring this case to a final resolution. It just drove her nuts that she didn't have the evidence she needed right now. However, it could surface someday—like in ten years, when somebody opened their mouth and actually spoke up.

A lot of old cases were eventually closed that way, but she didn't want to wait that long. And it wasn't about her ego; it really wasn't. This wasn't about having the greatest number of cases closed or being the top detective. This wasn't about being the best or proving herself to the rest of the team. This was all about getting these assholes behind bars. And, even then, she used the plural term.

She frowned at that, wondering why, and let her mind roam freely as she ran, her body starting to get excited about the next curve, the next hill. Something was addictive to that ebb and flow of nature, as the hills twisted and turned. It was very different running here than what she was used to. Often she was on a track at a gym or on the sidewalk, where everything was pretty evened out. Here, it wasn't even at all, and she was really glad when she narrowly avoided stepping into an unexpected pothole in the path, thankful she had come without Simon because he could have easily gotten hurt on the rougher terrain.

They had done fine the other day, but she hadn't known about his knee. She wondered how often it went out and whether it was something they could work on with conditioning—because she would really like to run like this more often. With him. She'd come alone by choice today, but, as she thought about the couples who were victims in these joggers' cases, couples who had run together and couples who had run apart, she wanted to be a couple who ran together. She'd have to talk to him about it when she got back.

Maybe today, while they were at the beach, they could talk about what they could do to build up the strength of that knee. She wasn't any pro on this stuff, and, as a matter of fact, he seemed to be much more into it than she was. But still, there was always that sense of wanting to know more about what he was doing, as long as he didn't feel like she was pushing him. She had a feeling that too much pushing from either one of them would be the end of their relationship.

She frowned, her mind automatically going from bits and pieces, trying to figure out just what in this relationship she was working so hard to save, when she realized it was everything. She was doing her damnedest to try and keep him in her life and to not step out of bounds in any way that would upset him. There was just so much to love about it all. So much to love about him.

And that was the part that got to her because she realized that she was hooked on him. She shook her head. "Really not a good idea," she murmured. And, of course, there was no smart, rational answer for any of that. Because you did what you did, and it didn't matter how any of it worked because, in reality, you were caught up in the emotions, and, while you were hooked, that's the only thing that counted.

She'd been in love before a few times—or at least had thought so. It didn't matter, and they apparently didn't mean a whole lot, when they fizzled out so fast that she wasn't even sure how she got there. It's not that she had fallen in love and then had fallen out. After the first flush of love, their relationships, their jobs, and their lifestyles had finally all collided. She worked to try and make everything fit but finally realized that she didn't care to work at it anymore.

The point when you feel like your relationship is just too much of a pain in the ass is also when you'd rather just get the good sex because the rest of it was too much work. And then, when the good sex was no longer great but just average and soon became mediocre, you're asking yourself why you were even still there. At least she did.

It may have made her sound shallow, and she didn't mean it that way, but it became a hindrance in her lifestyle, then something that was an irritant, and finally, when she realized she was ignoring her boyfriend's incoming texts, she knew it was already over. And yet, with Simon, it wasn't like that. He was different. He was exciting, and it hadn't taken very long for her to get hooked on him. Though a part of her was definitely worried about that.

Like where would they be three months from now? Would they be out here running together, or would she be sneaking off because he was pissed off but she wanted to run anyway? She hoped not; she hoped that something was there to sustain them further.

The fact that they each did their own work thing was good, right? She didn't even really know or understand what he did in his job, just as he was new to her detective world. This whole psychic thing should have been enough to keep her away from him for a long time. But now here she was and didn't quite know what to do with it. So far, she had just ignored it all, except to utilize whatever information she could gain from his visions. Again, that didn't make her sound very good.

She wasn't trying to be difficult; she wasn't trying to be anything other than herself. But being herself often seemed like it wasn't quite good enough. She winced at that because it brought up remembrances of her mother all over again. Her mother had knocked her down from the get-go, even as a small child, blaming her for everything, but especially for the loss of her brother. And that was another thing that really bothered her.

She'd always kept herself so busy at work that she hadn't had a chance to hunt down her missing brother, and that really bothered her. There had to be something that she could do to find him. But, so far, she kept coming up blank. Like the case that she was currently working on kept turning up without evidence, and that added to her frustration. She never wanted to be a person who walked through the world being completely ineffectual. And yet that seemed to be exactly what this jogger case was doing to her. She shook her head at that.

"Run faster," she murmured, "run, run, run."

The mantra went over and over in her head, as she ran faster and faster and faster, absolutely loving the blood pounding through her system, the sense of freedom, and the strength that poured through her veins. It was an incredible feeling. As she plowed her way up yet another hill, she slowed at the top and kept jogging, but took stock of her surroundings. She was miles away from the car park at this point. Still another thirty minutes of running probably. She smiled, wondering if Simon was awake yet, and how he would feel when he found out that he was alone.

⌘

ALL SIMON HEARD was the woman saying, "I'm going for a run." And the man reaching out to say, "Don't."

He smiled, knowing that the woman would get back into bed with her lover. Only this time she got up and headed for the door. Simon wanted to call out to her, saying, "Don't. Stay, stay with him."

But she was silent as she dressed quickly and moved to the front door. Something was familiar about her, something about her body frame. Now everything about her seemed familiar, and, as she opened the door, the lights from the hallway flashed on her face, and he realized it was Kate. He shot awake almost instantly.

He sat up, his heart slamming against his chest. "What the fuck?"

He tried to take stock of what had just happened, but it was a little too crazy for him to even sort out. Was it Kate that he had seen in his dreams or had he dreamed it all because he knew she had wanted to go for a run this morning, and now she was overpowering his dreams? At that, he turned and looked at the bed beside him, then bolted to his feet and checked out the rest of his apartment. No sign of her. He raced to her gear, noting that most of it was still here, as he dug through her belongings, not giving a damn for her privacy—until he realized her running gear was gone.

He snatched up his phone and called her. When she didn't answer, he sent a text immediately. **Where are you?**

She sent an answer back. **Running.**

At the sight of her answer, his heart slammed back into his chest, giving his body a chance to breathe again.

He sagged onto the bed. "Holy shit." He scrubbed at his face. When a text came back, he looked at it sourly.

Why?

Because I didn't know you would go without me. I wanted to go with you, and you know it.

And I didn't want you hurt.

That was her response. He stared at it in disgust. "What am I now?" he murmured. "An invalid who can't go for a run with you? Just because my knee occasionally pops out of place is not a big deal. I've been running with it for years."

But he wouldn't type all that on his phone and get the message across correctly. He was just pissed enough that he didn't even want to think about it. The dream—vision?—wouldn't leave him. It was all enough to make him sit here and contemplate his options. Feeling that sense of urgency rising, he bolted to his feet, that sense of adrenaline driving through his psyche. He quickly got up and dressed in his running gear, then raced to his vehicle.

He drove toward the running path, when he realized that he didn't know where the hell she was running. Why was he even in a panic anyway? She could have just been doing laps around False Creek. He snatched his phone and called her again, and she didn't answer, yet again. Driving at an excessive speed and texting at the same time, he raced toward the damn place because, in his heart of hearts, he knew she was there. Stanley Park. But there was no reason for her to be there, and, as a matter of fact, there were one million reasons why she shouldn't be there, particularly alone.

He sent her a text. **Where are you?**

Her answer didn't help clarify anything. **Ten minutes from the parking lot.**

Are you there, where the murders were?

When his phone rang, she said, "Yes, I'm just here for a run." She was out of breath, and almost a powerful joy filled her voice.

"But you're fine?"

"Yes, of course I'm fine. … Why?"

He snorted.

"Look. It's okay," she said.

"It's not fucking okay," he roared into the phone. "You're out there, just asking for trouble."

"And it's what I do," she replied, her voice getting stiff.

"It might be what you do," he bit off, "but it's not what you do without backup." At that, he could almost sense the wheels in the back of her mind turning.

"No," she said, "you're right. Normally I wouldn't be doing this alone."

"Right," he snapped. "I should fucking be there with you."

"I'm sorry. … I was thinking of you."

"And making me feel like I'm less than?"

She didn't ask for clarity about *Less than what?* which was a damn good thing because that would have pissed him off even more. He couldn't handle anyone playing games. One thing he loved about her was the fact that she didn't play games, which was why this behavior was driving him nuts.

"I don't get it. You fucking know better."

"I just wanted to come for a run," she explained.

Honestly enough truth was in her words that it made him pause.

"Seriously? You're not there to try and trap this asshole?" he asked.

"No," she replied, "honestly, I wanted to come for a run, and I now just realized how much location matters in real estate because this is a hell of a running path. I can see why people are paying these prices in the real estate market for the opportunity to be here."

"It was stupid thing to run by yourself," he snapped.

And once again her voice stiffened. "It's not stupid," she snapped back. "I wanted to go for a run."

"Well, so the hell did I," he snapped. "It feels like you snuck out on purpose. Like you were trying to get up there, deliberately going to that location, knowing full well that you shouldn't be there alone. You had to know I would be pissed about it, but you did it anyway because my anger apparently didn't matter to you."

"I honestly didn't think about coming here," she explained. "I was surprised to find myself driving in this direction because I wasn't initially planning on it. I looked around in your area, but I didn't really know where to run or how long the paths were, and I didn't want to go on just another cement-city run. My shins really don't like that."

"And I get all that," he said, softening his voice. "It just would have been nice if you hadn't cut me out."

"And I didn't think I was cutting you out," she replied, trying for a balanced tone of voice.

He appreciated that because he was *very* off balance himself. "The fact that you're even talking to me about it is good because I woke up with another one of those horrible nightmares."

"Oh, that explains it."

"Explains what?" he asked, as his temper snapped and rattled again.

"Why you're so pissed off. Obviously you're getting more of these vibes about the murders, and that just makes you think I'm in danger."

"You *are* in fucking danger, Kate. Have you forgotten that somebody followed you home last night?"

"Well, that won't do them much good, will it?" she asked. "Considering they followed me to your house, not mine."

"And what if they followed you to the running path?"

"Well, I didn't see anybody, and they would have had to sit there all night, and that's quite a stakeout."

"But not impossible, is it?"

"No," she replied slowly, "it's not impossible, but they'd have to be very dedicated."

"Dedicated is one thing," he noted. "You have killers out here who would do anything to avoid spending the rest of their lives in jail."

"Maybe, but that doesn't mean that's the way it'll work out for them."

"You're the one trying to stop them, so you are the prime target here," he stated.

"No," she disagreed, "that's not true. That would diminish the value of the whole team."

"Who is the one driving this case?"

"All of us," she snapped, "and you won't make me think that people are directing this at me and only me."

"And yet they are. Do you think anybody else on your team got followed last night?"

Silence came from the other end.

He checked his watch and realized that he shouldn't be more than a few minutes away from the parking lot he was heading to. He could have been pulled over anytime in the last twenty minutes for speeding, but he didn't give a damn. He would have told them a cop was in danger. The fact that she didn't seem to think she was in danger was the part that he and she would really have to talk about.

"I don't know," she finally replied, "but that would just be people getting the wrong end of the stick."

It took him a moment to realize what she was talking about. He groaned. "It doesn't really matter, does it? You can't just keep taking these chances."

"I'm not taking chances," she argued. "Look. I'm almost done with my run. I should be back there soonish."

He pulled into the parking lot and asked, "Where are you?"

"About a mile and a half to go, I think," she said, in-between her breaths.

"From the parking lot that you normally park in?"

"Why?"

"Because I just pulled in," he stated. As she started to speak, he heard a "Son of a—" and then her half scream and some thuds. "Jesus Christ!" He bolted from his car, clicking the fob, locking up, as he ran. "What's the matter? Kate, what's the matter? Where are you?" He took off running, not even knowing if she was up or down or around. Instinct took him on the same path, right where the murders had been. "Run, dammit. Run."

"I'm trying," she finally said, "and somebody's after me."

"Run to the parking lot," he replied. "I'm coming toward you. I'm on the high road."

"I'm running. I'm running."

"But remember," he murmured, "you could be running into a trap."

"Shit, it wasn't supposed to be like this. I'm alone."

"Yeah, well, somebody doesn't give a shit. They want you out of the picture, and they want you out now. Can you see who it is?"

"Can't check now," she noted breathlessly. "He's running behind me."

"Run, run, run, dammit!"

And then there was silence at the other end.

CHAPTER 16

KATE COULDN'T BELIEVE what had just happened. Somebody had tried to smack her on the side of the head with some stick. She was running as fast as she could, thankful that there was just enough light to actually see the path better and better. She realized that the path she was on would take her right up to where the double murders had happened. Knowing that she was likely being driven into exactly the same location, she tried to think quickly, but, in her mind, she was looking for an alternative route, though pretty heavy brush was in this area. She didn't dare get caught in a hand-to-hand combat situation because she didn't know whether he had a weapon or not. But, if that's all she had, she would take it.

Her eyes darted from side to side, as she raced flat-out, trying to get closest to the parking lot and Simon. She had no doubt he was racing toward her just as fast. A corner was up ahead, and she realized that just down below was where the second couple were taken out. As she raced straight up into that corner, she darted off to the side, diving full length into the brush and rolling up on the other side, where she immediately hid behind a tree.

She studied the area around her, hearing footsteps and the heavy breathing of her pursuer. He went around the corner, and he stopped, and she heard him swearing on the path behind her.

"Fuck, fuck, fuck!"

She twisted, trying to look, but couldn't see who it was. She couldn't see anything, except the man's leg. She waited and waited, trying to sneak around the corner. She would come up against Simon here any minute. And then she heard a man's voice.

"No fucking way you're getting away from me this time," he yelled. "Get out here."

She raised her eyebrows at that, wondering how often ordering your victim to come out and get shot would work. She didn't know if he had a gun or not, so she snuck down on her hands and knees and crept under the brush. She knew that he was close, but could he actually see where she was? Did he know this area well enough?

"I know where you are," he yelled.

And, dammit, he did appear to be approaching her.

"I've got a fucking handgun," he called out, "and I'm not afraid to use it."

She swore under her breath, silently looking at the trees, wondering if she could at least climb and get up out of the way. But there were no easy branches to climb up on, and climbing wouldn't be a silent process. He'd shoot her in the back before she got anywhere.

"You just had to keep sniffing around, didn't you?" he yelled. "You couldn't just leave it. You know those bitches needed to die. Nobody should be allowed to have bitches like that around," he roared at the top of his lungs.

She heard other footsteps in the distance. She didn't know how far away they were. She hoped her attacker didn't either. Except that, if he did, it would help send him on his way, and that wouldn't make her happy either. This had to stop, and it had to stop now. She just didn't know what the hell she was supposed to do, considering she hadn't brought her weapon with her.

Switching her position, she peered through the underbrush until she could see the path itself. No sign of him. The path was empty.

"Shit," she whispered under her breath. She heard running footsteps, as another couple jogged on the path toward them and took off in the opposite direction, both of them laughing and talking. But they were just at the start of their run it seemed, so it wasn't too hard on them yet, and they could continue to speak at the same time. But where the hell was Simon? She snuck a little bit closer, looking underneath the brush. And just then she heard a voice behind her.

"There you are."

And she froze.

* * *

SIMON RAN IN an all-out sprint, trying to find where the hell she was. He thought he knew which path she was on; he swore he knew which path, but it looked like he was one below her, and just enough distance separated them that he couldn't tell what was going on. He heard a voice yelling somewhere. But he heard no shots, no second voice. So, at the moment, it looked like it was just the one attacker. He heard another couple run off on a different path. He quickly retraced his steps and realized that a hook off to the left went higher up the hill. He hadn't thought that's where the murders were, but, for all he knew, that's where Kate was. At least it would give him a better vantage point.

With a stitch forming in his side and his lungs gasping for air, Simon continued to pound up the hill, until he got to the top, where he could look around. And down below somehow, he wasn't even sure how, he saw a man standing there, flailing his arms up in the air, talking to the trees. Simon frowned as he studied that. And then he saw the path that he'd missed.

He carefully retraced his steps, coming out on the path just down below the tree-talking man. The jogging couple were already past Simon and past the other guy, the pair happily heading off down the path on their morning run. Simon checked the parking lot, and nobody else was coming or going that he saw. He made his way toward the man, running as if he were just out for a casual jog. He watched as the man darted into the trees and hid. Simon continued past, totally ignoring him.

As soon as he got around the corner, Simon slipped behind a tree himself. There he waited and then carefully backtracked through the brush, trying to give as wide a berth as possible and to not make a sound. Then he stopped, as he saw no sign of either of them.

He pulled out his phone. With it on Silent mode, quickly sent her a text. **I'm here. Where the hell are you?** And when no answer came, he pocketed his phone and crept forward ever-so-quietly.

Then he heard a man speak.

"There you are."

He froze because the voice sounded so damn close by. He turned and looked around but saw no one. Taking a chance, he stood up, but again nobody was visible. With the brush and bushes as high as they were, there was no shortage of places to hide here. With every step Simon made, something broke and snapped under his feet. A tree was right beside him, so he quickly grabbed a low branch and swung himself up, which made a little bit of noise, but it wasn't terrible. He hid in the branches as he studied the area, moving the tree fronds around gently, trying to see where Kate and the attacker were.

At least he assumed it was an attacker, but, for all he knew, it was just a crazy man out having a talk with his psychosis because he forgot to take his medication. It wouldn't be the first time, and it wouldn't be the last. The morning light was starting to get brighter and brighter, and he thought there would be a lot more runners at this hour, but it was Saturday, and maybe people were more inclined to sleep in on the weekends, instead of getting out here and hitting the path.

After he heard the man's voice, he heard a woman call out.

"You missed me."

And he swore it was Kate.

A weird laugh came from the brush. And then a man bounded onto the path. "Well, you're here somewhere," he yelled. "I can hear you. Come out, come out, wherever you are." He practically chortled. "You know I can't let you live after this."

Complete silence came afterward.

Simon didn't know what he could do, but, thinking instinctively, he closed his mind and opened up his senses, sending out a message. *Run. Run down the hill, away from this asshole. Run, damn it. Run.*

Almost as if she had actually heard the message, Simon heard sounds of somebody bolting down the hillside, running flat-out, and halfway sliding through the brush.

The man stood in the pathway and started yelling, "No, no, no! You can't go that way. You have to go up here." And he headed after her.

Simon wasted no time. Jumping off the limb, he headed down the same path with the man in front. If the guy got a hold of Kate, at least Simon wouldn't be far behind.

His knee took a beating as his feet hit that first landing and then skittered even faster down the hill. Kate and her attacker were leaving quite a pathway, and that was good because, if anybody could help right now, they needed to know where the hell this would all end up. He wanted to call for backup for her sake, but he didn't have a chance, and he didn't dare take time out to make a call. He would have had to stop and find a way to balance because they were literally sliding down the side of the hill.

Up ahead, he heard the man roaring, but his words were indistinguishable.

No way to speed up, but, hell, no way to slow down either. The only thing Simon could do was let his body weight throw him down the hillside. When he came to a sudden stop on top of a large rock down at the bottom, he was stunned for a moment, the wind knocked out of him. And then he felt a gun at his neck. He slowly rolled over to see a man standing above him, the gun now pointed at his temple. He looked up at him in surprise. "What the hell, man?"

"Why are you following me?"

"I thought you were hurt. I thought you were in trouble," Simon said, trying to come up with an excuse. He slowly lifted himself to his feet, limping ever so slightly as he stabilized himself, holding his stomach where it had plummeted hard against the rock.

The man just stared at him. "You weren't chasing me?"

"Shit no, I was just out here for a run, and I heard yelling and saw you go down over the hill."

The guy looked at him uncertainly. "Do I know you?"

Simon immediately shook his head. "No. I don't think I've ever met you before." Looking at the gun, he said, "Would you mind putting that thing away? I'm really not here to hurt you." Then he took a step back and winced. "Shit, there goes that knee."

"Man, the fucking knees are the worst," the man noted. "My knee has been buggered up for years."

"Are you running on bum knees then?" Simon asked, with feigned surprise.

"Well, I thought I could try it today," the man stated, taking a couple more hobnob steps, favoring his knee. It may have been sore, but it sure as hell wasn't as bad as he was making it out to be. "But, *nah*, I can't run anymore," he said.

"Sorry, I was thinking that mine was better too." Simon bent down, putting his hands on his knee, and gently massaged it. But he kept his eye on the gun and a wary eye on the man. Straightening up, Simon continued. "Look. I gather you're having a shitty day. I'm sorry. I didn't mean to upset you or anything." He motioned at the gun. "I think, right now, I'm about done with running." Simon hobbled a couple steps toward the parking lot, trying to look as unthreatening as possible. "Are you okay if I just, like, go to my car?"

The guy looked around, then at the gun, and finally nodded. "Yeah, beat it."

And, with that, Simon took several more hobbled steps. As he turned to check out the guy once more, he saw him studying the area—looking for Kate. Simon heard a slight rustle off to the side, and the gunman had a big grin on his face, as he jumped across. "I found you."

A startled noise came, and Simon knew it was Kate.

Suddenly she bounced up, and, with a free leg, she kicked the gun out of his hand. It went flying harmlessly off into the bush, actually closer to Simon than he'd expected. He dove into the bush after it, wanting to make sure that the asshole didn't get his hands on it again. As he rose to the surface, he saw the two of them facing off against each other.

"Charlie, really?" she said. "Why the hell did you have to kill those two women?"

"You know why," he snapped. "Both of them deserved it."

"You destroyed two families."

"No, they were destroying their families, just like they destroyed their husbands. You know the guys both used to run, right?"

She shook her head. "I knew Agnew did, but I didn't hear that much about the other one being a runner."

"They were both runners, and they were both my friends. All of us used to go out running in the mornings," he said. "But those bitches slowly picked them off, one at a time, and ruined their lives. They turned them from these big robust, healthy men into the fucking mice they are now," he declared, with a sneer. "Women like that shouldn't be allowed to live."

"It's not your call to make," she said. "And why this elaborate set up?" she asked.

"I put a line up, and, hell, they'd run right into the branch. I've actually seen that happen here on the pathway," he noted. "A couple people have completely beaned themselves on branches."

"And you thought it would be a good way for them to die?"

Simon wondered the same thing because he sure as hell wouldn't count that as a normal methodology for killing somebody. But then he just about missed the next part of this discussion, and he had to refocus. What he heard made his blood run cold.

"And you're next."

CHAPTER 17

Kate stared at Charlie, the president of the running club, who she had spoken to several times. "I don't understand," she murmured, trying to get him to talk a little more. At least he didn't have the gun on him now. But that didn't mean there weren't weapons around this place or that he didn't have something booby-trapped.

He shook his head. "Some of the guys in the club used to think it was funny. They actually did that to a couple of young women, who were getting all the attention from some of the guys in our club. They took those women out immediately. One branch hit one of them and broke her nose. She went home, bawling her eyes out."

"And the second woman?"

"She tried valiantly to continue running, but then she got hit by a branch too." Charlie shook his head. "I'm the one who caught on to the rope on the other end of it and saw what they had done. They just sneered at me and said that, when life was a competition, you had to do everything you could to win. Then they laughed and took off. I didn't tell the cops or anybody because, really? What the hell would I say? So what? They smacked a couple of women with some branches. Later, as I watched how Robin and Jenna treated everybody in the club—and how it was getting worse and worse—I knew I couldn't let it go on anymore. There was just no way. They had to be stopped."

"Okay," Kate noted calmly, balancing on the balls of her feet, ready to lunge at any moment. "What about the other couple?" she asked. "What the hell did they do that they had to die for? Your hatred was for the two women. What about that innocent couple you killed?"

"It was twofold in that case," he replied. "One was to cover up the first two deaths. Obviously I had to do that." He gave a one-arm shrug, pointing at her, as if to say she should have figured that out. "But the other thing is that the woman was starting to talk to her husband exactly the same way that these two bitches had talked to their husbands. She started to put him down, anything to make him feel like an idiot. She even put out a leg and kicked him when he was on a path because he hadn't gone around a branch that she had wanted him to go around."

Kate stared. "Seriously?"

He nodded. "Yeah, you could tell she was just a younger version of Jenna and Robin. Like, holy shit, what's wrong with the women in this world?" he asked. "It used to be that, you know, women were all sugar and spice and everything nice."

"Well, I don't think that was ever the case," Kate said quietly. "Unfortunately for you, you seem to have come across some of the more unpleasant ones."

"You think?" he quipped. "Just like my own fucking wife."

And, for Kate, that was the core of it. "Did she treat you badly too?"

"Of course she did," he snapped, "because that's what women do. It's not a case of *people* are like that. It's that *women* are like that. Everything is all nice and beautiful, and then, the minute something bad happens, they blame you for everything. They turn into these absolutely miserable people. Someone you would never ever think could ever do something like that, but suddenly they turn against you, like vipers."

"I gather the divorce was ugly?"

"No, it was more than ugly. She made all these accusations about me being abusive, physically and verbally. Never any medical reports for evidence, nothing at all, but she got a woman judge."

"Oh my God," Kate murmured.

"I ended up not getting anything out of my marriage, and she got it all. But worse than that," he said, his voice filled with pain, "she got my sons." He shook his head. "I wouldn't have cared about anything else. The bitch could have had it all," he declared, "but she didn't have to take my sons. And then she did even worse than that." Charlie glared at Kate with such fury in his eyes. "She turned them against me and told them all kinds of lies. And they were lies," he stated. "I never laid a hand on her. I never yelled at her. She was just like the rest of them bitches. She was the one always yelling at me."

Turning his face, pointing to a long scar on his cheek, he went on. "You see this scar?"

She nodded slowly.

"She did that. With a knife no less. A kitchen knife. She lost her temper." He added, "I never told on her either. I never did."

"Maybe you should have," Kate suggested.

He glared at her. "You know how many people would have laughed at me then?" He roared, "They all would have said I was weak. How it was stupid to be abused by a woman. That I should tune her up, like she deserved. But I couldn't do it. I was raised to never hit a woman. How the hell was I supposed to do anything and hit her now?" he asked, shaking his head. "I hated her. God, I hated her," he repeated, "but I never ever touched her. Even after all she did. And she's still out there, walking around, being the same old bitch she always was, which apparently I couldn't see before we got married. Oh no, she was just pretending to be this absolutely gorgeous woman who supposedly loved me." Tears were in his eyes at this point. "But she never did, … no, she never loved me at all. Once she got her sons, that was it. She got the house too. She got everything. And me? What have I got?"

He shook his head. "I got a fucking scarred-up face and nothing else. It shouldn't be allowed. You know that, right?" He started to get angry again. "Somebody had to do something."

"And you thought that was you?" Kate asked.

"Well, it's not as if you would do anything about it, would you?" he sneered. "No way you would stop Jenna from hitting her husband. You know she used to do that, right? Jenna used to beat the crap out of her husband, and he didn't do anything to deserve it. But everybody thought he was abusive. No, no, no, it was the other way around. He was the one taking all the shit from her. I told him once that he shouldn't stand for it. And he just looked at me, horrified that I actually knew. I told him once that I understood. But he didn't really understand what I did understand."

Charlie's words started to get jumbled up.

"I realized then just how bad it was. I mean, I've watched those two couples for years. And the bitchy wives had just gotten worse and worse and worse," Charlie said.

"Relationships are supposed to make you better together. Those two, Jenna and Robin, they had a vile evilness within them that you could never imagine. And everybody suffered. I'll tell you that the world is a hell of a lot better off without them."

"So you decided that you would become judge and jury and that you would carry out the maximum sentence, *huh?*"

He nodded. "Damn right, I did. Somebody had to." Charlie glared at Kate. "You cops wouldn't touch them. The judges wouldn't touch them. My wife got away scot-free for being the bitch she was and left with me with nothing. Nobody could touch her now," he snapped. "I figured it was up to some of the men who have taken all the abuse all this time to put a stop to it."

"Did they know about your plans? The husbands, I mean."

"*Nah,* not really. One time I told Agnew that I might just do something about it. But that was after they were all having a bawling session, where all these guys were talking about how bad it was. But I didn't come right out and tell anyone I would do that. I think Agnew might have wondered though."

"You think that had something to do with his attempt to commit suicide?"

He thought about it and nodded. "You know? It could have. Guilt would eat at him, especially if he thought I would do that, but I didn't tell him. I didn't tell anyone. No, no. He needed some time to get his head together. He needed time to heal. Man, that bitch took the stuffing out of him, tore it all apart right in front of him, and threw it on the ground and stomped on it. There wasn't a whole lot left of the real Agnew for him to deal with the aftermath."

"Suicide is like that. You think the world's better off because you're such a loser."

"Somebody needs to build that kid back up again and tell him that it wasn't his fault. It was all that damn wife of his."

"And the other couple?"

"I already told you," he said, with a dismissive wave of his hand.

It bothered Kate that two lives were deemed so unimportant that they were picked to die because a wife may be having a bad day, or maybe they had a bet going that day, or maybe she was kicking her husband. Maybe she was doing something else, and Charlie thought that she was kicking him because he was coming from that perspective where everything was so bad and so ugly, and that's all that women did. It really bothered Kate, but this wasn't the time or the place to share that with Charlie. Plus, she also didn't need to set him off either.

"I still think it's sad," she told Charlie quietly, "that you snuffed out two more lives because you just figured they were headed down that pathway."

He shrugged. "Once I killed two, I was already headed for life in prison anyway. What's two more?"

She winced.

He nodded. "You ever kill anybody?"

"Yes, in the line of duty," she replied, tilting her head to the side. "I'd like to think it was justified."

"You know something?" he said, with a big fat grin. "I do too."

"Will you come down to the station with me peacefully?"

"The fucking hell I will," he snapped. "You'll have to

work for it." And, without another word, he turned and bolted down the pathway to one of the dead-men runs, which went straight down the damn hill.

Swearing, she raced after him.

Simon called out, "Kate, I've got the gun."

"Stay up there," she ordered, but she knew he wouldn't. That he'd found the gun was great though because then she didn't have to worry about some innocent bystander finding it and accidentally shooting themselves. But this trip down the mountain was bullshit. It was hard. It was fast. It was slick. And she knew that she would have a hell of a time with it. Yet she would not let Charlie get away though.

She knew where to find him potentially, but he could also have another bolt hole, and anything that delayed getting him into custody was just another chance for him to kill somebody else. Four deaths in this scenario were enough. It made a sick sense, but it all came back to his bad divorce and losing his family. So many times it was based on some simple trigger like that, something that ended up pushing people over the edge. She wasn't even sure exactly what the trigger had been in this case. Maybe Barry's divorce. There could have been a lot of small ones that built up to it.

Up ahead, dust and branches whipped past, and an almost crazy laugh came from Charlie.

She yelled, "Stop it. You'll hurt yourself."

"Who fucking cares?" he asked. As he came to one particularly bad corner, he turned and looked back at her. "You can't even keep up," he said, with a sneer. And, at that moment, he stumbled and cried out.

She watched in horror as he fell, tumbling overhead, down the rest of the path. She stopped and waited, but he hit hard at the bottom, and he didn't move. She made her way down as fast as she safely could, and, when she got to the bottom, she raced up to him, then reached down to check for a pulse.

As she heard other noises, she looked up to see Simon, a gun in his hand, coming down behind her. She looked up and shook her head. "He's dead." Actually she hadn't even needed to check his pulse because his head was at such an odd angle. "He broke his neck," she added, straightening up and gasping for breath. "God damn. What an ending to this mess."

"Well, you got your man," Simon stated, as he held out the weapon.

She looked at it and took it from him. "This is not how I wanted my day at the beach to go."

He looked at her in horror.

She nodded. "Now that I've caught him, you know I can't take off."

Simon glared, and she nodded, but then he smiled. "So how about tomorrow?"

She looked at him with hope. "Can we take a rain check?"

"Absolutely we can take a rain check," he replied, "but you'll want to call this in. I'm not even sure the path is safe up there because, for all we know, this guy had a booby trap set for you."

Kate nodded. "He was trying to direct me to a certain place." She wiped the dust and dirt off her face. "So I wouldn't be at all surprised." She pulled her phone from her back pocket and called it in. She looked over at Simon when she was done. "Thank you."

"For what?"

"For distracting him," she said. "It allowed me to get

into position."

"And what about the instructions?"

She looked at him, startled for a moment, and then she frowned. "*Instructions?*" she asked cautiously.

"Yeah, what happened that caused you to go bolting down the hill?"

She grimaced. "It was just this drive, this need, this—I don't know—this voice in my head, telling me to *Run, run, run.*"

He gave her a fat smile and nodded. "That was me."

She stared at him in shock. "No, no, no, you don't," she said. "No way in hell you'll convince me that you were talking in my head."

"Remember the vision that I had about the runner who, *uh*, was convinced to stay in bed and to not go out that day?"

She nodded. "Yeah, what about it?"

"Well, this morning I had another vision of her sliding out of the bed and taking off, even though her partner asked her not to."

She frowned. "So is she here?"

"Well, that's why I came running. And I admit I may not have caught it the first time, and I sure as hell didn't recognize it until now. With that person and that vision, the one who I connected to was the probable next victim," he stated.

She frowned and asked, "Yeah, but who was it?"

He reached up two hands, grabbed her on either side of her shoulders, and gave her a slight shake. "It was you. I saw your face in this morning's vision, and then realized you'd taken off on me, without even letting me know that you had gone running. That's why I came racing after you." She looked up, shock and horror rippling through her.

"Seriously?" she asked.

He nodded. "Seriously."

"Holy crap. That doesn't sound like a good thing."

"What? That I connected to you?"

"That we're so close that we connected at all." He looked at her for a long moment, not saying anything, making her feel like she'd just messed up big-time. She shrugged. "Look. I'm not saying that it's a bad thing."

Simon shook his head. "That is *exactly* what you are saying."

She frowned. "I don't know what I'm trying to say. I'm tired, exhausted really, and it's a little freaky to think that we connected through these abilities that I'm still trying hard to admit even exist," she muttered.

At that, a smile broke across his face. "Ah, so it pushes your buttons again and your boundaries as to right and wrong in reality."

"Sure," she said. "Doesn't it yours?"

"Well, it did," he replied, "but I have to admit that I'm starting to get used to it."

"Yeah? What happened to make you accept it?"

He added, "Realizing and understanding just how much good I can do with it. Because, my dear, I know you'll tell me that it's all bullshit, but there's a really good chance that having connected to you on this case kept you from being the next victim. So, the fact of the matter is, you didn't become a victim, whether that was by your hand, by my hand, or whatever combination you want to discuss," he suggested. "But the bottom line is, you're fine, and, if I hadn't had that vision, I don't know that it would have ended that way."

She looked up at him, not even sure what to say.

When she did go to open her mouth, he placed a finger against her lips. "Don't even start. We won't talk about it right now. We won't argue about it. We'll just let it rest. Because I know what I know, and you don't know what you don't know. And, until you're ready to accept everything that I've already got to this point of accepting," he noted, "we'll just be on opposite sides of the coin. For right now, let's just accept the fact that this is a good day because we both survived."

At that, she smiled up at him. "You know what? That is something I can get behind. And, as long as tomorrow's beach day still happens," she added, "I'll be totally okay with however this works out."

He looked down at her and smirked. "I'd give you a kiss right now, but have you any idea how dirty your face is?"

She groaned. "No, I really don't, but I didn't think it would matter to you."

He laughed and said, "Good point."

And, with that, he gathered her into his arms, and he kissed her, softly at first, then hard and passionately. When she finally came up for air, she heard catcalls around her. She lifted a hand and said, "Well, no thanks to you guys, I'm alive, thank you very much. And this asshole on the ground is our killer."

At that, Rodney came running down the last bit of the hill. "Seriously, he's the one, *huh*?" He looked at the dead body and asked, "Who the hell is he anyway?"

"He was a friend of the husbands," she explained, "and the president of the running club they all used to belong to. He had developed a really big hatred for women. But, just like a lot of other runners, this one finally met his match and, through his own actions, came to the end of the road.

And I, for one, am damn glad. Now we can clean up this mess and take care of business. I've got a shit ton of reports to write and a few other things to do, and then I am taking a couple days off."

Rodney looked over at her, then grinned. "Aren't you supposed to go to the beach today?"

"I wish I could." She reached up a tired and skinned hand, wiping her face. "We're pushing it off to tomorrow. So, I want everything wrapped up today, so I get Sunday off."

"I think we can manage that." Rodney laughed. "Especially now."

"Yeah, *especially* now." Kate turned to Simon and said, "It'll be a long day, so you may want to go home."

"I think I'll hang around for a while," he told her. "I'll just sit here and watch you work, if you don't mind."

She looked at him, opened her mouth.

He shook his head and said, "Don't. I came close to losing a lot this morning, so just bear with me and let me sit here and watch for a while. When you least expect it, you'll turn around, and I'll be gone, headed off to start my day." He stared at her for a long while. "But, for the moment, I just want to know all is well."

And, true to his word, when she looked around about an hour later, she saw no sign of him. She turned to Rodney and asked, "Seen Simon lately?"

"*Nah*, I haven't seen him in a while."

She smiled, then looked down at the coroner, Dr. Smidge.

He looked up at her and asked, "Is this the end of it?"

"Uniforms are checking the running paths for more booby traps but haven't found any. So, yes this is the end of it," she stated. "Well, let me say, it's the end of this one anyway.

He gave her a glare and nodded. "And, no doubt, tomorrow there'll be another one."

She hoped not, but unfortunately it was all too likely. Maybe, if she were lucky, it would wait until Monday.

EPILOGUE

Monday Morning

WHEN KATE WALKED into the station Monday morning, the sergeant looked at her and frowned.

"Thought you were taking a couple days off."

"I didn't ask ahead of time," she noted, "and I did take yesterday off, which I needed badly, but I wasn't sure about scheduling more."

"You've got a lot of hours piled up," Sergeant Colby told her. "So why don't you take a few days?"

"Maybe." She shrugged. "I could finish off a few things that I didn't quite get done on Saturday, then maybe work this week and plan on taking a long weekend—if that's okay with you?"

"It's fine by me," he said. "You're doing a great job, you know?"

She looked at him in surprise because words of praise were very scarce from him. "Thank you, sir," she replied.

She walked into the bullpen to the others standing up and cheering. "What's that for?" she asked, embarrassed by the attention.

"Well, we couldn't decide if we should say, *Good job* or *Cheers* or whatever," Lilliana explained. "But you know? You seem to have accepted some of Simon's work. Rodney told us all about it. He heard it from Simon apparently, about his visions that connected to you."

Kate winced at that. "I'm still not real comfortable with that whole thing."

"Another thing," Owen added, as he walked toward her and gave her a hug. "You took a hell of a beating on that hill, but you held your own. So, *Yay for still being alive.* Not to mention the fact that you closed the case with four murders, and you got it all done within eight days."

She smiled. "Thanks, guys. I have to admit it was pretty nice to have it come to an end, without anybody else dying. I mean, obviously Charlie died, and, for that, I'm sorry. However, if there had to be an ending, that's a good one to have, I guess. So, please tell me there are no new cases and that it'll be an easy week, and then I can take a long weekend."

They all burst out laughing. "We caught one last night," Lilliana said. "If you're up for it, we got a couple gang fights out in lower Hastings again."

She winced. "What is with that area?"

"Hey, it's just one of those tough areas of town."

"Knives, I suppose?"

"Yep, two sliced out, one dead."

She asked, "Open-and-shut?"

"Yep, sounds like it."

"Okay, perfect," she replied. "That sounds like the case I could use right now."

"Right," Rodney agreed, "and don't worry. There'll be another crazy one coming your way pretty damn soon. There's always somebody in the department who catches the weird and wild and wonderful."

She looked at him and asked, "Am I it then?"

"You so are." Rodney laughed.

Just then, the woman staffing the front reception desk walked in. Audrey, who was still here on a maternity leave coverage, announced, "We've got a woman in the front here who's looking to talk to Detective Kate Morgan."

Kate looked at her. "Why me?"

She shrugged. "She read your name in the paper."

"Oh God, no." Kate moaned. "The last thing I need is notoriety."

"Too late." Audrey gave her a bright, winning smile. "That horse has already left the gate, and you're not getting it back in again." She pointed behind her. "I put her into the first interview room. Don't take too long though. Looks like she might bolt." And, with that, Audrey left.

Kate turned and looked at the others, then saw the grins on their faces. "Did you guys set me up or something?"

"Hell no," Rodney stated, "but I'll come with you and talk to her, if you want."

"Yeah, sure, come on, partner. Let's go talk to her." She grabbed a pad of paper and a pen, then turned to look at the others. "I guess you'll have to handle that open-and-shut on your own."

"Yeah, I think we can manage that, if we need to," Owen teased. "Besides, this witness could be about nothing."

"We'll see." She walked toward the interview room and stepped inside to see a woman, her face and hands covered with scratches, looking like she'd been completely traumatized. Kate looked at Rodney with a shrug, then stepped farther inside, introduced herself. "Look. First of all, do you need a doctor?"

The woman gave her a haunted look. "No, I've just checked out of the hospital," she noted quietly.

"Okay then." Kate sat down and waited for the woman

to speak. As the woman nervously fidgeted, clenching and unclenching her scratched up hands, Kate finally spoke. "What can I do for you?"

"I'd like to report a kidnapping," she said.

"Okay, of whom?"

The woman looked up at her. "Me."

Kate leaned forward, so she was sure of what she heard. "You were kidnapped?"

She nodded.

"Do you know who kidnapped you?"

She shook her head. "No, but it was for a game."

At that, Kate froze. "What do you mean?"

"He kidnapped me, took away my shoes and socks, my pants and my shirt, and then said we would go outside, and he would have me walk—only to start and to stop whenever he would say so."

"What?"

She nodded. "I know. It doesn't sound normal. But I was blindfolded, and he would tell me to walk ten paces. So I'd walk ten paces, but I wouldn't know what I was walking into. Sometimes it would be into a thicket of a berry brambles. Sometimes into a river. And one time"—she stopped, and her breath hitched and hiccupped—"one time, it was into a rocky riverbed." She started to cry. "And then, whenever I would fall or get hurt, he would laugh and laugh and laugh. Sometimes he'd make me do it again and again."

"And how did he force you?"

"He had guns, lots and lots of guns," she said. "At least what I first saw. Then I had the blindfold on, and I never saw anything else again."

"Okay, did you tell anybody this at the hospital?"

She shook her head. "No, he dropped me off there and

gave me a message."

"A message? So what was in this message?"

The woman held up a piece of paper for her. "I don't know what it means, but he told me to give it to you."

Kate carefully took the paper from her hand and read the message out loud so Rodney heard. *"Kate, see if Simon can do this."* She flipped the paper forward and backward and then looked over at the woman. "Does this message mean anything to you?"

The other woman shook her head, with tears in her eyes. "No, I don't know anything about it. I don't know who Simon is, and I don't know what he's supposed to do," she murmured. "But I think it has to do with the game because he used to laugh all the time. He said something about *Simon thinks he's so fucking good, but I don't think he's got answers for this.*"

"And do you know who this Simon guy is?" she asked, her heart sinking, as she shot a look at Rodney, who now sat beside her, studying the note in her hand.

"No, but he made it sound like it was an old friend. Yet I got the feeling that maybe it wasn't so much of a friend as an old enemy."

"An enemy might sound better," Kate noted, "or at least a frenemy, a friend that became an enemy."

"Maybe," the young woman agreed, as she wrapped her arms around her chest.

Kate looked at her and frowned. "Are you sure you shouldn't be in the hospital?"

"He didn't hurt me," she whispered. "At least not this time. He said, if I didn't deliver the message, he'd show up, standing at the end of my bed, and I would know it's time to start the game all over again."

Kate winced. "Well, I sure as hell hope not. I think you've been through enough."

She nodded. "He did say," she added, then stopped for a moment and took a deep breath, which caught in her throat, before she exhaled noisily. "He did say that he likes to keep his pets."

Kate stared at her in shock. "What pets?"

The young woman looked up and stared at her, tears in her eyes, then replied, "I think he meant *human* pets. You have to stop him. Before he comes after me, please, please stop him."

Kate looked over at the young woman, now sobbing quietly, then got up, wrapped her arms around her, and whispered, "I will, sweetie. I will." And she sure as hell hoped that she wasn't lying.

I'll need Simon on this one in a big way, she thought to herself. Unfortunately he didn't yet know that he would play an integral part in this investigation because it could be all about his life. She knew that wasn't something Simon would be okay with, but he had to be, this time, because lives were at stake.

This concludes Book 5 of Kate Morgan: Simon Says… Run.
Read about Kate Morgan: Simon Says… Walk, Book 6

Simon Says... Walk: Kate Morgan (Book #6)

Introducing a new thriller series that keeps you guessing and on your toes through every twist and unexpected turn....

USA Today Best-Selling Author Dale Mayer does it again in this mind-blowing thriller series.

The unlikely team of Detective Kate Morgan and Simon St. Laurant, an unwilling psychic, marries all the unpredictable and passionate elements of Mayer's work that readers have come to love and crave.

Detective Kate Morgan isn't impressed with her latest case. A terrorized woman walks into the police station, with a message for Kate. Actually a message that drags Simon into the middle of it—no, make that front and center. A challenge has been issued, one that Kate is determined to solve, hopefully keeping Simon on the sidelines.

Blindsided, Simon doesn't understand the message or the hate being directed his way. And the last thing he wants to do is revisit his past. Yet being in the middle of one of

Kate's cases doesn't give him an option. If he can't get to the bottom of this, his life will be, once again, torn apart—all to appease a madman's new game.

But the answer, … when it comes, is closer to home than anyone realizes.

Find Book 6 here!

To find out more visit Dale Mayer's website.

https://geni.us/DMSSWalkUniversal

Author's Note

Thank you for reading Simon Says… Run: Kate Morgan, Book 5! If you enjoyed the book, please take a moment and leave a short review.

Dear reader,

I love to hear from readers, and you can contact me at my website: www.dalemayer.com or at my Facebook author page. To be informed of new releases and special offers, sign up for my newsletter or follow me on BookBub. And if you are interested in joining Dale Mayer's Reader Group, here is the Facebook sign up page.
http://geni.us/DaleMayerFBGroup

Cheers,
Dale Mayer

About the Author

Dale Mayer is a *USA Today* best-selling author, best known for her SEALs military romances, her Psychic Visions series, and her Lovely Lethal Garden cozy series. Her contemporary romances are raw and full of passion and emotion (Broken But ... Mending, Hathaway House series). Her thrillers will keep you guessing (Kate Morgan, By Death series), and her romantic comedies will keep you giggling (*It's a Dog's Life*, a stand-alone novella; and the Broken Protocols series, starring Charming Marvin, the cat).

Dale honors the stories that come to her—and some of them are crazy, break all the rules and cross multiple genres!

To go with her fiction, she also writes nonfiction in many different fields, with books available on résumé writing, companion gardening, and the US mortgage system. All her books are available in print and ebook format.

Connect with Dale Mayer Online

Dale's Website – www.dalemayer.com
Twitter – @DaleMayer
Facebook Page – geni.us/DaleMayerFBFanPage
Facebook Group – geni.us/DaleMayerFBGroup
BookBub – geni.us/DaleMayerBookbub
Instagram – geni.us/DaleMayerInstagram
Goodreads – geni.us/DaleMayerGoodreads
Newsletter – geni.us/DaleNews

Also by Dale Mayer

Published Adult Books:

Shadow Recon

Magnus, Book 1

Bullard's Battle

Ryland's Reach, Book 1

Cain's Cross, Book 2

Eton's Escape, Book 3

Garret's Gambit, Book 4

Kano's Keep, Book 5

Fallon's Flaw, Book 6

Quinn's Quest, Book 7

Bullard's Beauty, Book 8

Bullard's Best, Book 9

Bullard's Battle, Books 1–2

Bullard's Battle, Books 3–4

Bullard's Battle, Books 5–6

Bullard's Battle, Books 7–8

Terkel's Team

Damon's Deal, Book 1

Wade's War, Book 2

Gage's Goal, Book 3

Calum's Contact, Book 4
Rick's Road, Book 5
Scott's Summit, Book 6
Brody's Beast, Book 7
Terkel's Twist, Book 8

Kate Morgan

Simon Says... Hide, Book 1
Simon Says... Jump, Book 2
Simon Says... Ride, Book 3
Simon Says... Scream, Book 4
Simon Says... Run, Book 5
Simon Says... Walk, Book 6

Hathaway House

Aaron, Book 1
Brock, Book 2
Cole, Book 3
Denton, Book 4
Elliot, Book 5
Finn, Book 6
Gregory, Book 7
Heath, Book 8
Iain, Book 9
Jaden, Book 10
Keith, Book 11
Lance, Book 12
Melissa, Book 13
Nash, Book 14

Owen, Book 15

Percy, Book 16

Quinton, Book 17

Ryatt, Book 18

Spencer, Book 19

Hathaway House, Books 1–3

Hathaway House, Books 4–6

Hathaway House, Books 7–9

The K9 Files

Ethan, Book 1

Pierce, Book 2

Zane, Book 3

Blaze, Book 4

Lucas, Book 5

Parker, Book 6

Carter, Book 7

Weston, Book 8

Greyson, Book 9

Rowan, Book 10

Caleb, Book 11

Kurt, Book 12

Tucker, Book 13

Harley, Book 14

Kyron, Book 15

Jenner, Book 16

Rhys, Book 17

Landon, Book 18

The K9 Files, Books 1–2

The K9 Files, Books 3–4

The K9 Files, Books 5–6

The K9 Files, Books 7–8

The K9 Files, Books 9–10

The K9 Files, Books 11–12

Lovely Lethal Gardens

Arsenic in the Azaleas, Book 1

Bones in the Begonias, Book 2

Corpse in the Carnations, Book 3

Daggers in the Dahlias, Book 4

Evidence in the Echinacea, Book 5

Footprints in the Ferns, Book 6

Gun in the Gardenias, Book 7

Handcuffs in the Heather, Book 8

Ice Pick in the Ivy, Book 9

Jewels in the Juniper, Book 10

Killer in the Kiwis, Book 11

Lifeless in the Lilies, Book 12

Murder in the Marigolds, Book 13

Nabbed in the Nasturtiums, Book 14

Offed in the Orchids, Book 15

Poison in the Pansies, Book 16

Quarry in the Quince, Book 17

Revenge in the Roses, Book 18

Silenced in the Sunflowers, Book 19

Lovely Lethal Gardens, Books 1–2

Lovely Lethal Gardens, Books 3–4

Lovely Lethal Gardens, Books 5–6

Lovely Lethal Gardens, Books 7–8
Lovely Lethal Gardens, Books 9–10

Psychic Vision Series
Tuesday's Child
Hide 'n Go Seek
Maddy's Floor
Garden of Sorrow
Knock Knock...
Rare Find
Eyes to the Soul
Now You See Her
Shattered
Into the Abyss
Seeds of Malice
Eye of the Falcon
Itsy-Bitsy Spider
Unmasked
Deep Beneath
From the Ashes
Stroke of Death
Ice Maiden
Snap, Crackle...
What If...
Talking Bones
String of Tears
Psychic Visions Books 1–3
Psychic Visions Books 4–6
Psychic Visions Books 7–9

By Death Series

Touched by Death

Haunted by Death

Chilled by Death

By Death Books 1–3

Broken Protocols – Romantic Comedy Series

Cat's Meow

Cat's Pajamas

Cat's Cradle

Cat's Claus

Broken Protocols 1-4

Broken and... Mending

Skin

Scars

Scales (of Justice)

Broken but... Mending 1-3

Glory

Genesis

Tori

Celeste

Glory Trilogy

Biker Blues

Morgan: Biker Blues, Volume 1

Cash: Biker Blues, Volume 2

SEALs of Honor

Mason: SEALs of Honor, Book 1

Hawk: SEALs of Honor, Book 2

Dane: SEALs of Honor, Book 3

Swede: SEALs of Honor, Book 4

Shadow: SEALs of Honor, Book 5

Cooper: SEALs of Honor, Book 6

Markus: SEALs of Honor, Book 7

Evan: SEALs of Honor, Book 8

Mason's Wish: SEALs of Honor, Book 9

Chase: SEALs of Honor, Book 10

Brett: SEALs of Honor, Book 11

Devlin: SEALs of Honor, Book 12

Easton: SEALs of Honor, Book 13

Ryder: SEALs of Honor, Book 14

Macklin: SEALs of Honor, Book 15

Corey: SEALs of Honor, Book 16

Warrick: SEALs of Honor, Book 17

Tanner: SEALs of Honor, Book 18

Jackson: SEALs of Honor, Book 19

Kanen: SEALs of Honor, Book 20

Nelson: SEALs of Honor, Book 21

Taylor: SEALs of Honor, Book 22

Colton: SEALs of Honor, Book 23

Troy: SEALs of Honor, Book 24

Axel: SEALs of Honor, Book 25

Baylor: SEALs of Honor, Book 26

Hudson: SEALs of Honor, Book 27

Lachlan: SEALs of Honor, Book 28

Paxton: SEALs of Honor, Book 29

Bronson: SEALs of Honor, Book 30

SEALs of Honor, Books 1–3

SEALs of Honor, Books 4–6

SEALs of Honor, Books 7–10

SEALs of Honor, Books 11–13

SEALs of Honor, Books 14–16

SEALs of Honor, Books 17–19

SEALs of Honor, Books 20–22

SEALs of Honor, Books 23–25

Heroes for Hire

Levi's Legend: Heroes for Hire, Book 1

Stone's Surrender: Heroes for Hire, Book 2

Merk's Mistake: Heroes for Hire, Book 3

Rhodes's Reward: Heroes for Hire, Book 4

Flynn's Firecracker: Heroes for Hire, Book 5

Logan's Light: Heroes for Hire, Book 6

Harrison's Heart: Heroes for Hire, Book 7

Saul's Sweetheart: Heroes for Hire, Book 8

Dakota's Delight: Heroes for Hire, Book 9

Tyson's Treasure: Heroes for Hire, Book 10

Jace's Jewel: Heroes for Hire, Book 11

Rory's Rose: Heroes for Hire, Book 12

Brandon's Bliss: Heroes for Hire, Book 13

Liam's Lily: Heroes for Hire, Book 14

North's Nikki: Heroes for Hire, Book 15

Anders's Angel: Heroes for Hire, Book 16

Reyes's Raina: Heroes for Hire, Book 17

Dezi's Diamond: Heroes for Hire, Book 18

Vince's Vixen: Heroes for Hire, Book 19

Ice's Icing: Heroes for Hire, Book 20

Johan's Joy: Heroes for Hire, Book 21

Galen's Gemma: Heroes for Hire, Book 22

Zack's Zest: Heroes for Hire, Book 23

Bonaparte's Belle: Heroes for Hire, Book 24

Noah's Nemesis: Heroes for Hire, Book 25

Tomas's Trials: Heroes for Hire, Book 26

Carson's Choice: Heroes for Hire, Book 27

Dante's Decision: Heroes for Hire, Book 28

Heroes for Hire, Books 1–3

Heroes for Hire, Books 4–6

Heroes for Hire, Books 7–9

Heroes for Hire, Books 10–12

Heroes for Hire, Books 13–15

Heroes for Hire, Books 16–18

Heroes for Hire, Books 19–21

Heroes for Hire, Books 22–24

SEALs of Steel

Badger: SEALs of Steel, Book 1

Erick: SEALs of Steel, Book 2

Cade: SEALs of Steel, Book 3

Talon: SEALs of Steel, Book 4

Laszlo: SEALs of Steel, Book 5

Geir: SEALs of Steel, Book 6

Jager: SEALs of Steel, Book 7

The Final Reveal: SEALs of Steel, Book 8

SEALs of Steel, Books 1–4

SEALs of Steel, Books 5–8

SEALs of Steel, Books 1–8

The Mavericks

Kerrick, Book 1

Griffin, Book 2

Jax, Book 3

Beau, Book 4

Asher, Book 5

Ryker, Book 6

Miles, Book 7

Nico, Book 8

Keane, Book 9

Lennox, Book 10

Gavin, Book 11

Shane, Book 12

Diesel, Book 13

Jerricho, Book 14

Killian, Book 15

Hatch, Book 16

Corbin, Book 17

Aiden, Book 18

The Mavericks, Books 1–2

The Mavericks, Books 3–4

The Mavericks, Books 5–6

The Mavericks, Books 7–8

The Mavericks, Books 9–10

The Mavericks, Books 11–12

Collections

Dare to Be You…

Dare to Love…

Dare to be Strong…

RomanceX3

Standalone Novellas

It's a Dog's Life

Riana's Revenge

Second Chances

Published Young Adult Books:

Family Blood Ties Series

Vampire in Denial

Vampire in Distress

Vampire in Design

Vampire in Deceit

Vampire in Defiance

Vampire in Conflict

Vampire in Chaos

Vampire in Crisis

Vampire in Control

Vampire in Charge

Family Blood Ties Set 1–3

Family Blood Ties Set 1–5

Family Blood Ties Set 4–6

Family Blood Ties Set 7–9

Sian's Solution, A Family Blood Ties Series Prequel
    Novelette

Design series

Dangerous Designs

Deadly Designs

Darkest Designs

Design Series Trilogy

Standalone

In Cassie's Corner

Gem Stone (a Gemma Stone Mystery)

Time Thieves

Published Non-Fiction Books:

Career Essentials

Career Essentials: The Résumé

Career Essentials: The Cover Letter

Career Essentials: The Interview

Career Essentials: 3 in 1

www.ingramcontent.com/pod-product-compliance
Lightning Source LLC
Chambersburg PA
CBHW072045190726
48294CB00005B/1418